Dr. Radford —

Shadow and Light

by

Carol Koris

Thank you to all of your help! I hope you enjoy my story!

CK

TELEMACHUS PRESS

Cover designed by Telemachus Press, LLC

Cover art:
Copyright © iStockphoto/5547138/AnkNet

Published by Telemachus Press, LLC
http://www.telemachuspress.com

ISBN: 978-1-942899-49-5 (eBook)
ISBN: 978-1-942899-50-1 (Paperback)

Version 2015.11.20

10 9 8 7 6 5 4 3 2 1

Shadow and Light

Prologue

Maggie Miller gently rocked the developing tray and stared at the emerging image, the glow of the safe light giving the picture an orange hue. She stood perfectly still in her darkroom, willing the results she wanted onto the paper that floated in the developing bath. She focused on the features of the face as they began to appear: the close-cropped hair, graying at the sides, and the strong masculine chin. This was the part of photography she loved best—watching an image develop like a spirit from the nether world coming through, right to her, right onto her paper.

The black and white photo of her husband, Brian, became clear, concrete. It was a smiling face, but just a face. What Maggie had been hoping for was not there. She had taken the shots at one of Lilly's soccer games. Without Brian realizing it, she had turned the camera on him. She wanted his warmth and caring in the picture, knowing how watching Lilly always gave him a unique smile—unconditional love of a parent for a child—that softened his eyes, and gave the beginning wrinkles the look of rays around the sun.

She swished the paper around the developing bath with plastic tongs, then gently pulled it out to drain. A loud knock on the door startled her, and the paper fell back into the bath.

"Damn." Maggie picked the photo up and drained it again. The knock came again, this time less urgently. "What?" Maggie yelled through the closed door.

"Mommy?"

Maggie couldn't help but smile. Who else would be in the darkroom? Maggie and Lilly, her eight-year-old daughter, were the only ones home. Brian, a pilot, was on a four-day trip to South America.

"Lilly?" she said as she put the print into the stop bath and set the timer for ten seconds.

"Yeah, it's me."

"I know." Maggie smiled and heard a giggle from the other side of the door.

"The buzzer went off—the chicken's ready."

"Hold on." Maggie drained the print once more, put it into the print fixer and set the timer for six minutes. She looked at the large clock on the wall, 5:20, and then to the negatives she had hoped to process. Once again, she'd run out of time. The rest of the film would have to wait for another day.

"Do you want me to turn the buzzer off?" Lilly said.

"Thanks, and turn the oven off, too. I'll be right out."

"Can I roller blade until dinner's ready?" Lilly's voice was muffled right up against the door. Maggie could picture her daughter—her face positioned right between the edge of the door and the doorjamb, her lips almost touching the space where they met.

"Dinner *is* ready, Lilly. I just need to put the salad together."

"Please, Mommy?" Now her lips were pressed against the door, the words being pushed through the wood the way Lilly would have liked to come through herself and beg in person.

Maggie looked around the darkroom and understood the desire for a few minutes of squeezed-in pleasure. She walked over to the door and opened it a crack.

"Is it okay?" Lilly said. Her face was as close to the door as it could get. Her pale-green eyes seemed luminous with the reflection of the amber glow, and blond curls, escaping from a clip at the back of her neck, were surrounded by the natural light flooding in from the hall skylight.

Maggie studied her daughter for a moment and saw all the things she wanted to capture in her pictures: anticipation, excitement, a zest for life.

"I'll be out in ten minutes, then you can go. Turn off the oven and open the door so the chicken won't over cook."

"'Kay."

Maggie knew Lilly would've agreed to anything for a few minutes of speed on her roller blades. She turned and started to run away.

The timer buzzed behind Maggie. "Hey." She puckered her lips for a kiss.

Lilly ran back to her mother and kissed her quickly while making a loud "mwah" noise.

"Ten minutes," Maggie said.

"Thanks, Mom. You're the best." Lilly ran off down the hall.

"And get the stuff out for the chocolate chip cookies," Maggie yelled after her. She got no answer and listened to the footsteps get further and further away, then closed the door and took the print out of the fixer, not bothering to agitate it. She drained it and put it on the drying rack to refer to once she developed the negative again. She looked at the pictures hanging on the drying line, each one evenly spaced from the next. Maggie turned her focus back to the picture she had been working on and tried to see what she knew she wouldn't. Where was the man that helped her through her mother's death the year she gave birth to Lilly? The man that took the night feedings with pumped breast milk so she could sleep? The man who could sit with Lilly for hours on end teaching her math and never becoming impatient?

Her pictures were good, her business was booming, her clients happy, but she couldn't quite make that leap that made a picture take your breath away. She had set a goal of having published photographs by the time she was thirty-five and was only a year away from her deadline. She wanted the kind of pictures that told a story, captured a question, or gave an answer in one snapshot. All Maggie had captured were two eyes, a nose, and a mouth. She glanced at the unprocessed negatives and undeveloped film. Maybe later, when Lilly was in bed, she could come down and play some more. That's how she thought of her time in the dark room—play. It didn't pay the bills, it didn't clean her house, but this kind of photography was her reason for picking up a camera in the first place. To catch those moments on film that not just let you see another person, but let you know him.

Maggie stared at Brian's face and thought of Lilly's eyes, of how alive they always looked. If she used a little dodging on the lower half of his face, the eyes would be brighter, not perceptibly, but enough that they would pull the viewer to that part of the picture. She reached for another piece of paper, and then remembered dinner. The picture would have to wait.

Maggie checked the caps of the chemical storage bottles and the paper boxes before turning on the lights. She placed each negative back into its labeled-and-dated sleeve and each of the film cartridges into the canister they were neatly lined up next to. Brian once said her fanaticism with her sorting and filing methods made her film cartridges and canisters look like soldiers waiting at attention. She had finished college with a degree in accounting, and even though she'd only worked for a firm for two years, some of the precise thinking still stayed with her. Maggie liked to date, time, and label where her shots were taken so she could go back if a setting photographed particularly well. Maggie glanced at the clock. It was almost six.

A couple hours for dinner and Lily's homework, then she could come back and work. Maggie left the darkroom and tried to switch gears from photography to dinner. The chicken would surely be dry by now. Some sliced tomatoes and mushrooms to add to the salad and dinner would be ready.

"Lilly, I'm in the kitchen," Maggie yelled in the hallway as she walked into the kitchen, the smell of roasted chicken hitting her nose. She smiled as she saw the flour canister, chocolate chips, pecans, and measuring cups and spoons lined up on the counter. Her attention was drawn to a note taped to the door of the microwave, just above the open oven door.

Ten minutes are up. Come get me when your done.

Hearts and smiley faces were sprinkled on the page, but Maggie still noticed "you're" was misspelled and vowed to spend more time on Lilly's homework, after the cookies were baked. Maggie shook her head. She had said she'd be out in ten minutes, not that Lilly could go in ten minutes. She never let Lilly go outside when she wasn't in earshot of her call. She put on two oven mitts and placed the chicken on the straw trivet that Lilly must have placed on the counter. Just as she set the chicken down, she was startled by a loud honk and the screech of tires. "Lilly." She turned and ran to the front door. When the doorknob wouldn't turn, she realized she still had the oven mitts on. She threw them off and yanked open the front door.

She squinted through the bright South Florida sun to see a black Honda Civic sitting at the end of her long driveway, with a figure squatting near the street. Lilly was sprawled motionless on the pavement. As Maggie started off down the driveway, she felt as if she were looking through the wrong end of a telephoto lens; the faster she ran, the further Lilly seemed to be from her.

As she reached her daughter, she saw that Lilly's left arm was turned the wrong way from her elbow, her hand hyperextended. But what scared her even more was the stillness of Lilly's body.

"I didn't hit her, Mrs. Miller. I swear," the boy said.

Maggie recognized him as Tim Schiavone, a tall, thin boy from a few doors down who had just gotten his restricted license.

"I didn't hit her." He was yelling now. "I thought she was going to come into the street, so I honked. I'm really sorry. I didn't mean to scare her." He shook his car keys at her, held them out as if they were evidence. "I honked, then she kind of slipped and fell."

He went on and on as Maggie knelt down next to Lilly. "Lilly." Maggie tried to get into Lilly's line of sight but her eyes were half closed, and she didn't seem to be seeing anything. She stroked her cheek. "Lilly, can you hear me?"

"I swear it was an accident," Tim repeated.

Maggie looked up to his face, which was now bent over looking at Lilly. "Do you have a cell phone?" she said.

"Yeah. I didn't mean to—"

"Call 911."

The boy stood still.

"Give me your phone," Maggie yelled. Her fingers hit and missed 911 twice on the tiny cell phone before she got it right. She screamed her address into the phone, then at the operator as he told her to calm down. Maggie held the phone out to Tim. "Stay on the line until they get here." She could feel her chest heaving as she knelt next to her daughter and saw the pool of blood near her right knee. The unique smell of blood hit her nose, and she tried to breathe through her mouth. She wanted to pick up her daughter and hold her tight to her body, pull her back into her womb to protect her. Lilly looked like a rag doll, unmoving, with appendages going in the wrong ways. Maggie reached down to pull Lilly to her, but then remembered her first aid—the child shouldn't be moved in case there was spinal injury.

"I'm really sorry, Mrs. Miller." The boy paced from the car to Lilly.

Maggie looked up at his frightened face. He was no more than a child himself, but she had no energy to console him. "Will you go get your mom for me?" she said. The boy shook his head, appearing happy to have a reason to leave, and ran down the street.

Maggie moved the hair out of Lilly's face, stroked her cheek the way she sometimes did to wake her in the morning. She listened to Lilly's breathing. She breathed every time Lilly did, exhaled very time her daughter did, as if she could control the process. Breathe, Lilly, breathe. Her arm was broken, there was a cut on her leg, and it had to be a concussion because she wouldn't wake up.

When Maggie was ten, her grandmother had slipped into a coma after a stroke. Her father would bring her to her grandmother's house three times a week. Amidst the stale smell of the old woman's cluttered house, Maggie would stand next to the bed, holding the frail, veined hand and tell the dying woman about her day, detail by detail. Her father had said her grandmother could still hear her, even if she couldn't answer. Maggie put her lips next to Lilly's ear and spoke softly, continuously, telling Lilly how she loved her, how everything would be okay, help was on the way. Her lips brushed Lilly's ear as she said her arm would be as good as new soon, and they'd be back in the kitchen baking cookies in no time. And they would use macadamia nuts, Lilly's favorite, for the very next batch. Finally Maggie could hear the ambulance in the distance, the wail of the sirens getting more and more insistent. It was a sound she usually hated because it only came when something was wrong, but this time she was glad it was getting closer. She looked to the street, and when she looked back down, she realized Lilly had no helmet on.

***

The days in the Pediatric Intensive Care Unit after Brian and she were told Lilly's subarachnoid hemorrhage had left her brain dead were a blur to Maggie. She vaguely remembered the rhythmic whoosh of the respirator her daughter had been on, the beep of the machine that monitored her heartbeat, and the coldness of the sterile hospital room. But she would never forget the moment her daughter's heart began to slow unexpectedly, before they had had to decide whether or not to pull the plug. Brian had gone home to shower, and she was alone with Lilly. When the nurse came to ask Maggie if she would like to leave the room, she quietly told her to call Brian, then asked the nurse to leave them alone. She crawled into her daughter's bed and held her one last time. She ran her hand over Lilly's soft skin, held the unmoving hand, stroked her cheek. Maggie spoke softly to Lilly, telling her all the things she would have told her over the so many years she was being robbed of. The beeps got slower and slower, Maggie's voice lower and lower, and, finally, both stopped. Maggie would have lain there forever had Brian not come in to gently tell her the nurses would have to take care of Lilly now.

The police, the investigation, the neighborhood boy were a blur to Maggie. But she couldn't forget the sound the garbage disposal made when the tiny pieces of the note that appeared in her mailbox, written in a lanky scrawl, apologizing for scaring Lilly, were ground to nonexistent.

The relatives, the funeral, the praying every night that she would wake up from the nightmare she was living were yet another blur. But she would never forget the well-meaning uncle standing in front of the small white coffin who told her she could always have more children.

The fact that she didn't give Lilly permission to go outside became a blur, but she would never forget the instant she realized Lilly's head was lying unprotected against the pavement.

The multitude of photography appointments she canceled, telling the office that her assistant Donovan could handle them were a blur. But she couldn't forget that she was in the darkroom playing with her photographs when Lilly got hurt, and now Maggie refused to pick up a camera.

The thousands of pictures of people she had taken over the years became a blur, but she couldn't stop seeing her daughter, lying as still and silent as a photograph on the end of the driveway.

Life became a blur, making Maggie weary with the things she couldn't remember and those she couldn't forget. As the days dragged into weeks, Brian tried to get Maggie back to her "normal routine," as he called it. She liked to snuggle next to his body in bed and pull her favorite blue sheets up over her eyes. But watching the pointless trivia of Jeopardy or the pessimism of the news made her walk away from the television. On the one layover she had attempted with Brian on his flight to Los Angeles, they had to get him out of the cockpit to coax her from the small airplane lavatory where she would have spent the whole flight had they not discovered her. She felt like a marionette; he a puppeteer pulling her strings. She told him she couldn't do life's dance right now and he became impatient. She knew he just wanted to move on, that was Brian's way. To Maggie, every scene in life was an overexposed shot, but it didn't matter since she wasn't looking anyway.

Maggie reached down for the comforter. Brian was in San Diego on a three-day trip, and there was no one to tell her to get out of bed. The ache followed her like a shadow, larger sometimes than others, but always a part of her. As she pulled the comforter over her head, she realized that shadows don't really disappear in the dark; you just can't see them.

Chapter One

Two of the four overhead lights were out on the vaulted kitchen ceiling, giving the room a dingy look. "We need to fix those," Maggie said. She motioned upward when Brian, who was leaning against the sink, looked over.

Maggie, standing next to the stove in a blue flannel bathrobe, flicked a few drops of water into the frying pan. When they disappeared in tiny puffs of smoke, she laid thick pieces of honey-cured bacon across the pan. They immediately began to shrink and sizzle, and a salty, meaty smell hit her nose.

"It's been a long time since we cooked ourselves a late-night snack," Maggie said. The clock on the wall read 11:21 PM. She forced a smile Brian's way.

Brian, still in his uniform minus the tie and jacket, cracked a hard-boiled egg on the stainless steel sink and peeled it. "It's nice to have you awake when I get home from a trip," he said, smiling. "The only thing nicer is having you come with me."

Maggie used to enjoy the time alone with Brian on the day or two getaways in the different cities on his layovers. Now they were alone all the time.

"Tell me again why you can't come to San Fran with me this weekend?" Brian said.

Maggie tore a piece of paper towel off a new roll and put it over the plate she had set next to the stove.

Brian walked up behind her. "It will do us good to get away for a while." He circled her waist with his hands, reached down and kissed her neck.

"That city's so full of people." She turned around to face Brian. He looked ten years older since Lilly's death four weeks ago. He had been prematurely gray for years, but now with the lack of sleep and stress, he could easily be mistaken for fifty-seven rather than the forty-seven years old he was. She ran her finger along the light stubble on his cheek. "I should work."

Brian dropped his hands to his side. "You haven't worked since the accident." He walked back to the sink.

Maggie shrugged her shoulders. They never said "Lilly's death." It was always "the accident."

"I haven't felt like it," she said. "All those happy people."

"Weddings and bar mitzvahs are usually happy occasions." Brian opened and closed the empty egg-slicer. "You have all those bookings."

The smell of burning bacon crept through the room. Maggie pushed the pan off the burner and went to Brian. She put her hands on his arms, felt him flex his muscles under the polyester shirt. "Donovan can handle it," she said. "He's worked for me for over a year now."

"Donovan is just a kid."

"He's older than I was when I had Lilly," she said. She watched him turn his head at the mention of Lilly. "My business is fine."

"Is it?" Brian looked into her eyes. "I think you need to get out more, Maggie."

Maggie walked back to the stove, put the pan back on the burner. She moved the bacon around with the fork. "I get out."

"Grocery shopping is not what I mean."

"This bacon is scorched."

"You need to spend time with people. You won't even let me make plans to have dinner with friends anymore."

"Do you think we can still eat it?" She stabbed a piece with the fork, picked it up, and looked at it closely, then dropped it back into the pan.

"At least *go* to your studio, even if you don't do any of the photography."

Maggie walked to the refrigerator. "I wonder if we have any more. I hate burnt bacon." The cold air swirled around her as she rummaged through the shelves, then the drawers.

"Donovan can't keep doing the work of two people. It's taken you five years to build up your reputation."

Maggie stood up and saw smoke coming from the frying pan. "Now it's really burnt." She yanked the pan off the stove, pushed past Brian and put the whole thing into the sink. Water sputtered and grease flew as Maggie turned the faucet on full blast. A grease splatter hit her eye. She rubbed her fist into her eye. "I'm not ready."

Brian closed his arms around Maggie. "Hurts?"

Maggie clung to Brian, burrowing her face into his chest. The scent of his Eternity cologne mixed with starch from the cleaners and six hours in the cockpit covered the burnt smell. She deeply inhaled the smell that had always meant comfort, because it meant he was home, then turned her head up to his. He brushed his lips against hers.

"It's time you got back to life," Brian said.

"It's only been four weeks." Maggie could feel herself tense at being pushed. Only four weeks and three days, if today was Wednesday, which she thought it was. "Besides, it's not a matter of time. It's a matter of how I feel."

"I don't know what to do for you," Brian said.

"I'm fine."

"No, you're not."

Maggie pulled away. "So I'm not." She walked across the room. "I'm not some problem for you to solve." She rubbed her eye again. "Why do you have to try and fix everything?"

"What does that mean?" Brian's eyes narrowed as he stared at her.

"It means that whenever something is wrong, you try to fix it," Maggie said.

"And that's a bad thing?" He waved his hand in the air. "I do it every day at work."

"Our life is not a goddamn scheduled flight."

"I don't get you." He shook his head. "I'm wrong for trying to make you feel better?"

"Not for trying. For not stopping." She tightened the belt on her robe. "For not letting me feel bad. I don't know." Maggie ran her hands over her face. "Whenever I tell you what's wrong, you tell me ways to fix it. Then expect you me to. What if I just need to feel bad?" She stared at his confused face.

"Why would you want to do that?" Brian looked at her as if she had proposed flying a plane without wings. "Why not try to feel better?"

"It's not that easy," she said. She searched for words that would explain how she felt. "It's what I'm feeling, where I am."

Brian's posture was rigid, his arms crossed against his chest. He looked as if he were ready to get into the cockpit and give orders.

"Land the plane," Maggie said in an exaggerated voice. "Just for a minute, stop trying to be in control. Just *be* with me. Our daughter's dead. Where's the control in that?"

Brian walked across the kitchen and sat down at the table. Maggie moved a chair so she was directly in front of him. On his face, she saw the fight going on inside of him. He looked around the kitchen, his face becoming loose, then his muscles tightened again. His eyebrows shifted up and down, answering internal questions. Finally, he fixed on her face and said, "That was cruel."

"I don't mean to be cruel." Maggie searched for words. "You want me to pretend I feel better so life can continue on its merry way."

"I don't want you to pretend."

"I can't do what you do. You put it out of your mind."

"What's the alternative? Dwell on it?" he said. "How can I work like that?"

"Isn't there a middle of the road for you?" She put her hand on his face and ran a thumb under the dark circle under his eye.

Maggie saw in that moment how different they were. She always spewed her emotions like the hot grease that flew in the kitchen, and he always held them close for fear they would burn him if he let them out. She stood from her chair and sat on his lap, encircling him in her arms. She hadn't seen him cry once since Lilly died.

"Go to work and be in control, and then you could let it out when you're home, when you're with me," Maggie said.

She saw the look of panic in his eyes; then the shield of control fell over his face. She pulled him closer to her. She pictured herself a raging river and Brian piling sandbags, the same ones he used for himself, to hold her back. She realized she could no more push him than he could stop her. With his head nestled in her neck, she smoothed his hair.

"Can you just hold me then, when I need to let it out?" Maggie said. "Instead of telling me not to?"

He shrugged and pulled her close. "It hurts me to see you hurt."

"But I do hurt, Brian. I hurt so badly."

"I can't watch it." He shook his head. "Not on top of everything else." His voice cracked, and she thought for a moment that he was going to cry.

"It'll be okay," she said. She didn't know why she said that. She didn't even believe it. She rocked him the way she rocked Lilly when she got hurt. Or used to. She pulled him closer to her. "Let's go to bed." She kissed the top of Brian's head. They both stood. The pan of burnt bacon and grease sat in the sink. The sliced eggs were crusted over. Bread stood in the toaster waiting for the heat that would make them crisp. Salt, pepper, and mayonnaise stood lined up. "Screw it," Maggie said.

They ascended the stairs one at a time, arms around each other. On the second floor, they passed the guest room without a word, then Lilly's room with a palpable silence. Once inside their bedroom, Maggie closed the door to the rest of the house and went into the bathroom.

Her reflection staring back from the mirror looked like a Diane Arbus portrait—a freak. Arbus called the people in her photos freaks, but then explained they were people who had met their tragedy early in life, knew from the get go what life was about. They learned early that life could deliver a blow that you may never come back from, so these people dropped the facades and didn't bother to live like the rest of us. Didn't even pretend there was a "normal."

Maggie's hair was pulled back into a ponytail; she hadn't washed it that day. Nor had she blown it out or curled in weeks. The miracle cream she'd found in her makeup bag had cracked in a poor attempt at camouflaging her dark circles. Her eyebrows were bushy without the maintenance plucking. She ran her hand over her dry skin. Maggie didn't even pretend to know what normal was anymore. She brushed her teeth but didn't bother to wash her face.

In bed, Maggie rested her head on Brian's shoulder and closed her eyes. She tried to push the picture of Lilly at the end of her driveway out of her mind, and in an attempt to clear her thoughts, she imagined herself diving deep in the clear blue waters off the Bahamas and regulated her breathing to deep, even breaths. She pulled air into her lungs through her mouth, then gently blew it out. She tried to imagine the colorful pink and orange coral, the big bright fish that would be swimming around her. But she couldn't seem to picture them. Instead, she descended in murky water with the heavy tank and BC pulling her deeper. The gauge was getting low, and she was getting farther and farther from the surface.

Chapter Two

Maggie squinted through the scorching July sun that beamed down on her windshield, looking for signs for the Turnpike South, and then glanced down at the hand-written map on the seat next to her as she drove along the quiet one-way street in Ft. Pierce. She suspected she was lost, but figured eventually she'd find the street she needed.

She'd just finished her first shoot in seven weeks. While Donovan had been doing all of her work up until now, the appointment she had just finished had been made over a year ago with long-time clients. They had moved two hours north of her home but still insisted she do their wedding pictures. It had gone just fine. Simple stuff. Lots of gaiety, food, and relatives. And children.

I just wish life was as it had been. The phrase started going around and around in her head, as it had for the last seven weeks, pressing against her temples, the way the tires of her Ford Explorer pressed on the asphalt as she drove, trying to find her way. Maggie made a few more turns, wishing her car had a GPS or at least a compass. Finally, up ahead in the distance, she saw an overpass, then signs for the Florida Turnpike. North to Orlando, or south to Miami—towards home.

Maggie and Lilly had always joked about just getting on the Turnpike and going north all the way to Disney World to see Mickey Mouse. There had always been some reason they couldn't: Dad waiting at home, schoolwork to be done, pictures to be taken. Maggie pulled her car to the right and got on the entrance to the Turnpike going north. She opened her windows and let the hot air rush around her face. The atmosphere in the car felt thick due to the humidity, and when she took a deep breath, Maggie was sure she could smell the moisture.

An empty plastic bag in the back seat began to swirl around, lifted by the hot breeze. Maggie looked into her rear view mirror and watched the bag, as puffy as a jellyfish, buoy up, as she began to wonder for the millionth time: what if she hadn't been in the darkroom that day? What if she'd heard the honk sooner? What if Lilly had worn her helmet? What if any of those things had prevented the subarachnoid hemorrhage that had taken Lilly's life? The bag began to float toward the rear window. A loud honk made her realize she was drifting over into the next lane of traffic. She pulled the car back into the right-hand lane, closed the back windows, and decided she needed some coffee, some distraction from the monotony of the road and the torment from her thoughts. A glance at the clock told her that Brian wouldn't be home for hours.

At the next service plaza, Maggie pulled her car to the left and headed into the parking lot. She found a spot upfront and moved the air conditioning vent toward her face as she stared at all of the people going in and out of the entrance.

She was about to get out of the car when she noticed a boy and girl, both about eighteen years old, walking out of the building. The boy's hair was shoulder-length and carefully uncombed, his hand in the back pocket of the girl's jeans. The girl was talking and looking up at the boy, smiling, but the boy just stared straight ahead, ignoring her. Finally the girl turned her head away, her brows creased, her lips pressed tightly together as if to not let another word escape her mouth.

For a split second, the hope that Lilly would never date such an unkempt and inattentive boy flashed into her mind, but before the thought could even form, she realized the impossibility. Reality tightened around her heart like a noose, causing her to take a slow deep breath. She put her head down, telling herself not here, not now. She'd gotten good at stuffing the grief down when she needed to. She took it out late at night, when Brian wasn't around, and let it rush over her like the raging water from a broken dam. She would find the smallest rooms in her house, sometimes her walk-in closet, and sit with the door closed, even when no one was home. Somehow she felt the four walls, the restricted space, were the only way to confine her sorrow. But the large windows of her car would expose her grief to the world, and today she chose not to share.

When she lifted her head, a family of four walked out of the plaza doors, mother, father, and two daughters. The younger daughter, about Lilly's age, was stomping her feet and had her arms crossed against her chest. The girl stopped, and the family walked on for a few minutes when the older sister of about fourteen realized she was missing. Maggie noticed the pout on the young girl's face and reached around to the back seat for her camera bag, her camera still loaded with film used for the candid shots at the wedding. She looked through the lens of her camera as the mother knelt down next to the child. *You've already had a vanilla frozen yogurt. You can't have a chocolate one, too,* she might be saying. The child began yelling, and Maggie imagined it would be something like: *But I want it.* She opened her camera bag and quickly put her zoom lens on her camera. Maggie rolled down her window and aimed just as the girl hauled off and hit her mother. Shock, and then laughter, hit Maggie, and she had trouble keeping the camera with the heavy lens still, as she shot through the father coming over and picking up the child by the waist, carrying her off like a large bag of garden soil. All the while, Maggie focused in on the pain and anger on the young girl's face.

When they were out of sight, she lowered the camera, thinking of the fine line parents walk between appeasing and spoiling a child—what a difficult balancing act it is. She raised the camera to her eye and found an elderly couple moving slowly, he with a walker and she with patience. Maggie took a series of shots, then moved her field of vision back to the plaza door and waited.

A parade of people went by, and Maggie snapped a picture now and then, realizing that the sun was going down, and light to shoot was no longer optimal. Then a family approached the plaza: mother, father, daughter, and dog. As the group got closer, the father moved off toward the grass, dragging the little beagle with him. The mother pulled the little girl toward the entrance. The small girl, about three years old with shiny black hair that matched the color of the beagle's body, walked sideways, her arm outstretched for her dog. Maggie kept the two in the shot for as long as she could—the beagle barking and the girl tugging. Then Maggie focused the zoom lens on the girl's face. Sadness pulled at her features like a draw-string, creating a puckered pout. Maggie captured the upturned face, the pleading eyes, the silent cries. She shot through the twilight, knowing the pictures wouldn't come out well, yet unwilling to put the camera down.

Chapter Three

A few days later, Maggie walked into her strip mall studio, exchanged pleasantries with Gerlinde, her receptionist and right-hand woman, and then walked back to the work area to check on some pictures before she headed out to a Sweet Sixteen shoot at a home in Weston. She was surprised to find Donovan, her assistant photographer, sitting at the print table, his head bent over a stack of pictures. He turned and smiled when he heard her come in.

"What're you doing here? You haven't had a day off in weeks." she said. She watched him turn his head back to the photos, his almost snow-white ponytail bobbing behind him. Today, his black t-shirt accentuated his albinism, something she rarely noticed after working so closely with him.

"Julie has a nasty cold. I got her some soup and tissues and put her to bed. I left so she could take a nap," he said. He waved a handful of pictures. "These are the outdoor wedding you did the other day?"

Maggie nodded her head. "What a good husband."

"Interesting," he said.

"Your married life or my pictures?"

"Is this all of them? Do you need help deciding what proofs to show them when they get back from their honeymoon?"

"I already picked the best." Maggie started to gather the pictures into a pile.

"Where're the rest?"

Maggie held the pictures tightly. "These are the best."

"The picture of the groom feeding the bride has him stabbing her in the lip with the fork. Didn't they redo it?"

"Yes."

"And?"

"And," Maggie hesitated, then said, "I didn't get the shot."

"You didn't get the shot?" His voice was low, more astonished than accusing.

"I could swear I took the shot, but then when I looked for it, it wasn't in the sequence." Maggie flipped through the photos, laying them on the table. "It's not here. It's not on the negatives."

Donovan picked up a picture of the bride's mother. The elderly woman wore a ruffled, flower-patterned dress and was crying. A tree branch created a shadow over her face that Maggie hadn't noticed when she'd set up the shot. "Did her daughter just marry a serial killer?" Donovan said.

Maggie looked at the picture, then at Donovan's face where a small smile was escaping his lips. The impression of agony on the mother's face was undeniable. Maggie put her hand to her mouth but couldn't contain her laughter. "I didn't see it. I was trying to get the emotional-mother shot."

"Look at this one." Donovan flipped a picture on top of the pile. It was the traditional shot of the groom taking the blue garter off the bride's leg. The groom had the garter just below the knee and his smile was glorious. But looking closely, Maggie could see the all the way up the bride's dress to the crotch of her pantyhose.

Maggie bent over with laughter, then sobered, ready to cry. "I've ruined their day."

"Not if they're Diane Arbus fans. It brings new meaning to our slogan, 'We promise you'll never forget your special day.'" He held up a picture of the wedding party, and she saw that the ring bearer, aged five, was picking his nose.

Maggie switched back to peals of laughter.

"You two okay?" Gerlinde said from the door.

"Maggie's just redefining our photographic philosophy, is all." Donovan waved her away.

Donovan got up and steered Maggie to a chair. As she wiped her eyes, unable to decide if she wanted to laugh or cry, he piled up the pictures and turned them over. She looked at his amused face and started to giggle again. After a few minutes, she got up for a tissue and wiped her face.

"I haven't laughed like that in…" she searched her mind, "…too long. It would be worth it if it wasn't such a disaster." She plopped back down into the chair and rubbed her forehead. "What was I thinking? I thought I could do it. I'd promised them."

"I guess you weren't. You have a lot on your mind these days." After a few minutes of silence, Donovan went on. "These, on the other hand," he said as he reached for another stack of pictures, "are like nothing I've ever seen you do."

Maggie got up to see what he was talking about, then reached out her hand to grab the pictures when she saw they were the ones she'd shot at the rest stop the afternoon after the wedding. "I didn't realize I'd left those here." She shuffled the pictures like a deck of cards, unsure why she was embarrassed he had seen them.

Donovan shrugged. "I've already looked through them. They were lying here on the bench," he said. When she didn't answer, he got up from the stool. "I'd better get going."

Maggie looked down at the top picture. The little girl being carted off by her father was off centered in the frame, her features all squeezed together. Softly, she said, "They're bad, huh?"

Donovan walked toward her. "No. They're actually quite good."

A crimson blush filled his face as the same thought must have occurred to him that occurred to Maggie: He had described the pictures as both good and like nothing she'd ever done before.

"I meant they are good in a creative way that I've never seen you do before," Donovan said. He seemed to cringe. "I mean—"

"It's okay," Maggie said, cutting him off. "Just tell me why you think they're good." Maggie couldn't hide her excitement. She, too, had loved the pictures and had been back to the Turnpike plazas a few times since those had been taken. She had a darkroom full of film to process and develop.

Donovan reached for the pictures and shuffled through to one of the elderly couple: the woman, full face, eyes cast down, sadness mixed with resignation, and the man's head slightly tipped up, bushy unkempt eyebrows framing eyes glazed with pain. "You have captured what their life must be like—in one frame."

Then it wasn't just her wishful thinking. The pictures were good. She started to look for another picture to show him, then remembered her afternoon appointment. "Oh, damn," she said as she looked up at the clock. "I have that Sweet Sixteen in twenty minutes in Weston."

Donovan looked toward the wedding pictures on the workbench. "I'll go."

"You have the day off, and it's booked as my appointment."

"Julie and I aren't going to the IMAX because she's sick. I'll do the shoot. Why don't you take the afternoon off?"

"I thought I was the boss," Maggie said, laughing. "Why…"

Donovan picked up a picture from the wedding pile.

"Oh," Maggie said. She couldn't deny what was in front of her. "I'll be sure I'm focused." She said the statement almost as if it were a question.

Donovan nodded slowly, then said, "Take some time, boss. I'll do the shoot."

Maggie looked at the pale blue eyes that stared back at her. *Let Friends and Family Help You at a Time Like This* was the title of the chapter she had skimmed through last night with Brian in her latest grief book. Donovan, too, had a stake in the business that she had been sorely neglecting the last few months. If her business fell off, she wouldn't need an assistant. "Thanks," she said.

Chapter Four

Maggie sat in her car at the Ft. Pierce plaza, staring at the pink building with the bright blue roof, the checkerboard trim, and wondering why this was chosen to represent Florida. With Donovan's positive comments about her photos and the afternoon free, Maggie knew just what she wanted to do with her time, and it wasn't go home to an empty house. She had just been at the Ft. Pierce plaza two days ago, and her plan had been to stay closer to home today, but while she'd been driving, she realized that it was two months to the day since Lilly's death. She had already gotten to mile marker 130, way past West Palm, when she noticed where she was.

After circling the parking lot three times, Maggie finally found a spot up front, yet just a few spots over from the front door so as not to be conspicuous. She'd gone in for snacks, then settled in to watch as the inevitable parade of interesting people continued before her. Although some days were better than others, she always managed to get three or four rolls of pictures.

Maggie took her camera out of her bag just as a couple came out of the plaza, the woman walking just a few steps behind the man. He had long legs and took big steps. The woman seemed to hurry but couldn't quite keep up. Maggie raised the camera, and through the zoom lens, she saw the woman wore a theatrical amount of make-up. As Maggie snapped the shutter, the woman wiped the corners of her lips, which seemed to have a fresh coat of glossy lipstick on them. One hand arranged her hair while the other reached out and tried to catch the man's elbow.

Snap. What she liked with this couple was the pure anxiety on the woman's face contrasted by the oblivion on the man's. Snap. Come on, Maggie rooted the woman on. Walk faster. Maggie wanted to catch both faces in the same frame. She pulled back on the close up, hoping she could catch the emotion on an enlargement. The value of this shot was getting them together. By the time the woman caught up to the man, Maggie could only see the backs of their heads. Damn. Maybe it would make a nice solo shot.

Maggie watched the crowd, then couldn't believe what she saw next. A clown was walking up to the plaza. It wasn't the green afro, the red-polka-dotted jumpsuit, or the plain brown loafers with white crew socks that made her reach for her camera. It was the way the clown sauntered up to the door while his hand moved double time to bring a cigarette to his lips, smoke furiously pouring out of his nostrils. He paused at the door to finish his smoke.

Maggie cursed as she ran out of film and struggled to get a new roll in before the smoking clown disappeared. She quickly put the film on the little black prongs of the roller, threaded the film, and closed the camera. When she looked up, the clown was nowhere in sight.

Maggie was pleased when she got the clown on the way out, as well as the children who followed him like the Pied Piper. Cigarette in mouth, the clown stopped to give the children charms from his baggy pants pockets. She doubted she would top that today, but wasn't ready to head for home yet so she settled back to watch the crowd.

Maggie noticed the sun was setting and knew she didn't have much time left. Then a family came out of the plaza; the mother walked rapidly ahead, while the father, a thin man wearing a baseball cap, seemed to be pulling the daughter along. The daughter was skipping rapidly to keep up, her short legs no match for the man's long strides. Maggie raised her camera to her eye and snapped the three of them, then focused on the child's face. Perfect. Snap. The child had a mixture of excitement and fear on her face. Maggie wondered what the father had threatened the child with if she didn't hurry up. Snap.

Maggie suddenly remembered that when she was young, her mother would say: "Stop crying or I'll give you something to cry about." One more thing in life that didn't make sense. Maggie moved the camera to the father's face, but he was impassive. He seemed a little odd, unbalanced, a little too thin, an Arbus character. She took a shot of the father and child, then panned out to look for the mother, but she wasn't anywhere in sight. Maggie refocused on the child. Snap. Poor baby, Maggie thought. The little girl disappeared, and Maggie lowered the camera to her lap. The sun was going down, and it was time to go home.

Chapter Five

Maggie opened her front door, distracted by the fact that Brian's car was in the driveway. He wasn't due home until Friday, and today was Thursday. Her key was stuck in the lock and she was trying to get it loose.

"Hey."

Maggie looked up to see Brian leaning against the kitchen doorframe, wiping his hands with a yellow-checkered kitchen towel.

"Hey to you," Maggie said, finally pulling the key out of the door. She slid her camera bag off her should to the table in the hallway. "What are you doing home?" She walked over and hugged him.

"Equipment failure in Dallas. I deadheaded home to surprise you." He kissed her forehead, then released the hug. He pulled back to look into her face. "I called you a million times."

"My cell phone was off."

He raised his eyebrows as if prompting an explanation, and when she didn't answer, he said, "I made dinner. It's rather dry now."

"You know I only use my cell phone for work changes or emergencies," she hesitated, then went on, "or so Lilly could reach me."

Brian's face tightened as he turned to walk back into the kitchen.

Maggie followed Brian and watched as he took the lid off a large pot and began stirring with a wooden spoon. "Beef stew," he said.

Maggie walked to the refrigerator to get the pitcher of iced tea, then stopped and stared at a picture of the three of them at Flamingo Gardens, a local orange grove. "Remember how she loved to suck the orange juice right out of the orange with that plastic contraption they sold?"

"Sit down. Dinner is all ready," Brian said.

Maggie walked right by the set table to a wide drawer. She began to rummage around the space next to the silverware divider for the short plastic straw-like device. "She kept it in here," she said.

"I was going to make rolls to go with the stew, but there weren't any in the freezer," Brian said.

Maggie picked up a can opener and put in on the kitchen counter. "It has to be here."

"Iced tea, or would you like me to open a bottle of wine?"

Maggie piled a potato peeler on top of an egg whisk. "Where could it be?" She threw a lemon zester on top of the pile.

"Maggie, come eat dinner."

"It has to be here." She grabbed the contents of the drawer and began tossing them onto the counter.

"Stop, Maggie."

Maggie pulled the silverware divider out, and stuck in the corner of the drawer was the small blue orange-sipper. She closed her hand around the plastic tube and held it tight. She turned to face Brian.

"I found it." Bringing the tube to her lips, she said, "Remember how Lilly—"

"Stop." Brain slammed his hand on the stove.

Maggie looked up in surprise. "Lilly loves this."

"She hadn't used it in years, Maggie. Now put the damn thing down and come and eat."

"She used it all the time."

Brian looked from Maggie's hand, to her face, then out the window. "Fine," he said as he nodded his head. "Now stop."

Maggie watched as Brian's face became neutral, as if the circuit breaker that supplied its energy had been thrown. This happened every time she brought up Lilly. "Stop what, Brian?"

"Stop…" His voice trailed off and he walked to the table.

"Stop talking about her?" She watched him sit down and put a thin paper napkin on his lap. "As if she never existed?"

Brian rearranged the silverware next to his plate, moving the knife and fork one inch one way, then back the other way. "It's like rubbing salt into a wound."

Maggie stared at Brian. She walked to the table and sat on the chair next to him. "No, it's not. It's like immersing yourself in her memories." She reached out her hand to hold his. "It's all we have, Brian."

Brian pulled back his hand and stood suddenly, knocking the chair backwards. "Stop talking about her as if she's in the next room, as if she going to come home from school any minute." His voice got louder as he paced around the kitchen. "Stop talking about her as if she's still…" his voice trailed off. He came to stand in front of Maggie. "She's dead, god-damnit." He was breathing heavily, as if he'd just come back from a run. "Stop talking about her."

Maggie stared in surprise, Brian looming over her. He may as well have asked her to stop breathing. She stood to face him. "I can't."

"Well, I can't listen," he said. He turned and walked out of the kitchen.

Chapter Six

Maggie sat at the kitchen table, drinking her third cup of coffee and staring out the window at the lake. She and Brian had gone to bed without speaking, and this morning he didn't bother to wake her to say good-bye before leaving for his golf game. For the first time since she was married, Maggie regretted not having the kinds of girlfriends she had had in college. The kind you could talk to about anything. She had isolated herself with Brian, then been too busy with her life: her photography and Lilly. There were women she called friends, the wives of couples she and Brian went out to dinner with, but the few times she'd seen them and tried to talk about Lilly, their faces froze in forced and painful smiles, not even wanting to go where she would take them…to realizing what their lives would be like if fate had knocked on their doors instead of hers. Instead, conversations danced around the periphery of her pain, making her ache but never giving her the chance to purge.

She took one more sip of overly sweetened coffee and let her eyes move from the still, placid lake to the kitchen that looked as if a tornado had just pasted thorough. She didn't know where to begin. The house was in terrible need of attention. She wanted to tell herself that it was all the hours at the studio, the hours put into her craft, but the truth was she didn't care. What did it matter if there was lint on the carpet? What did it matter that there were dust balls on the tile? She'd even started naming them, instead of cleaning them up. In the entryway were the three blind mice— three balls of dust all the same size. She must be losing her mind. She had promised herself she would clean at least one room before she allowed herself to go to the darkroom. And even that was a mess.

Maggie turned on the television in the kitchen and started to unload the dishwasher: the same glasses, the same dishes, the same forks, every day. A derailed train, a University of Miami football player accused of hitting his wife, a child kidnapped on her way home from school. It was all the same. When Lilly died, there had been no television coverage.

Maggie reached for the bowl that stood out on the top shelf of her dishwasher as she turned to see an image of a child on the TV screen. She started to walk toward the television and the bowl slipped from her hand, hit the tile, and broke into pieces. Damn. She had become so clumsy since Lilly died, as if part of her brain had stopped working when Lilly's did.

On her knees, Maggie picked up one of the larger pieces. She ran her hand along the colorful pattern. She'd broken five dishes in the last two months, but this one was different. It was one of those dishes sold in the supermarket, a different piece each week, until you completed the set. This was a small bowl with scalloped edges and a garish red, blue, and yellow pattern. She had bought only one at Lilly's insistence. Lilly had said the bowl looked like an instant carnival and that it made her happy just to look at it. She had eaten her cereal out of it every morning. Maggie had eaten her own cereal out of it just yesterday morning, the first time she could look at it and not cry. Maggie held the sharp pieces tightly. "I'm sorry, Lilly." She shook her head and felt the tears coming.

Maggie turned when she heard an insistent voice on the television. "Please help. I cannot lose my daughter." A man's face was framed on the screen with several microphones near his face. The scene changed to a picture of a young girl with a ponytail, laughing, sitting on a swing. The camera closed in on the girl's face.

Maggie sat on the floor among the broken pieces and stared. "Lilly."

The screen switched to a car lot, and Maggie found out this was her last chance to buy a Honda at rock bottom prices from the largest dealer in the south.

Had the girl really looked like Lilly? She was younger, but her hair was blonde and something about her eyes reminded Maggie of her daughter. Looked familiar. Maggie stood up and went to the drawer that held the superglue. She rummaged around the accumulated junk and stopped when she saw the angel pin. Maggie picked it up out of the drawer and stared at it. It had a pearl for the head, and tiny crystal beads lined the wire wings. Lilly had made it for her last Mother's Day. Maggie'd worn it a few times and forgotten about it. She ran her finger over the wire wings, then pinned it to her blouse. The left wing was slightly larger and pulled the angel off balance. Maggie patted the pin in place, promising herself she would wear it every day, then continued to look for the superglue.

When she found the glue, she laid a paper towel on the counter and collected all the pieces of bowl she could find. She put them together like a puzzle, then began to glue them in place. When she was done, she had a bowl full of cracks and missing pieces. It would never hold cereal or milk again, but Maggie refused to throw it out. She looked at the half-emptied dishwasher, the sink full of dirty dishes, the shards of pottery she needed to vacuum off the floor. She walked across the kitchen and snapped the television off. The bowl was cradled in her arm as she walked down the hall to the darkroom.

Once inside she looked around at the disarray. Maggie placed the bowl on the counter. She would keep it in here from now on, where it couldn't get broken. She began to put the film, lined up and begging to be developed, into the bowl. When it could hold no more, she stood back and admired the bowl's new purpose. Cleaning up is cleaning up, she said to herself as she began to take some of the dried prints off the drying line. Then she glanced at the clock and saw she had plenty of time before she would have to start dinner for Brian when he got home from his golf game. Enough time to see what some of the pictures held.

Maggie put on *Kind of Blue*, a Miles Davis CD, turned the volume down low, and settled in at her workbench. She decided to start with the most recent plaza shoot. Maggie arranged everything she needed in front of her, then turned out the light and sat at her bench in total darkness. She uncapped the flat end of the film-canister with a can opener and trimmed off the film leader. The repetitious routine of developing film was soothing somehow. It was a process she used to do all the time without thinking, but today she let her hands feel the bow of the film as it slid between her right thumb and index finger. She slowly threaded the film onto the reel and sank it into the developing tank, conscious of her lack of ability to see what she was feeling. She sealed the top of the tank and turned the light back on.

Maggie blinked at the brightness, then set about finishing the developing process. She took the wet film out of the developing tank, squeegeed the strip, running the tongs from top to bottom in one stroke, then left it to dry. She turned her attention to film she had already developed, anxious to make some prints. She measured and poured the chemicals into the trays, arranging them in the order she would use them.

She cut the film into strips of six, switched on the safe light, turned the overhead light off, and put paper and negatives into the contact frame. As the contact printed in the amber darkness, she squinted at Lilly's pictures on her corkboard. After Lilly died, Maggie had placed her favorite photos of each year of Lilly's life in chronological order on the board so she had a timeline that showed her daughter from birth to present. She now wondered what Lilly would have looked like, been like, had she been allowed to grow up. First she saw her tall and beautiful with wavy blond hair, high cheekbones. Then she saw puberty: braces, breasts, pimples, and rebellion. What she wouldn't give to have one fight with Lilly over taking the car or getting a tattoo.

Silence surrounded Maggie, and she realized she had no recollection of the CD going off. She rubbed her hand on the small of her back, massaging the tightness out of the muscle. Hunched over her workbench and looking through the magnifying viewer, she laughed out loud when she saw the pictures of the "smoking clown." These were great shots, definitely worth enlarging. There were about twenty, shot in rapid succession, with great close-ups of the expressions of both the clown and the kids who followed him for the charms he produced from his pockets.

She moved to the next frame and saw a family with a small girl of about five. Then to the next frame with father and daughter, then on to a single shot of the little girl. She held the loop over the tiny picture and felt a glimmer of recognition stir in her brain, the eyes in the picture reminding her of Lilly. Then Maggie got a stronger magnifying glass and stared at the face of the little girl. She moved back and forth between the shots of the little girl, trying to remember exactly how she had moved, trying to see her in motion, not just in the still clips she had before her. The memory was there, but elusive, somehow.

Maggie grabbed the magnifying glass and the contact and went into the kitchen where she found Brian at the table reading the newspaper.

"I didn't know you were home," Maggie said. She glanced at the clock and realized Brian must have been home from his golf game for over an hour.

"You were working; I didn't want to bother you."

Brian had always interrupted her darkroom time, as if it were an inconvenience to him. She wondered if he was being nice, trying in his own way to make-up, or if he was still angry.

Maggie walked over to where he was sitting. "Thanks," she said, kissing his cheek. "Really." She put the contact and magnifying glass down on the table and grabbed the newspaper, riffling through it. She found what she'd come out to look for: an article about the missing girl who she had seen on the news, accompanied by a picture.

"Look at this picture, Brian." She sat down at the table and put her contact next to the black and white photo. She moved the magnifying glass over the thumbnail contact enlarging the girl's picture, then looked back and forth between the two. "This is her!"

"Her who?" Brian said as he continued reading the financial page.

"Brian, it's the little girl that's missing. I thought she looked familiar. Look."

She got up and took the financial page from his hand. In front of him, she set down the newspaper picture with her contact next to it. "Frame 24, this one." She pointed to the headshot of the girl and handed him the magnifying glass.

"I was reading, Mag," Brian said.

"Please, Brian."

Brian moved the magnifying glass over the contact, then over the newspaper. "That's amazing."

"Do you see it?"

"Yeah, the newspaper photo is full of dots. It's like pointillism." He turned his head with the magnifying glass in front of his eye like Sherlock Holmes.

"Brian! That's the missing girl."

Brian looked offended and turned around. "You used to like my sense of humor."

Maggie smiled. "Good try, Sherlock, now please?"

Brian looked back at the pictures. "I don't know, Maggie. They don't even have the same color hair. The blonde looks like Lilly." He picked up Maggie's darkroom contact. "Where did you take these pictures?"

Maggie's stomach tightened. She hadn't told Brian she'd been to the plazas every chance she had—even canceling appointments to go. She took the contact from him.

"I know, but look at her face," Maggie said. "Those eyes. It's her, Brian, I'm sure." Maggie's eyes darted back and forth between the two pictures. "I have to call someone. Is there a number with the article?"

Brian stared at Maggie. "You're too busy with work to come with me on layovers, yet you have time for your hobby."

"It's not just my 'hobby,' Brian," she said. "I love taking these kinds of pictures." She wanted to make him understand. "When I'm on a layover with you," she said, "I have to be up and perky because your whole crew is around and I'm the Captain's wife. When I'm out there at the plazas watching the world go by, no one can see me, and I just feel whatever I need to feel. It's different than just sitting in the house alone. I interact with these people."

"You talk to them?"

She shook her head. "I capture their expressions when they don't know anyone is watching. Honest expressions. Their faces and body language tell me their stories."

She looked at Brian's face. "I have other pictures if you want to see what I mean."

Brian shook his head.

"No, you wouldn't."

Brian stood up. "I've got to go. I have to leave for my poker game in thirty minutes. I'd better go shower and change."

"I never made dinner," Maggie said. Brian waved his hand in a dismissive way. She watched him leave the kitchen and sat down at the table, shaking her head.

Then the article she came out to find caught her attention. The little girl was Mira Vega, the five-year-old daughter of a prominent Miami defense attorney, and she had been abducted while on her way home from school. The housekeeper said she had been making a turn on a quiet street in Coral Gables, as she did everyday, when a "bum" stumbled in front of her car and fell. Thinking she had hit the man, she got out of her car to see if he was okay. He then subdued her with a "chemical on a rag" and grabbed the child. The housekeeper was found, unconscious, on the street where the incident occurred. Another resident of the area said she had seen a suspicious man two days before while driving her son home. She'd forgotten about the man until questioned by police. There was no ransom note as of yet, but because of Nestor Vega's wealth and high profile in the community, police were not ruling out the possibility. A $100,000 reward was offered for any tips leading to the safe return of the little girl. As to whether or not Mr. and Mrs. Vega would host their upcoming annual fundraising gala for the Jackson Memorial Ronald McDonald House that was scheduled to be held in only one week, Mr. Vega had replied, "We hope our daughter will be safe at home by then."

Maggie stared at the newspaper. What were the odds that she would randomly capture a kidnapper on film? The only thing going faster than her thoughts was her pulse, and she tried to calm them both down. This was the same girl, she was almost sure. But then, Brian didn't think so. She moved the loop back and forth between the single shot of the little girl and the newspaper. Had Brian even looked long enough to make a decision? Or was he still annoyed with her? She would enlarge and print all of the pictures with the little girl in them, and then the similarities would be clearer. She gathered up her stuff and headed back to the darkroom.

***

Maggie decided to print an 8 x 10 of the solo shot of the little girl first. She immersed the exposed paper into the developer and set the timer for one minute. She was amazed at how fast a minute went by most of the time, yet, sometimes, like now, and when she had waited on her driveway for the ambulance, minutes could feel like a lifetime.

She rocked the tray too hard and developer splashed over the rim. As the image began to appear, Maggie became more and more convinced that this was the little girl. Her eyes never left the little girl's eyes as she lifted the paper with tongs from the stop bath into the fixer. Maggie held the newspaper photo next to the fixer tray. The hair was definitely different, both the color and the length. She analyzed the chin, the structure of the cheekbones, the nose. These were details Maggie stared at for a living. The two pictures were from different angles but there was so much similarity. She remembered the little girl being almost dragged by the man. And Maggie remembered the eyes—wide with excitement, looking around, taking everything in.

She finished the developing process and set the print to dry, then turned her attention to the rest of the sequence. She looked at the three people, the distance between their bodies, the angles at which they walked to each other. She realized she only had one shot of the person she had assumed to be the mother and was beginning to think she had been wrong. She knew—had used it in her work—how proximity or visual alignment could imply a relationship whether real or imagined. Maybe she had assumed it was a family when it was only the abductor and the child.

Maggie enlarged all the pictures containing the little girl, five of them in all, and confirmed the similarities to her memory of the TV clip and the newspaper photo in facial expression, eyes, and body movement in each one, wishing she had taken more. When she set the last one to dry, she glanced at the clock. It was 3 am. She was certain that with the enlargements and the easier-to-see details of the girl's face and eyes, Brian would see that this was the little girl when he got home, which should be soon. In the morning, she would call the number she had seen for Crimestoppers and find out how she could go about getting these pictures into the right hands. She stretched her back and then put her head down on her arm on the workbench, staring at the little girl.

***

In the dream, Tim Schiavone, the boy who had caused Lilly's fall when he had lost control of his car, was playing basketball on his driveway with a young boy with a red crew cut. The little boy jumped far too high to slam-dunk the ball, swinging on the rim for just a second. As he floated back to the ground, he turned his head to look at her, and she saw it was Lilly in disguise. Maggie had found her! All this time that she thought Lilly was dead, she had been here, right under her nose. She ran to reclaim Lilly, and as will happen in a dream, the two boys were suddenly riding in a convertible hearse. Tim drove while Lilly-the-red-headed-boy sat up on the back seat waving good-bye as if she were a beauty queen in a parade. As they passed Maggie, Tim hissed, "I fooled you, Ms. Miller." Maggie ran after the car while Tim continued to yell her name, calling her Maggie now, in a mocking tone.

Maggie woke, panting, as she felt Brian shake her. "Maggie."

"She's alive." She sat upright, her head pounding, then looked around the room, surprised to find herself slumped over the worktable in her darkroom.

"Who?"

"Lilly." Maggie's voice was barely audible. Maggie stared at the pictures she had developed, then over to the corkboard where Lilly's pictures hung. She rubbed her temples to ease her headache and wiped her eyes as she came fully out of the dream.

"Lilly?" He pulled Maggie to him. "Lilly's gone, Mag."

"It was so real, Brian. She was just down the street, but her hair was red and short and spiky, like she was on a funky MTV music video."

"Maggie." Brian tried to soothe her.

"I was calling her, but she just kept going, getting farther and farther away..." Maggie's voice caught, and she couldn't finish. Her stomach was tight, and she couldn't shake the fresh grief of realizing all over again that Lilly was dead.

"Stop, Maggie." Brian's voice was losing its soothing tone. There was an edge of command to it now.

"She was right there, Brian. I just wanted to hug her again." She turned her head up to him. "Just once more. Can you imagine how good that would feel?"

Brian pulled away from her. "There's no sense wanting what we can't have." Brian looked at the pictures on the workbench. "Have you been working all night?"

She nodded.

He kissed the top of her head. "Come. I'll take you to bed." He took her hand and tugged her toward him.

Maggie stood and started to walk out of the room, but then stopped. "Wait." She went back to the table and picked up the 8 x 10 she had developed of the little girl. "Will you look at this?" She handed him the picture.

He took it, looked, and nodded. "Nice. A little blurry." He handed it back to her.

"It's *her*, Brian." She handed him the picture from the paper.

Brian held the newspaper photo of the missing girl next to the picture Maggie had developed. After a moment, he shook his head as he tapped the newspaper and said, "This girl looks like Lilly. This girl," he tapped the photo, "does not. They don't look at all alike, Maggie."

"How can you say that?" She squinted through the headache. "Look at the eyes. They have the same eyes: Lilly, the red-headed boy, Mira…"

Brian's eyes went back and forth between the pictures. "I don't see it." He shrugged his shoulders.

"Look." Maggie held the two pictures up. "It's my girl. It's Mira—"

"*Your* girl?"

"Yes, yes," she said. Her voice was getting loud. "Look, Brian."

He turned away.

"You aren't looking," Maggie yelled, putting the pictures in front of his face.

Brian grabbed the pictures, crumpling them in his hands. "Stop."

"Stop," Maggie yelled back. She grabbed the crumpled pictures, pushing him away from her. "Give me my girls!"

Brian let go of the pictures. He held Maggie's wrists and stared at her.

"Let go of me," Maggie said as she struggled to pull away. When her eyes met his, she stopped moving.

"Let me get you to bed." Brian took the pictures and laid them on the workbench. He led Maggie to the bedroom, with her giving him no resistance. She was tired, her head pounded, and she had no fight left in her.

In the bedroom, Maggie sat on the edge of the bed with Brian next to her.

"Maggie," Brian said, turning her head so their eyes met. "Sometimes you see things just because you want to. You…" he seemed to be searching for words, then added, "fill in the blanks. Like the stories you make up to go with your pictures?" He arched his eyebrows as if she had no choice but to admit this truth. When she still didn't say anything he added, "Like the dream? That wasn't real, either."

Maggie opened her mouth to protest, then clenched her jaws together. Yes, she made up stories to go with her pictures, but not this time. And the dream… *No sense wanting what you can't have.* Anger began to swell inside her, taking over the fatigue.

"I don't understand you," she said. "I want what I want, and I feel what I feel, and I see what I see. Not what I'm supposed to want or feel or see. And I know when I make things up. The dream is made up. This is not." She could feel her heart pounding.

Brian pulled her to him. "Are you sure?"

Maggie saw the angel pin hanging off of her blouse, then she saw the image that had haunted her for six weeks: Lilly lying on the driveway, as still and motionless as a photo. Suddenly Lilly had a red crew cut. Maggie groaned as she remembered the dream of Lilly alive and living down the street all this time. She put her head in her hands. She couldn't stop seeing the boy with the red-headed crew cut turn his face to her, and it was Lilly's eyes that looked back. She leaned back on the bed. She was so tired. Lilly's eyes became the eyes of the little girl from the plaza shoot, and Maggie felt as if she were losing her mind. Then the eyes of the missing little girl looked back at her and she couldn't shut them out no matter how tightly she squeezed her own eyes closed. The headache was getting worse.

Brian lay down on the bed and held her. Flashes of eyes and hair colors began to mix themselves up in her mind and she remembered a book she had when she was young. There were three flaps to the book and she could interchange the forehead and eyes, nose, and mouth and chin of different characters and cartoon animals, each combination creating a different character. She had loved to put a princess's crown, forehead and eyes with a witch's nose and chin.

She wasn't sure about anything as she closed her eyes and willed the headache to go away.

Chapter Seven

Maggie slowly woke as she felt Brian's hand on her back, massaging just the muscles she had cramped while sitting in the dark room. She arched her back into the kneading; it felt so soothing. Brian's lips moved slowly on her neck and the kneading became more gentle as his hand moved to her waist, then her buttocks. Maggie moaned and arched further into Brian's hand. She was in that netherland between sleep and awareness and was trying not to come fully awake.

She could hear Brian's soft moan as he moved his hand around her hips to her stomach, caressing gently. He pulled her to him and she could feel his erection, hard against her back. He took her earlobe into his mouth, his tongue moving the soft skin back and forth, then sucking gently. He whispered, "Wanna make up?"

Maggie let the sensuousness of his touch mingle with her fatigue. She turned on to her back and stretched, separating her legs to let his hand, which had moved down over her panties, move between her thighs. She turned her head to meet his mouth, and while she hadn't forgotten the argument, she simply wanted to feel good for a while.

After unhurried lovemaking, Maggie fell back asleep. She woke to the smell of bacon and Brian standing next to her with a hot cup of coffee.

"I brought this for you." He smiled as he set it on the nightstand.

"Thanks." Maggie let the sheet fall off her naked body as she reached for the mug. "Mmm. It's good." She didn't mention that it didn't have any sugar in it.

"I'm making breakfast, too," Brian said.

"So I smell."

"Do you feel better?" he said.

She nodded her head. "You're always good to my body." As soon as the words left her mouth, Maggie wondered where they'd come from.

"What does that mean? I'm not good to the rest of you?"

Maggie hid her mouth behind the hot coffee mug. These days she wondered who was putting the words together and pushing them through her lips. She really hadn't meant to say that, yet, if she thought about it, lately it was true. Then she remembered her night in the darkroom. "I'm so excited about the pictures, Brian."

"Did you develop more?"

"I enlarged all of them, including the solo shot of the girl that I showed you." She put the mug down and shimmied up in bed, propping herself against the pillows.

"Hold on. Let me get the food," Brian said.

"Will you bring back some sugar?" she said as he walked out of the bedroom.

Brian came back with a wood tray meant for dining in bed. On the tray sat orange juice, a plate of scrambled eggs, crisp lean bacon, lightly toasted rye bread, and the sugar bowl.

"Thanks," she said as she picked up the catsup and hot sauce and sprinkled both over her eggs. She popped a half a slice of bacon into her mouth. "Won't it be cool if I can help find this missing girl?"

"Don't talk with your mouth full, Mag."

Maggie swallowed. "Aren't you going to eat?"

"I already did. I wanted to let you sleep as long as I could. I have to go." He pulled his uniform pants over his boxers.

"I thought your takeoff was at one."

"It is. It's almost eleven, sleepy head. You were up late." He squeezed her shoulder, then disappeared into the closet.

"I wanted to show you the rest of the pictures," she yelled.

"I'll see them when I get back." He emerged from the closet buttoning his shirt, his jacket slung over his arm.

Maggie swallowed a mouthful of egg, then washed it down with orange juice. "It's her. I know it is."

Brian popped his tie into his collar, then sat on the edge of the bed. He leaned in and kissed her deeply. "I'll be back in two days. Let's spend some time together when I get back, okay? We'll both put off our hobbies for a while."

"But..."

"We need it, Mag," Brian said.

When she heard the front door slam, she put a teaspoon of sugar in her coffee and reached for the portable phone. She called the studio where she caught Donovan as he was going through some equipment for his afternoon shoot. She wanted someone to be excited with her about the little girl, and Donovan would be a great second opinion.

Chapter Eight

Maggie sat in a large booth, waiting, and stared out the window of a small diner that was just down the street from her studio. It was noon and the sun was shining off the cars in the parking lot. Perfect picture weather. Lots of light and shadows.

She tapped the spoon against her coffee cup and looked around the diner. The décor reminded her of a fifties sitcom. The booth had dark green vinyl seats, and the tabletop was speckled Formica with a ridged silver edge. The sugar and condiments were in thick old-fashioned glasses. The salt and pepper shakers looked like antiques, each table with a different set.

She glanced out the window again, saw Donovan get out of his car, noticed his biceps straining against his shirt, and sat up straight in the booth, touching her portfolio that held the pictures.

Donovan rounded the booth and slid in across from Maggie.

"I can't believe you've never been in here before," Donovan said. "It's so close to the studio."

"I used to be very busy…" Maggie let her voice trail off and picked up a miniature Coca-Cola bottle and sprinkled salt into her palm.

A plump, elderly waitress, with thinning gray hair, ambled over, dropped off the menus, and winked at Donovan, saying she'd be right back. She looked as if she might have been waiting table since the fifties.

"I used to feel guilty when Ethel waited on me," Donovan said. "Like when my grandmother used to run around and bring me food but never sat down."

"I was just thinking that."

"Don't feel bad. This is her restaurant, and her children can't get her out of here. She loves it."

"Her children? How old are they?"

"Retired. Live in Arizona." His face broke into a wide grin. "Let her recommend some pie. You won't be sorry."

Ethel appeared at the table with a pad and pencil. "What can I get you, honey?" she said to Maggie. Her eyes were tiny lights shining through layers of wrinkled skin.

"What kind of pie would you recommend today?" Maggie said.

"Washington State. Just made fresh ones an hour ago." Ethel said.

"What kind is that?"

"Apple." She poked the pencil she had been holding over her ear and into the hair net that held her hair away from her face. "Where've you been, girl?"

Maggie wasn't sure where she'd been or where she was going, but simply said, "I'll try the apple."

"You?" She looked to Donovan. "It's Pacific Ocean day. I have your favorite."

Donovan nodded.

"I make the best Hawaiian pie in the universe." She winked at Maggie. "And two hi-tests."

"She didn't write anything down," Maggie said as Ethel walked away.

"She never does. Just carries the pad. I think it's an excuse to put the pencil behind her ear."

"What's Hawaiian pie?"

"Pineapple upside down pie with macadamia nuts. Ethel's life is food. She thought every state should have a pie along with a bird and flower. My favorite is Washington, D.C."

"I thought your favorite was Hawaiian."

"Not to eat. Just the name. 'Multi-nut pie.'" He smiled as if he'd named it himself. "Ask her for the state pie menu. There're only a few pies available each day, though. I come here a lot to study, after work. My wife talks a lot when I'm home." He smiled.

"What are you studying?"

"I'm getting my MFA in photography."

Maggie felt herself blush. In all their time together, she'd paid so little attention to Donovan's personal life. She was glad when Ethel put the pies and coffees in front of them. Maggie's came with a mountain of vanilla ice cream full of specks from vanilla beans.

"I didn't order ice cream." Maggie smiled up at Ethel.

"You don't need to, kiddo. It's a given. Who would eat apple pie without ice cream?" She walked away shaking her head.

Maggie put a piece of the apple pie in her mouth, followed by a small spoonful of ice cream. The hot and cold competed on her tongue. The tart apples and sweet cream flavors did the same. The message to Maggie's brain was that she was seven years old and sitting in her grandmother's kitchen. "Wow. Nothing like comfort food."

"Good?"

"Any better and God would be jealous." Maggie looked up. "That was my father's favorite line."

"So what's up?" Donovan said.

Maggie's hand went to her portfolio. "I need your professional opinion."

"Proofs?" Donovan looked around. "Why here?"

"They're not proofs." She moved the pie plate out of the way and pushed the crumbs into a pile. "Did you hear about that girl that was abducted a few days ago? From Miami?"

"Sure. Lots of press."

"I think I may have seen her at the Fort Pierce plaza—maybe with the abductor."

"No kidding? You've got shots?"

"Yeah." Maggie grinned. She placed the pictures on the table next to the photo from the newspaper. "Here's the thing, she doesn't look exactly like..." She let her voice drift off as Donovan took the pictures. "You look. I won't say a word."

Maggie watched Donovan's eyes the same way she had watched Brian's. Brian's eyes had scanned the pictures the way she'd seen his eyes scan the control panel of a small twin-engine plane. His eyes were ever watching for changes, for things that were wrong; he had been trained to see differences. Donovan's eyes rested on areas of the facial close-up for long periods, then she could see them move to the same quadrant on the other close-up. He was looking for similarities. He alternately shook his head, then nodded.

Maggie picked up her coffee cup and sipped the lukewarm liquid.

"This could be her," Donovan said.

Maggie dropped the coffee cup that was not quite to the saucer. Coffee splashed on the photos. She grabbed a napkin and began to dab the wetness. "You think?"

"Could be," Donovan said as he helped get the rest of the coffee off the pictures. "This one," he held up the newspaper clipping, "is a standard professional portrait shot. Posed, so it's hard to see the child in movement. Yours are in movement. But look." He got up and came around the booth to sit next to her. He placed Maggie's picture next to the newspaper photo, then picked up two napkins. He covered the girl's face in the newspaper photo from below the eyes down and from just above the eyebrows up. "Even when they tried to pose her, her eyes stayed alive. They show movement somehow."

Maggie turned in the booth to face Donovan. "I know. They're the same set of eyes. Lilly's were always alive, too. That's what I saw; I just couldn't describe it."

He nodded as he looked. "Maybe. With different hair color." He bent over Maggie's picture. His finger pounded on the little girls eyebrows. "Look, in your shot, her eyebrows look light even though her hair's dark."

Maggie grabbed the picture as the napkins fluttered to the table. "I never noticed that."

"It's hard to say for sure because you took them from so far away. If they dyed her hair they didn't bother to dye the eyebrows."

"How did I miss that?"

"You were looking elsewhere." Donovan continued to stare. "Have you showed anyone else?"

"Brian."

"And?"

"He thinks…" She waved her hand in the air and let her words trail off. "He thinks I 'see things I want to see.'"

"What does that mean?" he said.

"I had a dream about Lilly and made a comment about wishing she were alive."

"Doesn't he wish the same thing?"

"Brian's very pragmatic. He doesn't spend time wishing for things he can't have."

Donovan thought for a minute. "That's kind of sad."

Maggie nodded. "I know. I can't be like that." Her hand ran over the picture of the little girl. "Like in the hospital. Once they told me that Lilly no longer had any brain function, I knew she would never wake up." She looked to Donovan. "I really *knew* she wouldn't. But that never stopped me from sitting next to her bed, day in and day out, holding her hand and wishing for a miracle."

Donovan put his hand on hers.

Maggie looked down. "This picture looks a little like Lilly when she was younger." She pointed to the newspaper picture.

Donovan picked it up and looked at it. His face broke into a smile. "I can see that. The eyes. Both very impish." He put the picture on the table. "Some kids never lose that look no matter how old they get."

"If they get old," Maggie said.

Donovan closed his eyes and shook his head. "Shit. I didn't realize what I was saying."

Maggie felt the pain grip her. She looked at the eyes on the table. Lilly's eyes in another face. She tried to swallow but her mouth was dry.

"I'm so sorry, Maggie," Donovan said.

Maggie reached for the angel pin on her shirt and closed her eyes so as not to see the eyes on the table, but in her mind she saw Lilly's unseeing eyes on pavement and opened them again. She took a deep breath.

Donovan put his arm around her. "That was really dumb of me."

She looked at his face. His pale eyebrows, his blue eyes so full of emotion. Eyes like Lilly's and the little girls. Eyes that would always be impish as they enjoyed a bite of pie.

"It's not you," she said. "It's everything." She turned her face away. She didn't want to mention the fights she'd had with Brian. They sat in silence while Maggie held his hand tightly as if it would keep her anchored in the present. "Will it always be like this?" The words were so low she wasn't sure she'd said them out loud.

"You mean you're traveling along not thinking about it and, bang, there's this giant hole in the road that you never saw coming, and once you're in it you don't think you'll ever get out—again?"

Maggie turned back to Donovan. "How do you know how it feels?"

His smile was sad. "I didn't exactly fade into the background when I was growing up—despite how pale I am." He looked down at his hand.

Maggie saw the contrast in their skin colors. She'd never thought about what it must have been like for him as a child.

"I'm sorry," she said.

He squeezed her hand. "We all have holes in the road. The thing to remember is that we do get out."

"I'm so tired." His silence let her go on. "What if one day I just fall in a hole and never come out?" Her voice was low, and again she was surprised at the words she heard herself say. But she knew they were true.

"It's tempting, isn't it?" Donovan nodded.

"I'm not sure why I should ever come out." She shrugged her shoulders.

He held her.

"Really." She searched his face. "Why did you keep going?"

He thought for a moment. "I know how cliché this sounds, but just before, when we were laughing, didn't it feel good? You have to remember how it can feel, then pull yourself out for those times."

Maggie was unconvinced.

Finally Donovan said, "I had a great mom. She made me laugh and find the good moments. She told me to connect those moments, like that connect-a-dot game, to live my life inside the dots, and to disregard the rest. She said the picture would be clear someday, even if it wasn't at the time." He looked into her eyes. "Isn't there someone who makes you laugh?"

Maggie thought of Brian. "Not anymore. The one I laughed with, got really silly with, was Lilly."

"Then do it for Lilly. She would want you to laugh and live on."

Maggie began to blink rapidly.

"You would want that for her," he said.

Maggie nodded. She knew the drill.

"Can I try to help you out of this hole? Or should I let you be?" he said.

"Help."

He pulled her closer, and she let her head fall onto his shoulder. The sunscreen he had to wear everyday of his life smelled like the beach, and Maggie closed her eyes and pictured soft, white sand. She felt his words spoken softly into her hair, falling around her like gentle rain. "It really does get better, but I won't pretend it's easy. I won't say you'll forget. Thoughts of her will always cause an ambivalent stab in your chest. Anger for having lost her, but thankful you had her at all. The laughter comes back if you let it, and it doesn't mean you love her any less if you get on with your life."

The words weren't new to Maggie. She'd heard relatives say them to her mother when her father had died. But this was different. Mothers were not supposed to outlive their children.

Maggie realized Donovan had stopped talking. She opened her eyes, torn between embarrassment to be so close to him and gratitude for the comfort. She looked at the eyes in the pictures on the table, then closed her eyes again. "Please don't stop," she said.

He started again, his voice soothing and rhythmic, like ocean waves, and she listened. And somewhere in her heart she heard. Somehow the words were seeping into her parched spirit, rehydrating her with a small trickle of the promise of belief. She wondered how many times she would have to hear it before she believed that life could go on, but hoped someday she would.

Maggie had lost all track of time, then she felt Donovan squeeze her hand. She sat up and felt her face get hot.

"You okay?" he said. He blushed.

She nodded. "Thanks."

He nodded back, got up, and went to the other side of the booth.

Maggie began to gather up the pictures. "So it's her, right?"

"I'm not sure, Maggie," Donovan said. "It could be."

Ethel appeared at the table and poured Maggie some fresh coffee. "You kids want anything else?"

"No, thank you," Donovan said.

"I do," Maggie said.

Ethel put the coffee pot down, pulled the pencil out from behind her ear and poised it over her pad. "Shoot."

Maggie reached for Ethel's pencil and said, "May I?"

"Have at it, kiddo," Ethel said.

Maggie reached for the newspaper photo and looked at Donovan, the pencil poised over the little girl's hairline.

"What are you going to do?" Donovan said.

Maggie shaded in the hair with curling motions. She stopped the dark color at the girl's chin, where the hair stopped in the plaza shots. Maggie put her picture next to the doctored-newspaper photo. She told herself to be fair and honest, to see what she saw, not what she wanted to see. She had a sip of the hot coffee and looked around the diner, like having sherbet between courses to cleanse the palate. Then she looked down. She started at the nose then looked outward in a circular motion to the chin, the cheeks, the eyes, the brows and back down the other side of the face. She pulled out to see the frame of the face—the hair. She did the same with the second one, then turned them both toward Donovan.

"Now what do you think," she said.

Donovan looked from picture to picture for several minutes, then said, "It's close. I don't know if I'd bet my life on it."

"But would you bet hers?" Maggie said as she tapped at the newspaper picture, feeling goose bumps rise on her arms and knowing she had no choice.

Chapter Nine

Maggie sat in her car outside the Coral Gables Police Department and stared at the sterile looking beige building that seemed to have risen out of nowhere in the middle of busy streets. Its rounded corners and textured surface looked as if it had been designed to be business-like but she found it ominous and unapproachable. Her call to Miami-Dade Crime Stoppers had given Maggie the name of the detective who was handling the Vega kidnapping.

She tapped the steering wheel with her left hand as she rubbed the soft smooth leather on her portfolio with her right. In her mind she ran over what she would say. She had brought all the photos she had of the girl she believed was Mira Vega, plus a blow up of the man she was with—the possible abductor. The man's face wasn't very clear but she imagined their forensic artist would be able to do something with it.

A meter maid pulled up behind Maggie's car. Maggie reached into the center console, trying to decide how much change she would need for the meter. How many quarters did it take to bring a little girl back from the missing?

A light drizzle began to coat her windshield. Just like South Florida to produce a sun shower out of nowhere. She took a deep breath and got out of her car, keeping her head down and covering her portfolio with her arm. She locked her car, put eight quarters in the meter, and ran across the street. She reached out for the glass door, then realized the right side of the entrance was the fire department. To her left was the entrance to the police department. Once inside, she shook the rain off, clutching her portfolio close to her body as she looked around. Behind the reception window was a young female police office, watching Maggie's approach.

"I'm here to see Detective Hodges, please," Maggie said through the circle cutout in the glass partition.

"Is he expecting you?" the police officer said.

"No, but I have information on the Vega case. The kidnapping," Maggie said.

"What sort of information?"

"I have pictures that I believe are of Mira Vega and perhaps her abductor," Maggie said through the hole.

The receptionist took her name and asked her to wait, then she picked up a phone and made a call. A few minutes later Maggie was told to wait in the lobby, the detective would be down in a minute.

After thanking the receptionist, Maggie backed away from the window. Her heart pounded. She fixed her hair and wiped the extra moisture off her forehead, feeling her armpits sweat. She couldn't even imagine what it must feel like to be here if you were guilty.

After walking back and forth across the small lobby several times, Maggie heard the bell from the elevator. A short, stocky man wearing a pair of khaki pants, blue shirt and a shoulder holster walked toward her. He looked to be nearing retirement, or worn out from the job; Maggie wasn't sure which.

"Maggie Miller?" When Maggie nodded, the detective extended his hand, "Detective Hodges. You have information about the Vega case?"

Maggie nodded toward her portfolio. "Pictures."

The detective stared at her for a few minutes, then said, "Come upstairs."

They rode the elevator up three floors and walked through a small waiting room in silence. Detective Hodges led her through a maze of cubicles to one near the back. He motioned to a chair, sat down behind his desk, picked up a black mug with the faded logo from the TV show NYPD in white, and took a sip. His light brown eyes stared at her over the edge of his mug as he said, "What've you got?"

Maggie shifted the portfolio back and forth and began to speak. "I—"

"Sit," the detective commanded.

Maggie sat on the edge of the wooden chair. "I have pictures that I think can help in the Mira Vega case."

"Would you like to show me?" He put the mug on his desk.

Maggie felt her face flush and suddenly knew how innocent people could be made to feel as if they'd done something wrong. She looked down and fumbled with the closure on her portfolio. When she looked up she noticed the detective was following her hands. She willed them to stop shaking.

"I'm a professional photographer. I was at a service plaza on the Turnpike, in Ft. Pierce, and I believe I got a picture of Mira Vega, quite by accident." Maggie handed the pictures to the detective. "I think there may be one of the abductor, too."

Detective Hodges took a glossy eight by ten out of a fat folder on his desk. He put it down and started to look at Maggie's pictures, chewing on his lower lip as his eyes moved from picture to picture.

"I'm sure it's her," Maggie said, "but I guess you'll need to verify it." She smiled and sat back in her seat.

Hodges didn't return the smile, but looked down. "This child's a brunette." He waved the top photo in the air.

"Yes, but I figured he could have cut and colored her hair. Look around her eyes."

He nodded slightly, as if giving the thought the benefit of the doubt. When he got to the one with the thin man, he pulled it closer to his face. "Where'd you say you took these?"

Maggie's heart began to thump. "At a service plaza in Ft. Pierce."

"What were you doing there? I mean, how'd you come to take these pictures?"

"I'm a photographer. I do weddings, graduations, things like that. One day I was at a Turnpike plaza after an on-location wedding and noticed all the people: their clothes, their reactions. I took out my camera and started to shoot. I found I could get really candid shots in public places, raw emotions."

"So that's the day you took these?"

Maggie felt her face flush. "No. I've been back a couple of times now. Different plazas."

He nodded and continued to stare at the picture with the abductor.

When he didn't say anything, she continued. "You catch people off guard when they don't know you're doing it. See their expressions?" She slid up to the edge of the hard seat. "You don't get that in a posed picture. That's why she looks so different in that photo there." She pointed to the one on his desk. "I take shots like that all the time. Well, I try not to. I wish I'd gotten a clearer shot of Mira, but I didn't know at the time I'd need one." Maggie realized she was babbling and sat back and took a deep breath.

"Mira," he said. "You say her name as if you know her. Do you?"

Maggie felt her face blush. "No. I…" She squeezed the fingers of her left hand with her right. "I've been hearing her name a lot."

He nodded and stared at her for a while. Then he looked back down. "This kid doesn't look scared or nervous as if she's being held against her will," he said.

In person, Maggie thought the look was somewhat anxious. "She was skipping, almost as if being pulled along."

The detective continued to look through the pile. She noticed he chewed on his lower lip when he was thinking. She saw him look at the newspaper photo that she had colored in at the diner. He laid it between the picture from his file and one of hers. His eyebrows rose. He continued to the next picture, then he stopped biting his lip, and looked up at Maggie. She sat still and quiet. "Who's this?" he said. He flipped the picture over, and Maggie saw it was a picture of Lilly at age five in which Maggie had colored the hair dark, the same way she had penciled in the dark hair on Mira at the diner.

Maggie inhaled sharply. She squeezed her hands together and tried to hide her embarrassment. How had she left it in the pile? "That's my daughter Lilly. My husband thought they looked alike, so I wanted to see how she would look…" Her voice trailed off as she stood, reaching to take the picture. "I'm sorry. I don't know how that got in there."

The detective held on to the picture and put it next to one of Mira. "I can see it. In the eyes." He looked up at Maggie, who stood in front of his desk waiting for the picture of Lilly. "How old's your daughter?"

Maggie swallowed. "Eight. She was. She died…" Maggie pinched the fleshy part of her palm.

Detective Hodges nodded. "Sit." He shuffled through the pictures again as Maggie sat back down. "How'd she die?" He held up the picture of Lilly.

"Roller blading." Maggie looked down, then back up at the picture of Lilly with pencil-marked dark hair. The short haircut suddenly looked like a helmet. She closed her eyes and heard herself groan. "No helmet. Subarachnoid hemorrhage." When she opened them again, the picture was back on the desk.

Detective Hodges's face softened. "Must be rough. I have two girls." He shook his head. "I can't imagine."

"You don't want to."

Detective Hodges folded his hands over the pictures and leaned forward. The empathy in his eyes seemed genuine.

"Sometimes I think I see her," Maggie said, "—at the supermarket, on the street—but of course, it's not her. I even have dreams that she's still alive. I had a nightmare the other night that she was kidnapped…" Maggie felt her face begin to crumple as she pictured Lilly driving off in the dream and bit her lip. She shook her head as if the grief were droplets of rain she could shake off like a dog caught in a downpour. She willed herself to stay focused.

The detective looked away, down to his desk, then spread the pictures out. "How long ago did your daughter die?"

"May—two months ago."

"Do you take other pictures, at these plazas, besides little children?"

"Sure. Families, things like that."

He nodded. "Do they always have little girls in them?"

Maggie shifted in her chair. "What are you getting at?"

"I'll check it out, Ms. Miller, but this little girl has the wrong color hair, she looks rather happy, and, well, she does look like your daughter."

"Lilly doesn't even have the same color hair as that girl."

"Neither does Mira Vega." He held up his picture of the missing girl.

"You can't just dismiss me because my daughter died."

"The reward is only if it leads to her return," Detective Hodges said.

Maggie stiffened. "This isn't about the money. It's about finding that little girl." She pointed to the pile of pictures on his desk.

"Like I said, we'll check it out. When did you say these were taken?"

"The date's on the back." She stood up, flipped one of the pictures over, then sat back down. "July 17th."

The detective rocked back in his chair and put his hands behind his head. He stared at her, chewing on his lower lip. "I should have asked you that question sooner," he said finally. "Mira Vega was safe at home on the 17th." The feet of the chair thumped the floor as he brought it forward. "She didn't disappear until the 18th. This can't be her."

Maggie looked from his face to the pictures on his desk then back to his face, trying to understand. "What are you saying?"

Very slowly Detective Hodges repeated the information. "Mira Vega disappeared on the 18th, the day after you took these pictures."

Maggie looked around the cubicle, her mind searching for an explanation. "That can't be." Maggie knew this was the girl. "That can't be right."

"I'm afraid it is."

"This is Mira. I know it's her. Are you sure?" Maggie said.

"Am *I* sure?" The detective's eyebrows shot up.

Maggie's mind began to run through the events since she saw the missing girl on TV. Like a movie montage she saw Mira on the screen as she jumped off the swing, her ponytail bouncing behind her; she saw the little girl skipping out of the plaza, being pulled by the thin man; she saw Mira's eyes stare back at her and come alive in her developing tray. She had been so sure as she blew up the shots. Those eyes. She knew this was the girl.

"Ms. Miller?" Detective Hodges said. "Are you okay?"

"I can't be wrong."

The detective came around to Maggie and put his hand on the back of her chair, standing close, but not touching her. "I'm sorry. I know you wanted to help find this little girl."

"I wanted to save her." Maggie felt her body shrink into the chair.

"How do you take your coffee, Ms. Miller?"

She stared at him.

"Cream, sugar?" he said.

"Milk. Lots of sugar."

He grabbed the mug from his desk and disappeared. Maggie took the pictures off the desk and began to shuffle them. She put Mira and Lilly side by side. She stroked one cheek, then the next.

"Here." Detective Hodges held his NYPD mug out to her. "I washed it out."

She put the photos together in a pile and turned them over. As she sipped the hot sweet coffee in silence, "July 17," stared back at her. She looked away.

Detective Hodges made a few comments about the weather, her photography, but Maggie had nothing to say. She drank the coffee, feeling the hot liquid scald her throat, only to give herself time to gather her thoughts so she would be able to walk out of the police station.

"Mira is still missing," the detective said. "But the upside is that this little girl here," he pointed toward Maggie's pictures, "is most likely safe at home with her family."

Maggie tried to let that make her feel better, but somehow, it didn't.

Chapter Ten

The ride home from Coral Gables seemed endless. Every car on US1 seemed to want her to go faster, and every truck on I95 seemed to want to run her off the road. The decisive person that had made the drive south had disappeared, and Maggie entered her house feeling purposeless. She put her portfolio on the hall table and went to her bedroom. She kicked off her shoes and looked at herself in the dresser mirror. Mid-calf black skirt, a sleeveless, turtleneck cotton sweater. Even hose. She had dressed "professionally" so as to give herself more credibility. She had been so sure the girl she took the pictures of at the plaza had been Mira Vega. Maggie pulled the comforter down and got into bed. She pulled the sheets up to her neck and lay there. She knew she had to be at the studio in a few hours to interview a woman who had answered her ad for a part time photographer, someone who could help Donovan until she was ready to get back to work fulltime.

But she didn't want to think of that right now. Instead of the constant barrage of thoughts that had been filling her mind, she was empty. She would get up, she would take pictures this afternoon, she would smile, but all that, too, would be empty. She fell asleep as she repeated the word like a mantra: empty, empty, empty.

***

Maggie was confused as she rolled over. The phone was ringing, and as she opened her eyes, she felt how swollen they were.

"You okay?" Brian's voice reached out over the distance from California.

"Fine." Her nasal voice said into the phone.

"You don't sound fine. What've you been up to?"

Maggie felt a mixture of disappointment, fatigue, and grief surround her like a steam bath. "Not much."

"You sound terrible, Maggie."

"I was sleeping, I guess."

"It's noon your time. What are you doing sleeping?"

Maggie put the receiver close to her mouth as if she were about to tell a secret. "I'm not fine." She tried to inhale through her nose, but it was clogged from crying.

"Oh, Mag." Brian's voice held such genuine concern, such tenderness.

She wondered why it couldn't always be that way. Why were there things she could talk about and things she couldn't? She didn't think he really meant to be intolerant, but sometimes what she needed and what he needed didn't mesh. And she had learned that there were times when he couldn't allow himself to feel the hurt at all.

"I made a fool of myself at the police station." The words leaked out of her mouth.

"I don't follow."

"I took the pictures of the little girl to the police. It wasn't her." She rolled onto her back, her legs getting tangled in the skirt she still wore. She stared at the ceiling waiting for his response.

"You did what?" His voice sounded confused.

"I was so sure it was her, Brian. I enlarged all the pictures. It looked so much like her."

Silence blared from the phone receiver, and Maggie pictured Brian taking a deep breath, shaking his head. Then he said, "I told you it wasn't her, Mag."

Maggie felt the sting of embarrassment all over again. She rolled onto her side, the phone buried into the pillow. "Please. Don't be Mr. Right, right now. I feel stupid enough."

There was silence on the other end, and Maggie feared what would come next.

"I'm sorry, Maggie." She could hear his breathing. "I'm sorry it was hard for you."

She closed her eyes, thankful he had heard her. "I miss you, Brian." For the first time in a long time, Maggie meant it.

"Do you want me to come home today instead of tomorrow? I can call in sick for the last leg of the trip."

Just the fact that he was willing to do that made Maggie feel less empty. "No, honey. I'll be fine. But it means a lot to me that you would do that."

"I've missed you, too, Maggie." She knew he didn't just mean the three thousand miles that separated them now.

"I'll try to be better when you get home," she said, not even knowing what she meant by "better."

"You don't need to be better, you just need to adjust to the things that can't ever be the same."

"I know." Her voice was a whisper. "I'm just not sure I know how. I can't do it the way you do."

"Then do it the way you do. Hire two photographers. Go to the service plazas every day. Twice a day."

Maggie gripped the receiver. "Do you mean that?" Her voice broke.

"I mean it, but I don't want you to cry."

"I can't help it."

"I'll even come with you to the plaza the next time you go. If you want."

"You will?" Maggie began to smile. "Now you are making me cry."

"I want my Maggie back. I guess I need to try things your way."

"Thank you. And maybe the photographer I'm interviewing today will work out and we can take a few days away."

By the time Maggie hung up the phone she was afraid to look at her swollen eyes in the mirror. The last time she had cried when she was happy was when Lilly won the fifth grade spelling bee by correctly spelling "aperture."

Maggie went straight to the freezer with a washcloth to make a cold compress for her eyes. She rummaged through the refrigerator bin for a cucumber to add to her homemade eye remedy. There were onions that had gone soft and potatoes that were growing eyes, but no cucumbers. She slammed the door; she couldn't remember the last time she went down the produce aisle. Ice would have to be enough. She would rest for thirty minutes to try to get the swelling down on her eyes, then get ready to go to the studio for the interview. She turned the ringer off next to her bed and lay down.

Chapter Eleven

An hour later, Maggie woke up and walked into her bathroom to splash cold water on her face. She couldn't believe that Brian would come with her to the plazas. She didn't want him to watch her take pictures, what she wanted was for him to see what she saw. But as she dried her face, she knew he would never see what she saw. Maggie stared in the mirror. The cold compress, minus the slices of cucumber, had done nothing to reduce the swelling in her eyes. Thankful she was the interviewer not the interviewee this afternoon, she turned away from the mirror and started for the darkroom.

Brian would be bored in ten minutes at a plaza, a place where she could sit for hours. He didn't share her fascination with people, and she'd tried to tell him it was because he never developed an unrestrained imagination. He was brought up concrete—to see what was there, not what could be there. Life to Maggie had always been the psychological equivalent of an M. C. Escher print. She could always see the metamorphic possibilities in a situation, the distortions, the improbabilities. Every picture wasn't just worth a thousand words, but a thousand possibilities as well.

When she and Brian had first started to date, she would show him pictures she had taken and tell him stories about what the people were thinking or doing. He would ask how she knew. She'd tell him she imagined it was so. He would laugh and say there was no way to know what someone else was thinking. She agreed, but told him you could guess by what people did and how they looked what they *might* do. He'd replied, why bother?

Maggie opened the door to the darkroom and looked at the remnants of all her hard work perfecting the pictures so the missing girl could be found. How could she have been so wrong? Maggie stared at the pictures on the drying rack, at the sleeves of negatives she had left out, all dated and in order. Did she really only see what she wanted to see?

Maggie's gaze fell on Lilly's bowl that was filled with film. She picked up the bowl and ran her finger on the glued cracks that looked like lightening bolts, causing the already gaudy pattern to be even more garish. The bowl that used to hold milk and cereal now held her undeveloped film, while the overflow was arranged on the table. The old Maggie would never have been so disorganized as to lump all her film in a pile. She sat down on the chair next to the table and stared at what she saw. She looked from the bowl to the film and back again. She picked up a plastic canister and saw the date scribbled on the top: Ft. P/5-17. Ft. Pierce/May 17. The day she had taken Mira's picture.

She remembered back to the day the newscast about Mira had come on. She had been cleaning in the kitchen and had dropped the bowl, turned off the television, and brought the glued bowl here where it wouldn't break again. In her upset she had capped the canisters and put them all in the bowl instead of lining them up chronologically. What if she had put the wrong cap on the wrong canister? What if it was a Ft. Pierce shoot, but from the 19th, the second day she had been at that plaza? Was there a way she could tell?

Maggie knew that as proof of the date people sometime put newspapers in their photos. There was no chance of that. What if she checked the weather report? Maybe one day had been rainy and one sunny. But then, she never shot on rainy days.

She remembered the drive had soothed her the last time she was there—the second month anniversary of Lilly's death—the 19th of May. Was that the day she saw the little girl? She put her head in her hands. It was less than a week ago and she couldn't remember! She really was losing her mind.

The phone startled her. She didn't even remember carrying the portable phone into the darkroom.

"Hey, boss." Donovan's voice came across the wire.

Maggie looked at the clock and remembered the interview. "How's she look?" She stared at the cracked bowl, held loosely together; Her mind felt the same way.

"I'm not at the office. Stuck with a dead battery at my house. I'm waiting for Triple A. Gerlinde told me you were home."

Maggie's head fell. "Thanks for letting me know."

"Will you make it?"

"Yeah." Maggie looked around her darkroom, then down at her wrinkled clothes. "I'll make it."

Chapter Twelve

Maggie sat in her office and looked from the well-dressed middle-aged woman to the woman's pictures on her desk. The pictures were actually quite good. The woman had the standard shots that proved her capable of doing the kind of work Maggie did—a portfolio of wedding, graduation, and birthday photos—but the woman had also included some creative shots. Maggie picked up a series of shots that showed a man in a suit in front of a building. While the man was dressed the same in both pictures, he looked very different in the shots.

"What is this?" She held up the pictures.

"I wanted to show the difference in people before and after a stressful event, so I took pictures of people before and then after going into the Claybourne County Courthouse." She blushed. "It was a good idea but I only caught a few of the same people. I guess some went out a different exit. I hadn't thought of that."

"Nice."

The woman, obviously somewhat nervous, continued. "You know, the way people are so different after an emotional experience..." The woman continued to talk.

Yes, Maggie knew. She noticed the woman was dressed not unlike she had been this morning when she went to the police department. She looked down at her jeans and sweater, then back at the woman who was still talking. Maggie remembered her ramblings in front of the Coral Gables detective and felt an affinity with the woman, wanted to put her at ease. She smiled at her. "A before and after series."

"Kind of."

"It's not just emotions," Maggie said. "I've noticed how smokers slow their pace, but quicken the drags on their cigarettes before going into a building." She remembered the man dressed as a clown—as if the outfit wasn't outrageous enough, his smoking had also caught her eye. Later he drove away in a Volkswagen Beetle with "Bo Bo the Clown" and a phone number painted on both sides. He had been strolling into the plaza, smoking quickly. But on the way out, his posture was more erect, his smoking relaxed. "A smoking clown was an interesting contradiction, therefore an interesting picture in and of itself. But I did notice the pattern of his smoking change when he came out," she said out loud.

"Excuse me?"

Maggie suddenly sat straight up in her chair. The clown! He was on the same roll of film as the one with Mira—but there were only his exit shots, his "after." If she could find the shots of him going in, on the other roll of film, and verify the date, she could prove the roll with him coming out, as well as the shots of Mira, had been taken on the 19th. The day after she was abducted!

"This is great." She slammed the pictures on the desk.

"Thank you." The woman looked at Maggie as if she were crazy.

Maggie stared at the woman, but saw the smoking clown in her mind. She picked the pictures up and waved them in the air. "Yes, very creative." She looked at her watch. "You're hired."

"I am?"

Maggie sprang to her feet, handed the woman her pictures and turned to leave. "Gerlinde will give you the details," Maggie said as she headed for the door.

"I'll have to think about it." Maggie heard the words yelled after her, as she sped past Gerlinde telling her to have the woman fill out an employee packet.

***

Maggie sat in her darkroom staring at Bo Bo the Clown. The first pictures of the smoking clown were on the end of a roll that had already been processed. The negatives were dated July 19th. Maggie could hardly control her excitement as she ran to her purse to find Detective Hodges's card. As each ring went unanswered, she became more impatient.

"Be there. Come on." She looked at her watch. It was five. Was he gone for the day or out to dinner? Maggie listened to the recorded message asking her to leave a message, or dial "0" to get back to the operator. She did neither; she hung up the phone. She wanted to be able to explain herself clearly, in person, so she called back every ten minutes. After trying for over an hour, she decided to leave a message after all.

Maggie said her name and phone number, slowly, then began talking in a very calm voice: "Detective Hodges, I came to see you this morning. I had pictures of Mira Vega. Well, you didn't think it was a picture of her because I'd dated it incorrectly. I've since confirmed that I actually took the picture of the young girl on the 19th. That's one day after she was abducted, not the day before as we'd thought. I'd mixed up the rolls of film…" Maggie bit her lip. Her story was beginning to get confusing. "Let me just say, there was a mix-up and now these could be pictures of Mira Vega. I mean, they are pictures of her." She shook her head. "Please call me back so I can arrange to bring the photos back down to you." Maggie repeated her name and number and hung up the phone. "Shit." She shook her head. "I sounded like a loon!"

She walked around to her nightstand to grab a magazine to pass the time until the detective called. Novels were a thing of the past. She couldn't focus since Lilly died; pictures and short blurbs were all she could handle. Maggie noticed the message light blinking next to the phone and wondered when the message had come in. Then she remembered she had turned the ringer off when she had laid down to take a nap. When she pushed the play button, the first message was from a nasal southern woman about refinancing. She pictured the woman as Lilly Tomlin doing her "One ringy, dingy" routine and asking "is this the person to whom I am speaking?" Then she heard Brian's voice. "Hey, Mag. I decided to come home anyway, even though you told me not to. I would surprise you, but I've learned that doesn't work." She heard him laugh. "I should be home between six and six thirty. Can't wait to see you."

Maggie glanced at the red numbers on her bedside clock, then at her watch to confirm. It was now 6:20. She thought about their earlier phone conversation and how it had left her feeling more romantic than she had since before the accident. She remembered she hadn't shaved her legs this morning and decided to hop in the shower.

She would just sponge off her body, then shave her legs. Maggie looked at the shelf of shower gels and decided she wanted something soothing. She poured a large amount of lemon verbena shower gel into her hand and used a loofa to foam it up. She inhaled the smell as she rubbed the course loofa over her shoulder, remembering where she had been the first time she experienced the smell—at the La Samanna hotel in St. Martin with Brian on their ten-year anniversary vacation. She rubbed the loofa on her neck and breathed in deeply, remembering how Brian had washed her back, his hands gliding over her hips, then down her legs and back up again, until he had caressed every inch of her body.

She hoped they'd stop bickering. She knew statistics showed a high divorce rate between couples that had lost a child, yet she'd never understood how that was possible. She'd always thought the loss would bond a couple together, not tear them apart.

Maggie heard the bathroom door open, and then Brian slid open the shower stall. He stood completely naked, smiling. "Hey," he said.

Maggie smiled back. Brian got into the shower and kissed her lightly on the lips. Then he turned her around as he reached for the lemon verbena. He gently washed her back, his hands lingering as they worked her tense muscles. Maggie closed her eyes and let the smell and the gentle kneading seduce her.

Brian turned her around. He ran his hand over her dripping breasts and kissed her softly at first, then more passionately as she responded. Maggie could almost imagine they were back in that Caribbean hotel before their lives had been fractured.

"Let's make this last," Brian said. His erection rubbed her leg. "You finish up. I'm going to get out and open a bottle of wine."

"I won't be long."

After shaving her legs and touching up her bikini line, Maggie dried herself off and decided to put something sexy on. She hadn't worn any of her lingerie since Lilly died. Her stomach pinched, but she pushed it away. She quickly picked a red teddy that was a favorite of Brian's. As she pulled the teddy on she realized she had lost some weight and her breasts weren't as full as they had been. She pulled them slightly out of the cups, trying to maximize cleavage, cursing herself for throwing away the pushup pads the teddy had come with. When she was done, Brian still hadn't returned to the bedroom. She wondered if he was waiting for her somewhere else, now that they were alone in the house. She dabbed L'eau D'issey perfume, Brian's Mother's Day gift to her, on her neck, her wrists, between the cleavage, and on the inside of her upper thighs, then tiptoed out of the bedroom to find Brian.

If he were opening Pinot Noir, he would be in the living room at the bar, but if he went for the Chardonnay he would be in the kitchen. As she walked from the empty living room to the kitchen, she could hear Brian's voice, very low. She remembered the way he used to sing to himself when he didn't think anyone could hear him. She smiled and tiptoed quietly so she could surprise him. She wanted to see his face when he saw what she was wearing. As she got closer, she could hear him more clearly.

"She has been very distraught since our daughter died." His voice was low, conspiratorial.

Who could he be talking to? Maybe it was his mother, but then he wouldn't refer to Lilly "our daughter."

"I understand," he said. Silence. "I didn't think the picture looked like her, either."

She took a deep breath, listening.

"She really hasn't been herself," he said. "Let me talk to her."

Maggie was torn between being paralyzed by what Brian was saying, by wanting to see how far he would carry this conversation as long as he thought she wouldn't hear him, and wanting to confront him.

"Yes, I'm positive. She told me it wasn't the girl." Brian was saying. "Thank you, Detective. I'll tell her you returned her call."

Maggie could feel her face get hot and imagined it must be the same color as her teddy. How dare he? She walked around the corner and through the doorway into the kitchen.

"What did you just do?" she said.

Brian's face was tight, angry, but it softened as he looked at her breasts, her legs. "You look beautiful." He put the portable phone on the kitchen table and walked toward her.

"Who were you talking to?" She wanted to see if he would tell the truth.

Brian ran his finger over her bulging cleavage.

"Answer me." She pushed his hand away.

"Let's talk about it later. You look great and smell wonderful."

Maggie backed away. She put her hands on her hips. "Why were you talking to that detective?"

"He was returning your call." He tightened the belt on his robe and then looked her up and down again.

"He was calling *me*, Brian. What did he say? Does he want the pictures?"

"Can't this wait, Maggie?"

"No," Maggie said. "This is important to me. Besides, why would you want to make love to an incompetent?"

"I didn't say you were incompetent."

"Distraught." She waved her hand in the air. "Not the same person."

"I meant you were distracted and not as diligent as you used to be."

"Why is that any business of his?"

"This whole picture thing. You told me you were wrong. I think you need to stop so you can focus on our lives."

"That's what *you* think I need to do?"

"I'll open the wine," Brian said. "Relax." He started toward the refrigerator.

Maggie reached for the phone.

"I came home so we could have some time together," he said.

"How dare you speak for me."

Instead of answering her, Brian's eyes moved to her cleavage.

Maggie suddenly became aware of what she had on. Her breasts heaved with her anger. She felt completely exposed and ridiculous standing in her kitchen having an argument dressed in a red lace teddie. She turned to go back to the bedroom to get dressed. She would call the detective back in private.

Brian grabbed her arm, his eyes narrowed. "Why did you even go down there after we decided it wasn't the girl?"

Maggie shook her head. "You decided. I didn't." She started walking toward the bedroom, very conscious of the snaps on the thong that suddenly scraped between her legs.

"I think we need to talk," he said.

"We'll talk all right, but I need to put something else on."

In the bedroom she reached for her robe.

"Now you're not comfortable dressed like that in front of me?" Brian said. "I've seen you like that hundreds of times. With less."

Maggie slipped the robe on and turned to Brian. "I'm 'not the same woman,' remember?"

"The detective just told me your pictures were taken before the abduction," Brian said.

"That's the thing! I called him back to tell him I misdated the photos."

"Maggie."

"Look. I think when I capped and uncapped the canisters, I must have switched the tops on two of the rolls. So I dated the pictures I took to the police station wrong. But then I remembered the smoking clown and went back to check."

Brian stared.

"The smoking clown spanned two rolls of film. That's how I can prove I was wrong. The first pictures of the clown were dated the 19th and the second pictures were on the same roll as Mira which I had mistakenly dated the 17th. So now I can prove I took the pictures after the abduction."

Brian took a deep breath. She could hear the anger in his voice. "All you know is that you took both rolls on the same day. If you switched tops, it means another roll is wrong, too. How do you know you're right about the first roll?"

"I couldn't have taken them on two different days. The smoking clown couldn't go into the plaza on one day and come out on another! Don't you hear me?"

"You aren't hearing me." His voice was loud. "How are you so sure you didn't take them both on the 17th? Maybe the date of the first roll got switched, not the second."

"Because I know." Maggie's mind began to race, and she tried to remember why she had been so sure in the darkroom, but she couldn't seem to grasp it right now. "Besides, I can call Bo Bo the Clown and confirm he was doing an engagement in that area on the 19th." She spread her arms as if all were clear now.

"Don't you see?" Brian said. "You want this so badly that you're re-creating facts to fit your argument. Our minds can do that." He started to walk toward her. "Paranoids do it all the time."

"Paranoids?" Maggie sat down on the bed. "So now I've gone from distraught to psychotic."

"I didn't say that. What I meant was the mind is powerful." He sat down next to her on the bed.

Maggie jumped up. "And my mind is telling me those pictures are of the missing girl."

Brian sat quietly for a moment, then said, "Can't you let it go?"

"Let it go and let another child die?"

"Another child?"

"I can't just let her die." Maggie's voice got louder. "I have to save Lilly."

"Goddamit. Lilly is gone."

Maggie froze.

Brian ran his hands through his short hair. He grabbed Maggie's arms and spun her around. "You said, 'I have to save Lilly.'"

Maggie felt her body slump as Brian's hands moved her to the bed. He moved his hands over her arms and up to her face.

Her face tilted as she looked into his. "I didn't save Lilly. I let her get hurt."

"It was an accident." He pulled her to him.

"Mothers are supposed to protect their children."

"Oh, Maggie." Brian began to kiss her cheek, her chin, her eyes. "You were a good mother. Not everything can be stopped."

The emotions that had been with her since Lilly's death were all tangled in the back of her mind: sadness, resentment, rage. They stalked around her brain, caged like predators without a prey. "I have no one to hate—cancer, a murderer, an abductor. No place to put all this anger."

"Lilly's death isn't about hate." Brian looked into her eyes. "Don't feel that way."

It wasn't so much the words, but Brian's tone that made Maggie feel like a little girl who was being chastised for the wrong answer. "I feel what I feel." Maggie sensed the emotions retreat back into their cave. She knew the feelings didn't go away; they just hid to haunt her at unsuspecting moments, jumped out to torment her like monsters from under the bed when she was a little girl—only these demons were real. She squirmed on the bed.

"It's not productive," Brian said. "Just like this missing girl thing isn't productive."

"Stopping another mother from having to go through this is not productive?"

Brian stood up and walked across the room.

"What if someone could have saved Lilly, but it wasn't *productive*. Or convenient?"

"This missing-girl nonsense is turning you into someone I don't recognize," Brian said, stalking out of the room.

Maggie paced the width of the bedroom; her eyes fell on the angel pin sitting on her dresser. If someone had saved Lilly then that pin would not be the last Mother's Day gift she would ever receive. She stood still in the room as she wondered if she was even considered a mother anymore, now that she had become the inversion of the "motherless child" cliché. Lilly's death had left her a childless mother. She walked over, picked up the pin, and ran her finger over the uneven wings. "Your mother is always your mother, Lilly, even if one of you is gone," she said quietly.

Maggie nodded slowly as her hand closed around the pin. That's what she would do. If the detective didn't believe her, she would take the pictures to the little girl's mother. A mother would know her daughter, no matter what color hair she had.

"I have to do this," Maggie said. She wanted time alone to think. She took the robe off and then the teddy. She stopped when Brian walked back into the room and stood naked in front of him. "By the way, I *am* the same woman. Only maybe more so." She turned and grabbed clothes from her drawers and started toward the bathroom to get dressed.

"What does that mean?"

"It means I'm going to do what I have to do."

Brian followed her. "What are you going to do?"

Maggie closed the bathroom door. Then locked it.

"What are you going to do, Maggie?" He banged on the door. "You can't go back to the police. You're making a fool of yourself."

The words stung Maggie. She came out of the bathroom fully dressed and walked out of the bedroom to go watch TV. She needed to calm down and didn't want to talk anymore.

"I forbid you to go back to the police." Brian's voice was stern with a touch of desperation.

Maggie stopped walking. She stood still, then turned to face Brian. "You forbid me? *Forbid?*" She pronounced the word as if it were laced with bitters.

"I want this to end," Brian said. His voice teetered between a demand and a plea.

"You selfish son of a bitch. Some little girl might die so you can have peace in your life?" She turned and walked away. Instead of stopping in the living room, she kept right on walking. When she got to the front door, she grabbed her portfolio and kept going.

Chapter Thirteen

Maggie sat in the diner by herself. She had never been there alone, but she was tired of driving around and needed someplace different, yet familiar, to think. She had called the detective three more times and got his recording. She refused to leave a message. She wanted to talk to him in person.

Ethel approached the table, pad in hand. "It's late. Where's your partner in crime?"

"Home, if he's lucky." Maggie realized it was late for Ethel to still be working. "Why aren't you home?"

Ethel looked around the diner. "I am." She poised the pencil above the pad. "I could ask the same of you."

Maggie shook her head. "I needed…" her voice trailed off. "I needed pie." She could tell her smile was feeble.

"You're in the right place."

"I'll have the mixed nut—Washington, D.C. pie."

"No can do. I don't have that one today. Will pecan do?"

"Sure. I was doing some method eating. Feeling a little mixed up today."

"You're lucky if you have days when you don't." Ethel picked up the pad and left. She was back with a cup of steaming coffee, side of skim milk, then gone again.

Maggie stirred the milk into the coffee and added sugar. She thought of Brian and added a little more. She wasn't sure which she was angrier about:

what he had said to the detective or for forbidding her as if she were a child. The spoon clanked on the sides of the mug as she stirred in more sugar. Between her upset at the station, the date debacle, and what Brian had told them, the police thought she was a hysterical, grief stricken mother. She put her head in her hands. Well, she *was* grief stricken, but that didn't mean she wasn't right.

Maggie realized Ethel was standing next to the table. She'd put the pie down, but didn't leave. "You okay, kiddo?"

"Fine," Maggie said.

"Let me tell you about a needlepoint pillow I made. A stiff-as-a-board cow, on her back with her feet in the air. Words below it were: 'I'M FINE.'"

Maggie laughed. She put a forkful of the pie in her mouth. As she crunched down on the crisp pecans, her mouth watered at the sweet filling. She pictured Thanksgiving Day feasts of the past, then realized who would be missing this year. She closed her eyes because she had to, but made it dramatic for Ethel. "Mmm." She exaggerated the sound.

"You ain't fine, and that's okay. Just don't lie about it."

Maggie nodded. "You're right; I'm not fine."

"If you want to talk, I've heard it all." Ethel put her plump hand on Maggie's and the warmth surprised her. "Can I sit for a minute?" Ethel said. "These legs are getting old."

Maggie nodded.

Joints cracked as Ethel edged her way into the booth and her belly bumped up against the table. "I've never seen you in here without Donovan. That the problem? You two have a spat?"

"No. It's…" Maggie looked to the portfolio of pictures next to her.

"Know the good thing about telling something to a stranger? It doesn't come back to stare you in the face every day."

"You're no stranger, Ethel."

"No stranger than anybody else," Ethel said, then laughed. "Wanna talk?"

Maggie knew how much she wanted to talk. She needed to clear her thoughts. She nodded her head. "It's about something I have to do."

Ethel sat still.

"What I need to do is very important to me. My husband thinks I'm overreacting because…" She let her voice trail off.

"Donovan mentioned you recently lost your daughter."

Maggie nodded.

"This is a hard time for both of you." Ethel nodded slightly. "I know."

Maggie searched her face. "Did you lose a child?"

"Yes. But it was more common back then."

"But not much easier, I'd imagine."

"No."

An honest answer. Maggie liked that. "I know it's hard for him, too, but he *forbid* me from doing something. Said it was for my own good. What kind of a marriage is that?"

"He *forbid* you?"

Maggie nodded.

"Has he always forbid or granted you permission, or just since your daughter died?"

"He's never forbidden me, but then I never wanted to do anything he didn't want me to. I mean nothing important."

Ethel looked at Maggie as if making a decision. Then she leaned back into the booth. "Let me tell you a story. About pie. Many years ago, after I'd raised all six of my children, did all the cooking and cleaning for the family for thirty-one years, I wanted to do something for myself. Maybe open a bakery." She looked around the diner. "I didn't really know what I wanted. So, one night as we're sitting listening to the radio and I was crocheting one of those lace doilies I could do in my sleep, I said to my husband, 'I'm thinking of selling my baking.' 'No you're not,' he said. I put my steel crochet hook in my lap. 'I'm not?' I said. 'No,' he said. 'Because no wife of mine is going to get a job. I support this family.' I picked up that crochet hook and finished the doily in record time.

"I didn't say anything that night, or for a day or two. I thought about all the jobs I'd already done…the kids, the house, the laundry, the cleaning, the cooking. Now I wanted to do one that I wanted to do, and he says no? So I went to him and said, 'Why don't I have a say in what I do next?' He says, 'Because I'm your husband.' I say, 'What kind of relationship is this?'

He looks me right in the eye and says, 'It's a marriage. What does it look like?' Again, I don't say anything. I get the few things that I need together. He doesn't even notice. I call my daughter, who lived in Mississippi at the time, and tell her I'm coming. Soon.

"Then, I make his favorite pie—apple. But what I don't tell him is that I put citric acid crystals—you know, sour salt—that you use to make Tzimmes—in it. Lots of it. This pie is so tart that it made my mouth pucker when I put the tip of my pinky in and tasted it." She shook her head. "I'm still puckering, just thinking about it. I put it down in front of him…all warm, caramel-colored filling oozing out, the smell of cinnamon filling the air. He's reading the paper, reaches over and puts a huge bite into his mouth. He begins to gag, then choke. He swallows it down, looks at the pie, his eyes all bulging out, cheeks all pulling in, gulps down some milk. 'What the hell is this?' he says. I look him right in the eye. 'Apple pie, you bastard. What does it look like?'"

Ethel chuckled, her wrinkled face bobbing up and down. "I loved that line."

Maggie started to laugh, watching the glee on Ethel's face. "Did you end up leaving?"

"No." She shook her head. "I just needed to always know it was my choice, that if I stayed it was not because I had nowhere to go," Ethel said. "Everything is a choice, even doing nothing."

Maggie knew she could not choose to ignore this little girl. She looked at Ethel's wise face and wanted her opinion. As she reached for her photos, she said, "Did things get better with your husband?"

"Not over night. Let's say we redefined 'marriage' somewhat."

Maggie thought about it. The times she'd given in before weren't really that important to her. The things that were important to her, Brian had always gone along with. "This is the first time he's trying to stop me from doing something I think is important."

"Does he know how important it is to you?"

"He knows." Maggie pulled the pictures out of her portfolio and told Ethel the story. She ended with the conversation she overheard with Brian on the phone with the detective. "Now they'll never take me seriously. When I call they'll just placate me."

"He did that? He told them you're not the same person?" Ethel's face softened. "I can see why you're angry. But he probably thought he was protecting you."

Maggie rubbed her face with her hands. "He thinks I'm getting wacko about it. He thinks I'm seeing things that aren't there." Maggie's forefinger thumped the eight by ten. "What do you think, Ethel? Do you think they're the same girl?"

Ethel squinted at the pictures, moving her head from side to side. "Are you? Losing it?"

"I don't think so, Ethel. I know how I've acted, and I can see why he's worried, but I haven't been this focused since Lilly died."

Ethel reached for Maggie's coffee cup. "May I?"

Maggie nodded.

Ethel took a sip. "Cold, but damn good."

Maggie laughed. "You're beautiful, Ethel."

"Hell if I don't know it. Just took me too many years to figure it out."

Maggie looked at Ethel's puffy eyes, her kind expression. "You don't see the resemblance, do you?"

"Kiddo, these eyes don't see a lot of things they used to," Ethel said.

Maggie dropped her head and stared at her hands as she clutched the coffee cup.

"Besides," Ethel said, "what else can you do if the police won't believe you?"

"I can go to the mother. I know *she'd* recognize her."

Maggie felt uncomfortable at Ethel's silence as her eyes roamed the diner.

Finally Ethel said, "If it is the little girl and the abductor, there's a chance you could save this girl, or stop this guy from doing it again."

"I *know* it's her."

"All I'm saying is be sure." Ethel nodded to her, then said, "Or you'll stress an already tense marriage for nothing."

"You don't think I should pursue it?" Maggie's voice was incredulous. "It would be wrong to not try and help."

"I'm not saying that. All I'm saying is, some times there are no rights or wrongs, only decisions you can live with. Can you live with yourself if you let this go?"

"No. If I could have helped and she turns up dead…"

"Then there's your answer."

"Brian will be furious."

"The fence that separates the two sides of Hell: Damned if you do, and damned if you don't. Whatever side of the fence you end up on, make sure you can look yourself in the mirror every day because sometimes, doing what you need to do, can be a lonely place."

Maggie stared at the pictures on the table. "You're pretty wise."

"You don't live this long without something rubbing off on you. I've watched a few of my kids die, their kids. Your self's the one you have to learn to live with, the one you're sure to be stuck with till the end." Ethel had a sad smile on her face.

Maggie pushed the plate away from her. "Thanks." She looked around the diner. "I'd better let you go."

Ethel nodded.

"Just one more thing." Maggie grabbed Ethel's hand. Her voice was low. "How do you do it? Keep going after watching your kids die, your grandkids?"

Ethel squeezed Maggie's hand and let go, then eased out of the booth. She stood next to Maggie, nodded toward the table. Her wet eyes glimmered through pillows of wrinkles. "I do it for the pie, kiddo. It's as good a reason as any."

Chapter Fourteen

When Maggie returned home from the diner, Brian was already in bed. She let a slice of light from the bedroom closet escape into the room. Once she found her nightgown, she undressed in the bathroom, trying to be quiet and not wake Brian. She was still angry, yet she knew his motive had been in her best interest. She eased into bed and pulled the comforter up to her neck. Brian's head raised; he looked at her, then at the glowing red numbers from the alarm clock.

"You've been gone a long time," he said.

"I needed to think." Maggie knew she would tell him where she'd been when he asked. She had decided she would even use Ethel's apple pie story to open up the subject of his lack of support—and explain why she needed to keep going on the chance that this was the missing girl.

Brian turned over in bed.

Maggie waited for him to ask her where she'd been. Waited for him to say something.

Maggie lay on her back, staring into the darkness. She didn't know if she should try to convince Brian again about the pictures, or if she should just act alone. He'd gotten so angry. Then, she heard Brian begin to snore. She sat up, not believing he'd fallen asleep. After a few moments of listening to his snorting inhales and whistling exhales, she lay back down. Maggie tossed in bed, willing herself to relax, to fall asleep, as the red numbers on the alarm clock kept counting down the minutes toward morning. Finally, she couldn't lie still any longer.

Maggie rolled over and gave into her sleeplessness. She got up and went into the kitchen. She looked around the room and couldn't find the article that went with the picture of Mira. She went to the garage, to the recycling bin, and rummaged around until she found the section that the picture had been in. She tore the article from the newspaper and went back to the table. The Vega's address was not in the paper but the mention of the fundraiser gave her an idea.

Maggie went to the small room off the family room where the computer was. She couldn't remember the last time she had been online. After she signed on, she saw that she had three hundred and sixteen emails. She had no desire to read any of them, but saw that in the subject line of one was an announcement for an online guest book someone had posted for people to express their thoughts and condolences for the family concerning their "recent loss." Maggie immediately went to the top of the screen and redirected her computer to Google. What could anyone say about the death of an eight-year-old that could make any possible sense? They were sorry? Of course they were. That she was wonderful? Of course she was. That it was one of the most unfair things that could happen to a person? Yes.

She stared at the colorful letters that spelled out Google and thought they looked as if they had been written by a child. She typed in a search for Ronald McDonald House fundraisers. The search resulted in 2,370 items, so Maggie went back and refined the search to include Miami. This time she was down to one hundred and sixty-four, and on the first page, after checking out two hits, she got lucky. There was a link to a story under Entertainment Stories in "Miami's Community Newspapers On-line."

A small article about the upcoming annual fundraiser, "hosted by one of Coral Gables' most benevolent citizens, Nestor Vega," lavishly praised Vega for his generosity in giving back to the community. The article stated that while you had to purchase a ticket to share in the $500-a-head festivities inside the estate, for a small donation of your choosing, all Coral Gables' children were welcome to come by, meet Ronald McDonald, and get a coupon for a free Happy Meal. And, as customary, all former patients and families that had used the Ronald McDonald facility in the past would attend for free. The gala would be held at 216 Bayshore Drive, Coral Gables... Bingo! Maggie stopped reading and jotted down the address.

She switched to Mapquest and typed in the address. The red star appeared and Maggie immediately zoomed in. It looked as if the house was on a waterway that had direct access to the ocean. She printed out the map and felt a mixture of adrenaline and fatigue swirl through her body. She would call the detective one more time in the morning, and if he still discounted her pictures, she was off to see the mother.

She got back to bed, satisfied with her plan. The bed was comforting, and as she turned her back to her sleeping husband, pulling the sheets up to her chin, she found herself suddenly exhausted. She closed her eyes, imaging the excitement on Mira Vega's mother's face when Maggie handed over such valuable evidence. She only hoped it wasn't too late.

***

When Maggie woke, Brian was not in bed, nor anywhere in the bedroom. The memory of her mid-night search and the map leading to the Vega household made her anxious to get her day started. Her late-night anger at Brian slowed her steps when she smelled coffee as she approached the kitchen. She knew they needed to talk; she hated living with conflict, but maybe it could wait until she got the pictures to someone who could find the little girl. Brian sat at the kitchen table reading the paper. He looked up as she came in, then looked back down.

Silence was ringing through Maggie's head. She got a cup of coffee, took her time with the milk and sugar, deciding whether she should stay in the kitchen or just go back to her room and get ready for the day. As she started out the door toward her bedroom, she looked back at Brian. He never looked up, never said a word.

Maggie turned back and thumped her coffee mug on the table. Brian looked up.

"I thought we weren't supposed to go to bed mad," she said.

"Then why didn't you say something?"

Maggie felt her anger mount. "Why didn't you?"

"I talked to you."

"You commented on how long I was gone."

"You were," he said.

"You didn't say a word about the argument or try to resolve it."

"You usually do that."

Maggie nodded her head. "I hate going to bed angry."

"I know. I was surprised when you didn't say anything."

"Why didn't you check to see if I was okay?" Maggie said.

Brian shook his head. "I'm not sure what to do with you these days. Whatever I do is wrong."

The conversation felt like a dog chasing its tail. Maggie leaned against the kitchen counter. "I'm so tired, Brian."

Brian folded the newspaper and turned his body toward Maggie. "Is all this because I decided to save you some embarrassment and be honest with that detective?"

"Honest? In whose opinion?" Maggie paced across the kitchen.

"You told me it wasn't the girl," he said.

"I was wrong." She stared at him, feeling her face get hot.

"I know."

"I'm an adult and can speak for myself."

"You haven't been acting like one lately."

Maggie stopped pacing. "And who are you to decide that?"

"This is getting nowhere." Brian stood.

"I'm tired of having to explain myself."

"I'm tired, too," Brian said, "of being accused of being wrong for trying to make you feel better."

"Then stop. Let me alone."

Brian stared at her as if trying to see through her. "Maybe that's exactly what I should do," he said. "Let you alone for a while."

"What does that mean?"

He shook his head. "I can't take it. If you have the energy for this..." He let his words drop off, then turned to face her. "Either you drop this missing girl thing and focus on our marriage, or—"

"Or, what?" Maggie said.

"Or I can stay at the commuter pad that Gary Lustig has."

Maggie couldn't believe he was giving her an ultimatum. She walked to where he was standing at the window and looked into his eyes. "Brian, this girl could die if I don't come forward."

"You came forward. It didn't work. Face it." He put his face right in front of hers. "You can't save her, no matter how much you want to. Just like you couldn't save Lilly."

"You bastard!" Maggie reached out and slapped Brian's face. As she watched his shocked expression, she pulled her hand back and held it close to her chest, stunned by what she'd said and done. She'd never called him a name before, nor would she have believed she would strike him. She watched his face turn to steel. Regret pushed her anger down. "I'm so sorry, Brian." She reached out to touch his face. "I didn't mean to do that."

He grabbed her wrist. "I don't even know you any more." He shook his head as if talking to himself, trying to comprehend a difficult concept. "You can't adjust."

"Adjust?" The anger seesawed back up. She threw her hands in the air. "Is that what you've done? Like adjusting for a thunderstorm that's gotten in the way of your flight plan? Is that what our daughter's death is to you? Fucking interference on the radar screen? Go around it and continue on?"

"What else is there to do, Maggie?" He stood with his hands on his hips.

Maggie sat down at the table and put her head in her hands. "It's only been two months, Brian. I don't know what else there is to do, but for me it feels like the whole fucking plane has blown up." She looked up into his face.

Brian stared back. "Think about what you want, Maggie. I'll give you some time alone. Maybe it will be easier without me here to *control* you."

The mocking tone with which he used the word "control" made her vacillation between anger and sadness continue. He broke eye contact, and Maggie watched him turn to leave.

"You're right about one thing," she yelled as he walked out of the kitchen. "You don't know me. Because the last thing I want right now is to be alone." Or maybe the last thing she wanted was to be stopped from finding this missing girl. When he didn't come back, she walked to the dark room and didn't bother to turn on any lights as she closed the door.

Chapter Fifteen

Maggie's mind raced as her car sped south on I95 toward Coral Gables, toward the Vega house. Anger raged through her as she thought of Detective Hodges' reaction to her early morning phone call and her news that the pictures were indeed taken the day after the abduction. The detective started another lecture on how rewards were not awarded for clues, but only if they led to the safe return of the child. Maggie had interrupted him, hung up, and gathered her pictures together to take to Mira Vega's mother. What did Maggie care how the family got the pictures, as long as they got them?

Her thoughts bounced to the last twenty-four hours with Brian. She couldn't believe they had had the fight they did, and even worse, she couldn't believe he'd left and she had let him. She didn't remember them arguing much before Lilly died, yet now it seemed to be a common occurrence.

Her mood continued to sink as the exit numbers got lower and she got closer to US1. She missed Lilly so much. It was more than the fact that her daughter wasn't there; it was that she would never again be there. Maggie *knew* that in her mind—she just couldn't seem to *grasp* it. It was like the word you search for in your mind to complete a thought: you know you know it, you just can't get to it. Lilly's absence was an abyss in her life that she didn't have any clue how, if ever, she would fill.

Then anger took over Maggie's mind, again, when she thought of Brian's decision to give her time to think. She did nothing but think. That was as stupid as the parent who gave the crying child something to cry about. Didn't she have enough voids in her life right now? Why couldn't

the one person who should support her during this time be there for her?
She needed time to get back to "normal life," whatever the hell that was
anyway. And how much time and exactly what she expected to happen, she
didn't know; those were questions she needed answered to quantify an un-
quantifiable situation.

I95 turned into the slower lanes of US1. From her last trip to the Coral
Gables Police Department, she knew she was getting closer, and for now,
for this moment, she was glad Brian was not at home, having to be answered to. She didn't need to make excuses for where she was, and she
knew she would go even if he'd asked her not to.

As she veered to the right, Maggie glanced at her portfolio that con-
tained the pictures she would show Mira's mother. Of all the things she was
confused about, this was not one of them—this was the missing girl.

Maggie drove down the narrow, tree-canopied streets of Coral
Gables with the map she had printed from Mapquest, pinpointing the
Vega house in the development of Coral Reef. She'd been driving slowly,
in "The City Beautiful," as Coral Gables liked to call itself, and she had to
agree, at least this part was quite lovely. Some day she'd have to come
back when she had time. Maybe to visit Mira once she was returned safe
and sound.

She drove over a small bridge and to her left was a stone sign "Coral
Reef," with a guardhouse barring her entry. Maggie knew she had a 50-50
chance of being stopped and was ready. She remembered from her search
for her own house that privately owned streets must be maintained at sub-
stantial cost to the owners, but access could be barred for added security.
However, what still surprised Maggie was that publicly owned streets, those
maintained by all the taxpayers, could not deny access to, well, the public.
The guard gate was only a deterrent, not a roadblock.

She pulled out a manila envelope with her card stapled to the top.
Inside were assorted pictures of the catering halls and homes that had
housed the many events she had photographed. Maggie moved her car next
to the guardhouse and just behind the gate, and then opened her window.

"Yes?" A tall, muscular man in a uniform looked at her as he leaned
out of the guardhouse holding a clipboard and pen.

"I'm here to see Mrs. Vega," Maggie said, firmly. "About the fund-raiser." She waved the envelope in his direction as she checked her watch, as people tend to do when they have appointments.

Without asking another question, he nodded and the gate in front of her went up. As she drove ahead without having to offer another word, Maggie took this to be the first good omen since she had taken the pictures.

Maggie looked down at the map on which she had highlighted the route in red. It looked like one of those puzzles that held a treasure when you got to the center. She turned her car left and right following the snaking movement of her red pen on the map. Maggie's heart began to beat faster while her pressure on the gas pedal slowly diminished as she came around a cul-de-sac and saw the house.

Situated on a doublewide lot, with lighted tennis courts off to the side, the house was exquisite. Maggie didn't remember ever using that word to describe anything before—but this house defined the word. She passed slowly while the car behind her honked. Maybe City Beautiful, but not City Polite. She circled around the cul-de-sac and pulled off a short distance from the house. Stately palm trees bordered the house and lush foliage was placed for the utmost privacy—but the full front of the house was visible. She wondered which, if any, of the French doored-balconies led to Mira's room.

Short columns, connected by an iron fence seemingly designed to allow a view of the house, surrounded the property. Off to the side was a large ornate iron gate. There were three cars in the driveway, and for the first time Maggie realized that the little girl's mother may not be at home.

She drove onto the paved driveway, up to the speaker in front of the gate, and pushed the buzzer.

"Yes?" A tinny voice, female with a very heavy Latin accent, came through the metal box. "Can I help you?"

"I'm here to see Mrs. Vega."

"For what purpose, please?"

Maggie cleared her throat and spoke in her most resonant professional voice. "I'm a photographer. I have a picture of Mira that I believe was taken after her abduction, possibly with the person who has her."

There was a pause. "Please wait."

Maggie nodded to the machine and waited as the thick South Florida summer heat filled her car. She turned up the air conditioning. The gold leafing on the tall iron gate was the first detail Maggie found ostentatious. The pattern swirled around, curving to end in gold leaves. She tried to image what it would be like to photograph the shadows from the pattern as the sun hit the gate when a voice boomed out of the speaker, startling her.

"Why have you not taken this picture to the police?" It was a strong male voice with the slightest hint of an accent.

Maggie was ready for this question. "I did," she said. She fixed her gaze at the black speaker box as she spoke. "They seemed very busy, sir. I don't think they took me seriously enough." Maggie winced at the lie; they hadn't taken her seriously at all. "If this were my daughter, I would want to pursue this lead."

There was a pause, then, "How did you find this house?"

"You're having a public function here in a week. The address wasn't hard to come by."

"The reward money is not given for tips, only for a tip that leads to the safe return of my daughter." He said it as if he'd said it hundreds of times before.

Maggie felt frustrated as she realized she couldn't interrupt on a speaker such as this one. When he stopped talking she said, "This is not about money. It's about your daughter."

"Why should I believe you?"

"You don't need to. Let the picture speak for itself. What do you have to lose by looking?" Maggie waited. "I would take a few moments, if it were my daughter."

After a long pause, the speaker clicked. "Wait in your car. I will send someone to get the picture. Do not proceed into my driveway, or I will call the police."

"I understand." Maggie knew she wouldn't have time to explain, so she picked out the picture she had blown up of Mira's face. It was grainy, but if you held it away, you could see it was her. All she wanted was reasonable doubt so she could get in and talk to the child's mother and father, not drive away and have them discount her as the police had done.

Maggie saw the large, carved-wood front doors open, and a heavyset man walked down the driveway. She turned off her car and stood outside. The gate squeaked slightly as it swung open, and the man approached the car.

"Mr. Vega will look at the picture." He held out his left hand and pulled back his jacket with his right. The hand rested on the handle of a gun.

Maggie realized how vulnerable this family must be feeling and knew she must appear non-threatening at all costs, yet completely convincing. She held the picture up so the man could see it. "Please tell him to look closely. I believe her hair color has been changed to disguise her." She handed over the picture, along with one of her business cards, hoping to give her photograph credibility. "If he has at least a reasonable doubt that it is her, it's worth his time to look at the rest of the pictures I have."

The man nodded and walked away leaving Maggie to stand in the sun. She shaded her eyes and watched the man walk up the driveway, as the gate lumbered closed behind him. She paced up and down in front of the house and imagined the little girl playing on the lawn. In her mind she saw her doing cartwheels and tumble-saults. She imagined chasing the little girl while playing tag. But in her mind, as Maggie tapped the small shoulder, the face that turned around to became "it" was Lilly's. She got into the car, started the engine, and turned the air conditioning to full blast. She redirected the center vent at her head and closed her eyes as the cold air swept over her face.

When there was a tap on her window, she jumped, then turned to roll down the window as the man reached for the handle of her door and opened it.

"Mr. Vega would like to speak to you."

Maggie nodded and turned the key in the engine, creating sudden silence. She walked next to and slightly ahead of the man as the silence continued. Once through the gate, the walkway was lined with low, blue-flowering shrubs that perfectly accented the pink pavers of the driveway. The alcove that covered the front door reminded Maggie of a small hotel, yet the scarlet potted geraniums and matching bougainvillea somehow made the area intimate and inviting.

A woman in a housekeeper's uniform nodded as Maggie entered the house, and she was stunned at the change in ambiance. While the outside was warm and lush and enticing, the foyer was large, sparsely furnished and off-putting. Straight ahead was a bank of tall French doors that allowed a view of the spacious backyard and the canal that connected to Biscayne Bay.

The man had gone slightly ahead, and Maggie's footsteps echoed on the immaculate white ceramic tile as she hurried to catch up. As she passed the one piece of furniture in the alcove, a table full of photographs, she slowed down. Maggie stood still as her eyes swept over the collection dedicated to a small blond child. Maggie picked up a picture in a heavy silver frame, and the eyes of the girl from the service plaza stared back at her. The eyes of Mira Vega.

"Mr. Vega is waiting," the man's voice said from behind her.

Maggie felt a hand on her arm. She put the picture down, and as she walked away she saw, in her peripheral vision, the woman pull a dust cloth from her pocket and wipe nonexistent fingerprints from the frame. Maggie wondered what it would be like for a child to grow up in such a fastidious environment. The man walked her down a long hall and through open double doors.

Maggie found herself in a large library with built-in dark cherry wood bookshelves that covered all four walls. A ladder leaned against the shelves and reached to just a few feet under the vaulted ceiling. Sun streamed through a skylight, and in the light, in the center of the room, stood a man holding Maggie's picture. His shoes were polished to a high shine, his dark pants held a perfect crease, and his bright blue shirt was meticulously pressed. But the sleeves of the shirt had been haphazardly pushed up past his elbows and dark circles framed his eyes. His hair, although carefully combed, looked as if it hadn't been washed in days. Maggie wondered how he got up day after day with the uncertainty of ever seeing his daughter again. With Lilly, there had been no doubt of what the outcome would be as the small body lay in the intensive care unit bed. There was no bargaining, no pleading, no telling God you would trade the rest of your life for hers. This she could attest to as hell. She couldn't imagine loss coupled with doubt. Walking the line between hoping for the best and accepting the inevitable must be a special kind of torture devised by the devil himself.

The man put the picture down on a massive dark cherry wood desk that held a shine to rival that of his shoes. He walked toward her.

"Ms. Miller. It is a pleasure to meet you." He reached out his hand and rather than shake her extended hand, he enclosed it in both of his. "I am Nestor Vega." His smile was polite but held no joy, and his eyes seemed to read her face the way a blind person's fingertips would read Braille. Maggie remembered then; he was an attorney, an extremely successful one. "Thank you for coming," he said.

"Thank you for seeing me." Maggie put her portfolio down. "I lost a child, too, so I had to come." She winced at what her words suggested. She thought she saw his eyes begin to tear, but it disappeared so quickly that she wondered if she might have imagined it. "Do you agree that could be Mira, Mr. Vega?"

"Please, call me Nestor." He motioned her to a small leather love seat in a sitting area away from the desk. "Please," he said as he gestured to the chair. He remained standing while she sat on the edge of the seat and put her portfolio next to her. "In my business," he said, "I never make a decision before seeing all the evidence." He sat in a large overstuffed chair. "I understand you have more pictures." He leaned forward with his elbows on his knees, a starving man waiting for a morsel of nourishment. "Where did you take these pictures?"

Maggie reached into her portfolio and pulled out what she had brought. She had checked and rechecked the pile this time. "At a service plaza on the Turnpike." She handed him the pictures and watched his face closely as he examined them. His expression was what she imagined was his court face until he got to the last picture. His eyebrows deepened as he brought the picture close to his face. She had left the one with the thin man on the bottom of the pile knowing it would be a difficult picture for a parent to see—your child being possessed by an abductor. He let out a noise, but caught himself and his face once again regained control. He bit his lip as he looked at the other pictures again, then at the last one. Maggie could see, as skilled as he was, he was trying to keep his composure.

Nestor took his time putting the pictures into a neat pile, lining up the edges, then leaned back and crossed his legs, looking as calm as royalty that had received her for tea. "I thank you so much for taking the time to come. It was very good of you, but this is not my daughter." He folded his hands over the pile of pictures in his lap.

Maggie stared at Nestor's face. She could swear that he had said "not" in front of "my daughter," but she must have heard wrong.

"She is a very close match, yes, but I am afraid," he shook his head and held her eyes as he said, "she is not my Mira."

Maggie was aware of her eyes being held in his hypnotic gaze and felt for a moment that this man just might be able to convince her that Jack the Ripper was innocent. She broke eye contact. "Mr. Vega, I know this must be difficult." Maggie was on her feet and over to a table covered with photos. She picked one up and brought it to him. "This looks like the same girl to me." In the photo, the little girl wore a bright pink ski bib and a matching pink ski cap that covered her hair. Without the hair-color discrepancy it was even more apparent this was Mira.

For an instant, anger seemed to flicker across his face. Then she watched his expression fall into neutral composure. "Don't you think I would know my own daughter? That I would do anything to find her?"

"I don't understand," Maggie said.

"There is nothing to understand." Nestor walked to his desk and dropped the pictures, then turned in a choreographed movement. "I truly appreciate your concern, Ms. Miller, but this is not my daughter."

Maggie looked around the room trying to comprehend. His initial reaction to the photos had convinced her she was right. She couldn't have imagined it, yet, now he was negating everything she had witnessed.

Her eyes fell on another picture. It was of Nestor Vega, his missing daughter and her mother. The daughter's fair features were in striking contrast to both parents' dark hair and eyes. The composition intrigued her, too. The little girl sat on the father's lap while the mother stood behind the chair. An interesting shot for a man she would have thought to be a strong patriarch.

"A nice picture, no?" Nestor picked up the picture and looked at it. Then he put it down and turned toward her. "The little girl you have seen is very close in many ways to my Mira, but the hair color, the bone structure is so very different." His voice had taken on a tone that he probably used in court to convince jurors. "And how I wish," his eyes cast upward toward the skylight as if it were a direct channel to his God, "how I wish it were her. To know she was still alive."

Maggie's face got hot as he stared unblinkingly at her.

"You said you'd lost a child," he said. "Then you know a parent would do anything to get her back."

"You don't think this is worth pursuing?"

He put his hand on his chest. "A false lead, false hope. No, that would kill me yet again."

Maggie remembered the fresh pain every time she woke up thinking that Lilly was still alive. And yet, something seemed wrong here. The only other solution was that everyone else was right and that she really had lost her mind.

"You understand." He said it as a statement, then extended his hand. "Let me see you out."

Maggie grabbed her portfolio, avoiding his hand. "May I have my pictures?"

"Perhaps I could keep them. They are quite good. Maybe someday, when Mira is back home, I could call upon you for your services as a photographer."

Maggie stared at his face as he stared at hers. The pictures were fair at best, most of them grainy, one even out of focus, and from what she had seen around the house, he knew that, too. She brushed by him, walked to the desk and grabbed the pile he had put down. "I can do much better," she said as she held up the pictures. "When she returns." She slipped the pictures into the side pocket of her portfolio.

As she walked to the door, Nestor Vega put his hand on her elbow. She resisted her urge to move it and wondered if her animosity was as palpable as his hand. This man was experiencing something similar to what she had when she lost her own daughter. Empathy had compelled her to come. The house was filled with pictures of the little girl, and she was more convinced than ever that her pictures were of Mira Vega. Yet, here she was—being turned away, again.

At the front door Nestor turned to her and said, "You have been a good Samaritan for coming all this way. I thank you, even though you made the trip for nothing." He took her hand in both of his. "If there is ever a time I can return the favor."

She noticed that the smile on his face now looked genuine. She turned to leave, then felt compelled to try to convince him one more time. Perhaps ask to speak to the child's mother. She turned back suddenly. "Mr. Vega…" She stopped when she saw the smile had completely disappeared.

"Yes?" The smile returned, every bit as genuine looking as it had been before it disappeared.

She couldn't forget that he was an attorney, a very, very successful one. What he couldn't know was that studying faces was her business, too. "I hope you get your daughter back soon." She put on a wide smile, extended her hand, and turned away. She was almost certain he was lying, but the question that overwhelmed her was why.

Chapter Sixteen

On her way home, Maggie stopped at the studio to see if Gerlinde had any baked goods before heading off to her afternoon appointment. A tasty pastry sounded appealing after the morning she had had with Nestor Vega. There were none on the table in the break room, but she was surprised when she saw Donovan making coffee.

"What are you doing here?" she said to Donovan. "The schedule has you at an in-house family shoot."

"Two of the little girls had the chicken pox. In all the hubbub, they forgot to cancel," Donovan said. "Want some company on your shoot?"

Maggie hesitated, and she saw Donovan blush.

"Or, I could do it," he said, "and you could take the rest of the day off."

The offer was almost too good to pass up. She was still confused about Nestor Vega and wondered how she would concentrate on the shoot. Then she remembered the clients were ones she had worked with before and the park where she was to meet them was very soothing.

"A repeat client," she said. "I should go." It would be a short shoot in a quiet park, but she realized she would like the company. "Come along. I had a bad morning. I could use the distraction."

"The highest compliment. Donovan the Distraction." He smiled.

"I mean company." She smiled back and realized how comfortable she had become with him.

***

The shoot at Three Lakes Park went smoothly, especially when Maggie took a few of the suggestions that Donovan made, out of earshot of the clients, of course. They were loading the equipment into her car when Donovan said, "Are you okay? You seem distracted."

"I'm…" Maggie was about to say "fine" but stopped herself. She was upset about Brian and upset about Nestor Vega's reaction, but didn't really want to talk about either one. "I'm really not okay, but I don't want to talk about it. Is that okay?"

Donovan laughed. "Of course it's okay. It's not obligatory to share all your secrets." He looked closely at her face. "Do you have some time?"

Maggie looked at her watch. Now that she wasn't hunting down kidnappers or in her dark room looking for pictures, she seemed to have lots of time. Not to mention the recent lack of husband. "Are you going to take me for pie?"

"Not exactly." Donovan took the blanket Maggie used for on location baby shoots out of the back of the car and put it under his arm. He took her hand and began to lead her to a grassy area away from the trees. He spread the blanket on the ground and sat down. He patted the spot next to him.

"Should you be in the sun?" Maggie said.

"Probably not."

"Then what are you doing?"

"I want you to see something," he said.

"What?"

"If I tell you it won't be a surprise."

"How old are you?" she said playfully. "Only eight-year-olds say that."

"There are parts of me that will never grow up."

"Peter Pan Syndrome?"

He shook his head. "I could never get the flying thing right."

The mention of flying made Maggie think of Brian. She plopped down on the blanket.

"Close your eyes and lay back," Donovan said.

"Donovan—"

"You liked the pie, didn't you?"

Maggie smiled and closed her eyes. "It's not your job to cheer me up."

"Lay back and be quiet."

Maggie scooted to the end of the blanket and lay back.

"Open your eyes. What do you see?"

Maggie turned toward Donovan. "A very strange man."

"Not here," he said. He took her chin in his hand and gently moved her head straight. "There." He pointed to the sky and then lay back down.

"There's nothing there but clouds."

"Right."

Maggie felt a slight breeze blow over her body. She inhaled and let the tension of the last few days ease out of her. She could smell hamburgers cooking on a charcoal grill and thought how nice a picnic would be right now. Potato salad with lots of celery and mayonnaise. Crunchy and creamy. Salty potato chips. Baked beans with bacon on top. Crisp slices of onion on the burger. Lilly always preferred hotdogs, not too burnt. Maggie closed her eyes.

"Did you ever find things in the clouds when you were little?" Donovan said.

"Yeah." She remembered a hill in Nash Park in New Jersey where she and her father would look at the sky. She looked at the clouds. "My father called them Rorschachs in the sky. He pretended to analyze my answers."

"Then you know how to play."

"Once we sat there for two hours until I said I saw a dog. He said it meant there was a puppy in my future then took me home where my mother had a ten-week-old cocker spaniel waiting as a surprise. I named her Bailey."

Donovan chuckled. "Very nice."

"I'd forgotten about that day." Her eyes searched the sky for a resemblance of a puppy. "I never played that game again, after he died. I was ten."

"It's time you started again," he said softly. "Tell me what you see."

"That one looks like a cow," Maggie said. Her hand pointed to the two o'clock position in the sky.

"I predict there will be milk in your coffee today."

Maggie groaned. They lay in silence as the white clouds moved lazily overhead.

"When I was little, my mother told me I was a cloud that had fallen to earth," Donovan said.

Maggie turned onto her side to look at Donovan. His white eyebrow could be mistaken for little clouds above his eyes which were the color of the sky on a clear day. "She did?"

"She would point to the sky and say, 'There's Donovan. Oh no, wait, here he is.' Then she would tickle me. I would wait all afternoon until she did that."

Maggie laughed.

"It was the way she explained my color to me," Donovan said.

"Really?"

"I know she told me other things, but that was the one I wanted to believe. She said the sun and the clouds were archenemies and fought for dominance of the sky. The sun would burn up the clouds, so the clouds were there to chase the sun away. Since I was a cloud, she told me I must always protect myself from the sun with a hat, clothing, sunglasses, and sunscreen. If I disguised myself, the sun wouldn't recognize me as a cloud, and wouldn't burn me."

"I like your mom."

"When kids at school would make fun of me, I'd look at them and say, 'You don't know who I am,' and I'd walk away."

"How long did you believe that story?"

"What do you mean?" He looked at her in feigned horror.

Maggie smiled.

"I always knew it was a medical condition," Donovan said. "I just liked her story better."

Maggie looked at Donovan's pale skin, almost white hair. He was a handsome man with pleasing features: a strong chin, high cheekbones, a nose that was too thick for a woman but looked perfect on a man, and wide, open eyes that housed kind blue irises. The overall effect was of a photo that had been overexposed. She tried to imagine what he would have looked like with pigment.

As if he had read her mind, Donovan stared into the sky and said, "I dyed my hair once, put on that self-tanning stuff. I wanted to see what I would look like normal."

Maggie reached out and touched his upper arm. "You're not *not* normal, you're just different."

"That's what mothers say to children they love in spite of their 'differences.'"

This Maggie knew to be true. "How did you look? With the added color, I mean?"

Donovan turned his head to look at her, then back to the sky. "You're the first one I've told that story to who's asked me that."

"I'm sorry."

"Don't be. I looked like a ghost who'd been covered in caramel, and my hair dipped in chocolate. I couldn't do anything with the eyelashes."

Maggie laughed. "You're making me hungry." Then she thought of how cruel children were to each other. "It must have been hard when you were little."

"It's how I started taking pictures. When people would stare at me, my mother told me to stare back. I took her literally and picked up a camera. That made the difference—I was inviting them to look at me. But then they didn't notice *me*. Point a camera at someone's face, and all they think about is themselves."

Maggie'd noticed how differently people behave when their actions are being recorded. As if it didn't count if it wasn't caught on film. Shouldn't it all count?

"And it's a place to hide," he said. "I can look at anything, stare at anyone, and no one questions it."

"Does it still bother you? How people react?"

Donovan thought for a few minutes, then said, "I know now that I'm an anomaly. I'm walking proof that things go wrong, things we can't control. If something happened to *me*, something could happen to *them*." He shrugged his shoulders. "Most people don't want to be reminded of that on a daily basis. I've learned to accept their reactions and understand it's not me, but what I represent that they can't handle."

Maggie thought about what he said, of how people like to pretend they are in control. She thought of Brian's close hold on the reins of life. Was his fear that she was out of control? Yet, was there any control? If she had come out of the darkroom when she was supposed to would her child be alive today? Or would she have died while Maggie tossed lettuce, tomatoes, and cucumbers, every bit as senselessly? Lived, if Maggie had skipped the salad all together?

Donovan turned toward Maggie. "Some days I'd rather be a cloud," he said, nodding toward the sky. "Tell me what you see."

Maggie scanned the puffs in the sky willing herself to see a form in the undefined shapes. She couldn't see anything but clouds. She thought of the past few days. "What do you do if you see one thing, but everyone else tells you that it's not what it is?"

"Cloud forms are pretty flexible, Maggie."

Maggie lay in silence as a cloud moved over her head. She sat up. "I went to see the family of the missing girl."

"And?"

"The father said the girl I took the pictures of wasn't his daughter."

Donovan sat up and faced Maggie with his legs crossed. "You feel let down because you were wrong?"

"I'm not sure I *am* wrong."

"What do you mean?"

Maggie picked a blade of grass. "I know it sounds crazy, but I still think it's her." She put the tender end of the grass in her mouth and bit down like she used to when she was young. Then she thought of pesticides and spit it out.

"Wouldn't a father recognize his daughter?" Donovan said.

"That's just it; I think he did. It's as if at first he thought it was her, then he said it wasn't. I don't get it."

"I don't either. What does Brian say?"

Maggie groaned. "He has always thought I was over reacting. He told me to stop and was surprised when I went to the police."

"The police must have believed you if you got to the father."

"They didn't, exactly," she said. "I went on my own."

"To the family?"

"I got a little crazy in the police station, got the date I took the pictures wrong. The detective blew me off, then when I found the real date, Brian answered the phone and told him I'd been distraught."

"I'm not following. It's like trying to catch up on a soap opera after you haven't watched it for weeks."

Maggie laughed. "My life feels like a soap opera lately. So much drama."

"You've been through a lot."

Maggie nodded, then lay back down. After a few minutes she said, "Do you think…" She wasn't sure she should even put the question into words, because a question begged for an answer.

When she didn't continue, Donovan said, "Some times I think. Some times I'd rather just eat pie."

Maggie stared up at Donovan, his head surrounded by clouds. She thought of his mother. "I don't think I would have been as wise with Lilly as your mom was with you."

"Are you thinking of all that you'll miss?"

She shook her head. "I'd rather eat pie than think of that right now." She sat up. "I don't even feel like me anymore. I don't know who I am. I plan to say or do something, and I hear myself say things, do things, and I wonder where they came from."

"Sounds scary."

She stared at Donovan. She held the edge of the blanket tight in her fist. "Do you think Brian is right? Do you think I could be losing my mind?"

He seemed to be thinking hard, as if it were a possibility. "Maybe you're allowed to lose your mind—at least some. You have a big loss to get used to. Maybe it's a matter of being able to come back when you need to." His eyes narrowed. "Can you?"

"How would a crazy person know?"

"What do you think?"

"I've thought of nothing else since I left that house in Coral Gables. That I must be the insane one. I feel as if I know in my heart that man is lying, but it makes no sense why he would. At one point, I thought maybe he didn't want his daughter found for some reason. She looks nothing like him or his wife. Maybe he thinks she's not his. Or maybe he did to her what was done to that poor little beauty queen in Colorado."

"Is there room in your mind for the tiniest possibility that it isn't her?"

"None." She picked another blade of grass and put it in her mouth. She began to chew. "And that makes me insane, doesn't it?"

"Not insane."

"Could I want Lilly back so badly that my mind *sees* the little girl the way I want? Brian said our mind does that all the time—rationalizes our delusions."

"Does it matter about the little girl? It's out of your hands now."

"I've read enough psychology to know that a defense mechanism only works when it's unconscious," she said.

"Meaning what?"

"It means that it only relieves your anxiety if you are not conscious that you're using it. Like denial."

"I was a Psych major. I knew that part. I wondered why you said it," he said.

"It means that I should go home now, look at the pictures and that little girl should look no more like Mira Vega than she looks like you."

"If she turns into an albino, then I'll know you are insane."

Maggie laughed, but Donovan's expression became serious.

"Look, Maggie, that little girl does look like Mira Vega," Donovan said. "It was not your imagination, and it won't go away no matter how much insight you acquire."

Maggie felt as if he had just given her a present on her birthday. She reached over and touched his arm. "Thank you for saying that. I'm not just making up the resemblance, am I?"

"No, you're not making it up. But that doesn't mean it's the same girl."

"But at least I'm not insane." She threw her head back and looked at the sky. She looked back to Donovan and smiled broadly. As she stared at his smile, his pale features, his ponytail, she realized she wished he would reach over and hold her to comfort her as he had in the diner.

Donovan leaned in and kissed Maggie's forehead. She closed her eyes and felt his soft lips brush her skin. She opened her eyes to see him staring intently at her face. She felt her face flush as she noticed she had tilted her lips a fraction of an inch in his direction. She turned away as she realized it was not just a comforting hug she wanted. Maybe she was insane.

Chapter Seventeen

The next afternoon, Maggie walked into the studio and stopped at Gerlinde's desk, squinting her eyes at the vegetables in the rectangular Tupperware container on the blotter. "What are you eating?"

"And good afternoon to you, too," Gerlinde said, crunching loudly on a carrot stick.

"I'm sorry." Maggie dropped her portfolio next to Gerlinde's desk. "I've been into comfort food, and now my taste buds seem to control my mood."

"Carrot sticks and celery with low fat Ranch dressing for me."

"There goes my mood."

"Bill needs to lower his cholesterol so I decided to try to lose some weight at the same time," Gerlinde said.

Maggie shook her head in mock horror. "So we all have to suffer along with your husband?" She started toward her office. "I guess coffee with extra sugar will have to do me."

"It'll go great with the Vanilla Raisin bread I brought *you*."

Maggie stopped in her tracks. "Are you teasing me? Because on a day like today it could be grounds for dismissal."

"You couldn't live without me, honey. But, no, I'm not teasing. Soaked the raisins for a whole day in vanilla extract."

Maggie changed course and headed for the break room. She put her portfolio on the floor and unwrapped the half loaf of homemade bread that sat on top of the microwave. She brought it to her nose and inhaled. "This is heaven." Maggie dug out a raisin and put it in her mouth. The rich flavor of raisin was mixed with heady vanilla. "This is so good." She turned to see Gerlinde leaning on the doorframe, her face glowing.

"I know."

"Where's the rest?"

"Donovan stopped by and took a chunk with him."

"Mmm." Maggie was glad for the excuse to have the silly look on her face that Donovan's name seemed to produce.

"Now that you're in a food-induced good mood, you have an urgent message."

Maggie's stomach felt as if an elevator had moved suddenly. "Brian?"

"No. Some man named Nestor Vega has called several times and said you would know what it was about."

"When did he call?" Her mind was racing. Could he have changed his mind?

"Yesterday afternoon and this morning. You had your cell phone off. He didn't say it was urgent until the third call this morning. He got a little angry when I wouldn't give him your home or cell number."

Maggie popped the rest of the slice of bread she had cut off from the loaf into her mouth, then poured a cup of coffee. "Bring the number into my office, please." She headed for her desk. "The next appointment is in fifteen, right?"

"Change of plans," Gerlinde said.

Maggie stopped walking.

"I filled in an on-site shoot for this afternoon." She looked at her watch. "You have just enough time to have a snack and call this guy back."

Maggie continued to her desk and in a few minutes Gerlinde appeared with four pink message slips in one hand and a slice of vanilla raisin bread in the other. "His office and home." She handed Maggie the pink papers and took a bite of the bread.

"The diet?"

Gerlinde shrugged. "My cholesterol is fine." She walked out.

After dialing Vega's office and being told he was home for the morning, Maggie called the house and spoke to the housekeeper who told her Mr. Vega was working. When she identified herself, she was put right through.

"Ms. Miller. Thank you for returning my call."

"What can I do for you, Mr. Vega?"

"I was wondering if you could tell me exactly where and when the pictures you took were taken." Nestor said.

"Have you changed your mind about the possibility that it is Mira?"

"Are there any more besides the ones you showed me?"

Maggie noticed he hadn't answered her question. "It *is* her, isn't it?" She looked to the picture of Lilly on her desk and nodded.

"Ms. Miller." His voice was tense. She could hear him exhale, and with his next words she could picture the fake smile. "I'm not sure if it is my daughter or not. But I've been," he hesitated, "advised not to ignore any leads. So perhaps I could have the pictures back? And any others you may have."

"I'm afraid I showed you all of them." Who was advising him? The police, she wondered?

"The location?"

If it were the police then he would know where they had been taken—she had told Detective Hodges. Maggie wondered why she hesitated to tell him. She wanted the little girl found and yet he made her uneasy. Now she was sure he knew it was his daughter, so why the cloak-and-dagger routine? She decided to avoid his question, the same way he had avoided hers. "The police have that information. Have you called them?"

"It would be much more expedient if I could get it from you. They would have to plow through a pile of fake leads."

"That's a good point." The advice didn't come from the police then. "Who advised you to continue on this lead?"

"I don't think that should make any difference, Ms. Miller. You came to me, remember?"

Maggie tapped her desk. And you sent me away, she said to herself. "You're right, Mr. Vega," she said using his name in the same mock reverential way he used hers. "Let me go through my files, and I'll get back to you in a day or so."

"A day or two!" His voice boomed through the phone. "My daughter could be dead by then."

"I'll get back to you as soon as I can."

"Time is of the essence, Ms. Miller. Every day my daughter slips further away. Can I send someone to get them?"

Maggie bit her lip. "No. I'll call you. I have all your numbers. Good-bye, Mr. Vega." She hung up the phone without waiting for him to say good-bye. Maggie didn't feel one bit of guilt at the lie. Maybe that's how attorneys did it. She put her purse on her desk and dug out the card from the Coral Gables police department. The first time she tried Detective Hodges, he was away from his desk. She hung up and called right back, and this time he answered the phone.

"I don't know if you remember me, but I came to see you on the Mira Vega case," Maggie said. She kept her voice even, in control, trying to make up for the previous debacles. He didn't remember her until she refreshed his memory. The loss of her own daughter and the misdated photos seemed to be the threads that connected her to the case, and she feared that didn't help her credibility.

"When I first showed Mr. Vega the pictures—"

"You spoke to Mr. Vega? How did that come about?"

Maggie could see the conversation deteriorating if she tried to explain, and she didn't want to not be believed, again. "Look, Detective, I know you think I'm an unreliable witness and what my husband said didn't help, but we're talking about a little girl's life here. Please try to listen to the facts. Take me out of the equation."

"Talk to me."

"Mira Vega hasn't been found yet, has she?"

"No."

Maggie looked up to see Gerlinde standing in the doorway pointing to her watch, a reminder that it was time for Maggie to leave for her appointment. She mouthed "Thank you," then closed her eyes to think. "How or why doesn't matter, but I was at the Vega house. I'm a professional, Detective Hodges. I study faces for a living. All the pictures around the Vega house match the ones I took of the little girl at the service plaza, yet Mr. Vega says it's not her."

"Then he agrees with me, I'm afraid to say."

"That's what he says, but just now he called me," she counted the pink slips, "four times since I was there. He wants the pictures back, and he wants to know where I took them. When I asked him if he'd spoken to you about this, he became evasive."

"I don't know what you're implying, Ms. Miller."

"I'm not implying anything. I'm saying outright that this man's behavior is odd for someone who claims to want to find his daughter." She took a deep breath. "Let me start again. When I showed him the pictures, he obviously recognized his daughter, then he abruptly said it wasn't her. Now he is insisting I give the photos to him, not to you."

When there was no response, Maggie said, "Don't you find his behavior odd?"

"I don't mean to sound condescending," Detective Hodges said, "but I don't know any other way to say this but to be honest. I find it interesting that you want me to excuse your eccentric behavior after the loss of your daughter, yet you want this man to behave rationally while in the process of possibly losing his."

Maggie remained silent.

"Will *you* concede that fact?" he said.

Maggie nodded for a long time before the word came out of the mouth. "Yes."

"I know you want to help, Maggie. And I want to find the son of a bitch who has this girl, but I'm not sure fighting over Mr. Vega is productive."

"I don't want to fight." Maggie leaned back in her chair, the fight gone out of her. "All I'm asking you to do is look a little closer at the situation. I'd bet my life that it is the missing girl, and I don't understand why he would come to me instead of you if he were playing straight. If it's a lead worth following, it's one you should follow. The FBI should follow. Not me, not him."

"That's a valid point."

"Thank you for that."

"I'm not your enemy in this. We all want to find the girl."

"That's all I want." Maggie could hear papers shuffling, and she wondered if he was already blowing her off.

"Why don't you send him the pictures, and if he believes they are of his daughter, I'm sure he'll contact me. Fair enough?"

Yeah, right, Maggie thought to herself. "How about if I send them to you, and Vega can come into the station to see them?"

"Good," Detective Hodges said. The word came out as if he were lying about his wife's terrible cooking.

"Good," Maggie repeated in the same flat tone. "Thank you."

Maggie hung up and looked at the clock. She had spent more time than she had planned on the phone and wondered where the newly added on-site shoot was and how much time she needed to get there. She walked to Gerlinde's desk, looked at the booking sheet, then back to Gerlinde.

"We usually meet with first time clients in the office before we go to an on-site shoot," Maggie said. "Who is this? Did you meet her?"

"She came in to meet you without an appointment. Insisted she would wait for you. I told her she could talk to Donovan who was due back. She said no. So finally she just went ahead and booked. Gave me cash."

"Cash? Before the job?"

"I told her to go out on a job we require a non-refundable deposit so we don't waste our time if we get there and she cancels at the last minute. She gave me cash."

"What kind of shoot is it?"

"A family thing she said. She wanted natural surroundings. Said a friend of hers had used you." Gerlinde handed Maggie a client information card with a referral name on it that Maggie didn't recognize. "She lives further north, so I suggested Medallion Park, if that works for you." Gerlinde looked at the clock. "Guess you'd better head out."

Maggie handed the card back to Gerlinde.

"And one more thing," Gerlinde said. "She wants only you, not one of your 'assistants,' she said."

"Snooty?"

"British. They always sound snooty. She was dressed nicely and carried herself like she was used to money. I figured we could use some more referrals to build the business back up."

Chapter Eighteen

Maggie got out of her car at Pavilion 6 in Medallion Park, feeling the heat and humidity surround her. She glanced up to see that not a single leaf on any of the trees was moving, but even in the heat this was one of her favorite outdoor places to shoot. There was plenty of natural light at this time of day and the abundant trees provided shading if she wanted the play of shadows and light. She looked at her watch and realized that she was just on time. For once, traffic had been on her side.

It was a hot afternoon, and except for a few people jogging, the park was relatively empty. She knew the spot by the lake she would shoot and walked over to the area, leaving her camera bag and equipment in the car. There was a couple on a blanket right about where she might want to shoot. Maybe some pictures under the trees first, and if the couple didn't leave, she would politely ask them for the spot for a short while. She'd never had any-one refuse.

Maggie was staring up at the few clouds in the sky thinking of Donovan, as she always did when she saw clouds now, when she heard her name in a clipped British accent.

"Ms. Miller?"

Maggie turned to see a woman with a wide-brimmed hat and large dark sunglasses walking toward her. She wore a cream colored suit, with matching hose, her heels sinking into the grass as she walked. An unusual outfit for a park shoot, especially this time of year. The woman walked with confidence despite the mismatch of her shoes and the terrain and extended

her hand as if the privilege were Maggie's, who now understood how
Gerlinde had classified her as "snooty."

"Thank you for meeting me on such short notice," the woman said.
"I'm Sandy Jones."

"Nice to meet you, Ms. Jones," Maggie said.

"Please call me Sandy, Ms. Miller."

Maggie nodded. "I prefer Maggie. Shall we get started? Gerlinde told
me you wanted a family shoot." Maggie looked around. "Who will I be
photographing today?"

The woman looked at the couple on the blanket. "Can we talk in private for a moment, perhaps at your car?"

Maggie looked around. She never liked to be in a compromising position with strangers, even a benign looking woman. Maybe she was paranoid,
but better safe than sorry.

"How about over there?" Maggie pointed to the pavilion.

The woman looked around, then nodded. "Of course."

When they got to the shade of the pavilion, the woman took off her
sunglasses. Her eyes were a striking shade of green and would photograph
beautifully.

"It's really better to talk about the possibilities for the photographs
after I have seen your family," Maggie said. "It will give me a better idea
about what I can do for you. I have sample books in the car. I'll get them
for your family to see, if you'd like."

"Can we sit?" The woman sat at the wooden picnic bench, her posture
as straight as if she'd just take a seat at the opera. She waited for Maggie to
do the same before she continued. "You've recently lost a daughter," the
woman said.

Maggie swallowed. "How do you know that?"

"I have, too," the woman said slowly. "So I'm hoping you'll
understand."

Maggie felt that common bond strangers feel at a shared loss. Her
voice was gentle as she said, "Is this your first family picture since she's
gone?"

The woman's eyes moved from the sky to Maggie. "Have you ever had
a pain worse than the one of losing your daughter?" The words sounded

almost clinical with the high tone and clipped British accent, almost as if Maggie were on trial.

"No." Maggie tried to keep her voice just as clinical. "I can imagine how hard this must be." Maggie wondered what it would have been like if she'd had another child to care for after Lilly's death. How would she have managed?

The woman looked at Maggie for a long time. "Do you think you would have gone to most any lengths to save her, if you'd had the chance?"

Maggie pictured Lilly on the street, still and unmoving, and remembered her urge to pull the child back into her womb to protect her. Maggie's composure began to melt and her head began to hurt while she tried to stay grounded. She rubbed her hand over her temple and attempted to sound professional. "What I would or wouldn't have done doesn't matter. I can take pictures for you. If you need someone to talk to—"

"It's you I need to talk to. I see the pain in your eyes. It's fresh; it's raw." The woman's green eyes bore into Maggie. "It doesn't go away. I know."

Maggie stood up. "I don't know what you're doing, but—"

"Please sit, Maggie," the woman said. The voice was an octave lower and devoid of the British accent. "I need your help."

Maggie stared at the woman and let herself sink back down on the bench.

The woman took off her hat and ran her hands through short brown hair, then leaned over the table that separated them. "It was my daughter you took pictures of at the service plaza. The pictures you took," she hesitated, "to the police."

"Your daughter? Who are you?" Maggie's thoughts were jumbled. "Did Nestor Vega send you?"

The woman laughed softly. "In a way."

"He wants more information, yet he claims the pictures aren't of his daughter. Now she's *your* daughter." Maggie shook her head. "I've already called the police and told them I think something is very wrong in that house."

The woman's eyes widened, the smile gone from her face. "You've been back to the police? Do they have the pictures?"

"I called them and—"

"Then they don't have them?"

"No, but I plan to give them—"

The woman reached out her hand and clamped it over Maggie's wrist. "You mustn't."

Maggie pulled her hand away and got up. She paced the pavilion, wondering if she should call the police from her cell phone in the car.

"Maggie, please sit down." The woman's face was contorted now, her eyes full of fear.

Maggie stood next to the picnic table, but didn't sit. "Is this a ploy of Nestor Vega's to conceal those pictures?"

The woman turned to watch the couple that had been at the water's edge approach. She said nothing until they had passed. "No, this isn't Nestor's doing. I found my way to you through him, but I am not here on his behalf." She looked around the park. "Did you tell him you were coming here today?"

"I don't tell Nestor Vega my schedule," Maggie said.

"I'm sorry. I'm taking a great risk being here, talking to you. But I felt I had no choice. When I found out you had lost your daughter, I had to hope you would understand when I asked you to stop."

"Stop what?" Maggie said.

"Stop trying to find Mira. Stop going to the authorities, to Nestor with those pictures you have."

"Why would I do that?"

"Because I'm her mother, and I'm begging you to." She stared at Maggie. "My real name is Lydia Vega."

Maggie noticed the erect posture was gone, and the woman's shoulders slumped as she said the name.

"Mira, the girl whose picture you took, is my daughter."

Maggie crossed her arms in front of her chest. She studied the woman the way she studied proofs in her darkroom, examining features, looking for details. "You are not the woman in the pictures that I saw at the Vega house. You are not Mira Vega's mother." Maggie's voice had become loud, accusing. "Who are you?"

"Please sit." Lydia's eyes scanned the park. About fifty feet away, a man was throwing a Frisbee to a large German Shepard. "Don't make a scene. Mira's life could literally depend on what you do. I'll go slowly, and try to make you understand, but please don't call attention to us," she said as she leaned on the wooden bench. Gone was the confident woman Maggie had met. "Please? I will ask much of you, but for now…just your time, and I will pay for the session."

Maggie sat down. Money for her time was not the problem.

"Mira is my daughter," the woman said again, "and the pictures you took of her at the service plaza are of the two of us."

Maggie was surprised by the words. "She was with a man."

The woman managed a weak smile. "I'm flattered that I fooled you with my disguise, but now I must convince you otherwise."

Maggie shook her head. "I saw a man at the plaza, not you."

"And just a few minutes ago you saw a wealthy British woman, didn't you?"

Maggie stared at the woman's short, cropped hair, then at her features, the high thin nose that had looked very British to her a few minutes ago. She knew how a photograph taken out of context could lie—give an impression that was in no way related to reality. Could this woman's appearance be doing the same thing?

"Go ahead," Maggie said.

"Nestor and I were married six years ago and had one daughter. You went to our, his, house. The woman in the pictures is his new wife. He tells no one that she is the stepmother, because he likes to pretend I'm dead. That's what he had told Mira.

"I met Nestor Vega when I was touring with a Broadway production of *Dracula*. I was Mina—the lead. We were performing at the Miami Beach Convention Center, and he attended the opening night party." She looked off into the distance. "He was incredibly handsome, charming." She looked at Maggie. "What I didn't know then was that litigation is just another form of acting, and those of us who can act can fool you on demand."

"Like the British accent and demeanor."

Lydia nodded. "More importantly, the 'man' who left the service plaza with Mira. But let me finish. I was dazzled by the attention Nestor paid to me, the lifestyle, the money. I left the company, and we married just two months later. I thought I was living a fairy tale. We threw lavish parties in a magnificent home, we traveled, we loved each other, and we had Mira. It took me a just a short while to realize that Nestor enjoyed many of these same things with other women. Many women. In my defense, I was in love, I was happy, I was busy." She put her head down. "I was crushed when the truth sunk in. When we were together he treated me like a unique jewel he'd discovered and couldn't get enough of. He whispered things in my ear that would make me blush in public. How I believed it all." She tilted her head. "Have you ever thought you had it all?"

Maggie thought of her life just a few months ago. "Yes." Her voice was hushed, as if she didn't believe that answer could even possibly be correct.

Lydia nodded, as if she understood all too well. "Nestor in his way was sincere. He did love me, loved our life, but he also believed it was his right to have other women. It was part of his machismo. He couldn't see the harm in having women on the side as long as he made a home with me, with our child. He thought I was wrong for objecting." Her eyebrows rose. "He even wanted more children. He was so convincing that I questioned myself for a while. Then I realized it was not a life I chose to live, picturing my husband making love to other women." She shook her head. "I couldn't live with him like that no matter how much I did love him. Or maybe the problem was that I did love him. I told him it had to stop, or I wanted a divorce."

"And so you divorced?" Maggie said.

"It was a bluff in a way," Lydia continued. "I'd hoped it would stop him. I didn't want a divorce. I wanted my husband, the life I thought I had."

Lydia gazed at the lake, then looked back. "Instead, it made him angry. I'd always know he had a temper—I'd seen it with the house staff, but he'd never raised his hand to me." She looked down. "Before this. He was out of control. I tried not to make him angry, but we continued to argue. There was no compromise." She looked back at the lake. "When he began to let his anger affect Mira—she looks very much like me—I knew we had to leave."

"What did he do to her?" Maggie said.

Lydia turned her face away, as if running from the memory. "He would lash out—hit her," she said, her head still turned to the side. "I tried to draw his anger toward me, but," she looked up at Maggie with her green eyes watering, "anger's not a rational process. And I think he saw it hurt me more to see her hit than the actual blows he would deliver to me." She took a deep breath. "He broke her finger when she was two. She'd put her hand up to cover her face…" Lydia raised her hand close to her face, then closed her eyes and let the sentence trail off. Then suddenly she pushed her shoulders back and turned to face Maggie. "When I told him I was leaving and taking Mira with me, he laughed. Family," she paused and tilted her head slightly, "or the illusion of such, is everything to Nestor. He said he wouldn't be ridiculed by having a part-time daughter. Finally, he said I could go, but I had to leave her behind. I refused."

Lydia stood and reached into her purse. She pulled out a pack of cigarettes. "Do you mind?"

Maggie watched the woman's hand shake as she held the pack. "Go ahead."

Lydia took her time lighting the cigarette, then inhaled deeply. "I gave this up a long time ago, but then started again when I was alone." She took two more drags, then dropped it to the ground. "I never let Mira see me smoke." A very sad smile crossed her face. "I proceeded with the divorce." She stopped for a minute and looked at the abandoned cigarette on the ground. "You know what my husband does for a living. What you may not know, and neither did I, was the extent of the connections he has in the community with other lawyers and judges. I couldn't even find anyone to represent me at first. Then I found someone newly out of law school, idealistic, and she took the case. Nestor responded by filing for sole custody. I said I would reveal his temper, the fact that he struck us both. He told me I would never prove it. I began to realize it wouldn't have mattered if my lawyer was Houdini. I wasn't going to get a fair trial; I was going to lose custody of my daughter."

Lydia paused, fanning herself from the heat, then continued. "He threatened that if I didn't drop the divorce proceedings he would have me declared incompetent and deny me visiting privileges altogether. I didn't think it was possible." She took out another cigarette, held it between her fingers, but didn't light it. "Then, during the trial he produced witnesses, professionals, hired guns I believe they're called, who fabricated stories. He held all the cards. I was depressed, immobile.

"Then I thought, what would Nestor do? I began to think of ways to get out of an impossible situation. I demanded money for a settlement. Money was easy for Nestor. I convinced him that if I had money, lots of it, I would drop the case and leave him alone with his daughter. I would disappear." Lydia looked at Maggie. "I am a good actress, Maggie, yet I still can't believe he thought I would do it. I guess sometimes we believe what we want to believe.

"He agreed to the divorce under those terms—settled out of court. I would disappear for an outrageous amount of lump-sum alimony. It was hard to leave Mira, but I knew it was the only way I could get her back and for good."

"You left your daughter with a man who beat her?"

Lydia dropped her head and took a few steps away, shaking her head as if talking to herself. Then she quickly turned back, and the anger on her face surprised Maggie. "How dare you judge me. Do you think I would have left her if I had any other choice? I'm here now." She spit the words out at Maggie. "What good would I have done her locked away as a mental case? He would have stopped at nothing to keep her. I did the only thing I could: I moved away, invested the money Nestor gave me, and started putting my plan into place. When everything was ready, I would kidnap my own daughter and disappear."

"Then why are you here talking to me?" Maggie said.

Lydia wiped sweat off her forehead and laughed bitterly. "What's that old cliché about the best laid plans?" She walked across the pavilion, the heels of her shoes clacking on the wooden floor, and stood with her back to Maggie. Lydia turned slowly and walked very close to Maggie. Maggie could see Lydia's eyes moving across her face, as if looking for something.

Finally, in a very soft voice, Lydia said, "I walk a fine line between telling you enough that you believe me, and too much so that you can ruin everything." She took a step back. "Let's just say that things were about to change in Mira's everyday life, and my access to her would not have been possible. I was forced to move before I was completely ready."

Maggie tried to digest the story. She shook her head. "You admit you're a good actress. How do I know any of this is true? That this isn't a ploy to get me to back off?" Maggie looked at Lydia. "If you aren't here on his behalf, how could you know that I was at his house, that I've since had contact with him?"

"When you have power, you always have enemies, even if you don't know who they are. I have an ally in the house. How else could someone get a child as guarded as Mira?"

Maggie had wondered about that when she saw the protected life Mira lived. "The news said she was with the housekeeper when the housekeeper was knocked unconscious by a man, and the child taken."

"Yes."

"You hired someone to take her?"

Lydia shook her head. "The less you know the better it is for you. And," she hesitated slightly, "for my friend. I'm not the only one in jeopardy because of you."

"Even if I believed this outlandish story, what is it you want from me?"

"Stop going to the police and stop talking to Nestor. Destroy the pictures. They are the only thing that can link me to the kidnapping."

Maggie thought about the day in Nestor's study. Of how his face changed when he got to the last picture, the picture of Mira and "the thin man."

"Doesn't Nestor want her found?" Maggie said.

Lydia reached into her purse and lit the cigarette she'd been holding. "He wants us found," she said, exhaling a long breath of smoke. "But he wants to have me disappear and avoid any focus on him in the process."

"He thinks he can buy you off a second time?"

Lydia looked at Maggie. "I believe he will kill me this time." Her hand shook as she put the cigarette to her lips and inhaled. "Did you think it was strange that Nestor said the picture wasn't of Mira?" The words were laced with smoke.

"Yes."

"Did you wonder why?"

"For hours on end," Maggie said.

"He recognized me, but didn't want to admit it so he could never be connected to any mishap I might have."

"Why didn't Nestor just admit it was Mira, then, and keep the pictures?" Maggie said.

Lydia shook her head. "That's a good question. I can only guess that you caught him off guard, and once he said it wasn't her, how could he ask for them back?"

Maggie remembered the way Vega had casually dropped the photos on his desk, as if Maggie would simply leave without them. "He did," Maggie said in a low voice.

"He did?"

"Yes, before I left, he tried to keep them. I couldn't figure out why."

"Now you know why. He's used to people listening to him when he asks for things."

Maggie felt things should be clearer, but instead she felt more off-guard. She was perspiring more than usual and the summer heat seemed to weigh her down. "Why does he need my pictures? He knows what you look like."

Lydia shook her head. "I've had plastic surgery. I don't look the way I used to. He needs the picture for his investigators."

"But if you look different, how did he recognize—"

"Somehow he recognized me. I'm still not sure how." She dropped her half-smoked cigarette to the ground and crushed it with her foot. "I wish to God I knew." She kicked the cigarette butt into the grass, then looked up at Maggie. "But, don't you see? You have photos of what I look like now, which are also the only proof that I am involved. Those damn pictures. I've worked so hard, waited so long. If you hadn't taken those pictures, I would have been out of the country in a few days. Once Nestor or the authorities have a current picture, I can't risk going anywhere. Even a convenience store."

"And you want—"

"I want those pictures destroyed! If you give them to the police, my picture, how I look now, will be plastered everywhere. I'll never get out of the country with Mira. All my planning, the weight loss, the plastic surgery will have been for nothing. All because you were sitting at a plaza snapping pictures."

Lydia got up and walked around the table, sitting very close to Maggie. "This may have been some artistic endeavor to you, but this is my life. Mira's life. I cannot, will not lose my daughter again, and she must not go back to him."

Maggie tried to move away, but Lydia grabbed her arm.

"Don't you see?" Lydia pleaded, "Like it or not, you are my only chance here. I need you to say it was a mistake. Say you threw them out when no one believed you. Doctor them up so it's someone else in the picture. Anything, please."

Lydia's wild eyes were scaring Maggie. She tried to pull away. "You're hurting me," Maggie said.

Lydia's eyes zeroed in on Maggie. After a long pause, she let go of Maggie's arm.

Maggie rubbed her upper arm and stared at Lydia.

Lydia slumped onto the bench. "You can't understand because you don't know Nestor." She squeezed the back of her neck as she rolled her head front to back. "If he gets a copy of that picture…"

"You said he already recognized you. That he's already looking."

"He is. But he has no current picture," Lydia said. "And I look different enough that he knows I could slip by."

"What about the police? I've been to them."

"But you didn't leave my picture. Besides, Nestor has incredible power. He's told them there's no validity to your story, so he can find us first."

Maggie got up and started to pace the pavilion. She didn't know what to think. The story was outrageous. She wracked her memory, trying to remember that day, to remember the pictures, trying to superimpose this woman's face onto the thin man's to see if they were the same. She watched Lydia's movements as three Muscovy ducks walked up to the pavilion and

Lydia pulled a package of wrapped crackers out of her purse, scattering them for the ducks.

"I carry these for Mira," Lydia said.

Maggie couldn't place this woman in her pictures, and none of her movements were like the man she remembered at the plaza. "You still can't prove any of this is true," she said. "If Nestor Vega is as devious as you say, how do I know you're not part of an elaborate scam to get me to back off?"

"What do I have to do to convince you?"

"Why don't you just stay and prove that he beats her? He's unfit?"

"I tried that once, remember?" Lydia shook her head. "Only in fables does David win against Goliath." She said the words to Maggie as if she were explaining something to a five-year-old.

"Maybe if I saw the little girl; saw that she was safe."

Lydia shook her head violently. "It's not possible."

"Why? Because you don't have her?" Was this just another roll for this actress?

"I can't risk it. How do I know you won't set me up? Have the police waiting? Or worse, Nestor?"

"You came to me," Maggie said.

"But not with Mira. This is my only chance to get her away from him, and, with or without your help, I have to try." Her green eyes stared at Maggie. "I can't lose her again."

"I have no way to believe you. You've proven nothing—only spun a good yarn—that's all."

Lydia leaned so close to Maggie that she could smell the tobacco on her breath. "I hoped you would understand. What if you could have *your* daughter back? Would anything stop you?"

Maggie felt the sting of the remark. "No," she said finally.

"Then you do understand," Lydia said. "I'll do anything I have to."

Maggie stared at Lydia. She wondered what she would do if she faced the devil and was given the chance to have Lilly back. She knew. She would sell her soul. Maggie saw the desperation on the woman's face and wondered if it were real. "Then prove to me you are her mother and that she's safe and happy and where she should be."

Lydia stared back. "How do I know I can trust you?"

"You can trust me, if you're telling the truth."

"And if I am? Will you let this go?"

Maggie shook her head. "I don't know." She ran her hand through her hair. "I need time to think."

"Promise me one thing," Lydia said.

Maggie remained silent.

"When Nestor contacts you again, please, don't mention a thing about this meeting."

"What makes you think he'll contact me?"

"I know him. The only thing on my side is that he has no way of knowing that I know about you, about the pictures." She looked at Maggie and seemed to be making a decision. "This is my last chance." Her face softened. "I'm begging you. One mother to another. Please don't tell him I've contacted you."

Maggie stared at the woman in front of her who was pleading not to lose her daughter the way Maggie had pleaded with an unseen foe at Lilly's bedside. She recognized the pain. It was embedded in her forehead, etched around her eyes, tugged at her lips. It was the ineffable pain of losing a child. It was the variable that remained constant in this nonsensical equation she couldn't solve. It wasn't the words that made her believe this woman, it was the pain written on her face. Maggie didn't believe it could be faked. But then, even if the pain was real—was her story true?

Lydia reached out her hand and covered Maggie's with it. "I was right about one thing."

Maggie pulled her hand away. She wasn't ready for an alliance just yet.

The woman put her hand down at her side. "Even if you don't believe me, I can see you understand," she said. "And I am sorry for your loss."

Maggie, frozen in time, holding a still hand that now only existed in her memory, stared at the woman. After several minutes of silence Maggie stood. "Where can I reach you if I need to?"

Lydia shook her head. "You can't. I'll reach you."

Maggie sat still as she watched the woman put the sunglasses on her face and cock the hat on her head then walk away. Her posture seemed to get more erect the further she got from Maggie.

Chapter Nineteen

Maggie stared at the small pieces of paper that held the new messages from Nestor Vega. She moved the pink squares around her desk, arranging them in a line in chronological order, then positioning them clock-wise, according to the time of day he'd called. She'd avoided returning his calls because she didn't know what to say, what he would say. *When Nestor contacts you again, please, don't mention a thing about this meeting.* She couldn't stop hearing Lydia Vega's words in her mind. Maggie had just piled the messages in a stack when Gerlinde walked into her office and closed the door behind her.

"What's the matter?" Maggie said. She never closed her door.

"That man is here." Her head nodded toward the messages. "To see you."

"Nestor Vega is here?"

"He's in the waiting room. I told him you were busy, but he said he would wait until the end of the day if necessary."

Maggie stood and began to pace around her office. She stared out the window.

"Is this about that missing girl?" Gerlinde said.

Maggie nodded her head without turning around. A forceful knock on her door made Maggie turn to look at Gerlinde, who shrugged her shoulders. "He's the only other person here, unless Donovan's come in," Gerlinde said.

Maggie went to her desk and swept the messages into the top drawer. "Yes?" she yelled toward the door.

The door opened and Nestor Vega walked in. "I'm sorry. I am a persistent man. Not unlike yourself, Ms. Miller." He nodded to Gerlinde and extended his hand to Maggie. "Accept my apology for barging in. I had to see you. Again, perhaps, not unlike the day you came to *my* house and had to see me."

Maggie shook his hand. "Thank you, Gerlinde. Mr. Vega has found his way." She looked toward the man. "Sit, please."

Nestor Vega sat in one of the two chairs in front of Maggie's desk. Rather than sitting next to him as she often did with prospective clients, Maggie sat behind her desk, putting both distance and mass between her and the man.

"What can I do for you, Mr. Vega?"

"Nestor. Please."

"Nestor."

"I've called you numerous times, but..." He waved his hand in the air. "You must be very busy, so I came to steal a minute of your time."

"And now you're here." Maggie couldn't explain the thump in her chest, why this man was making her nervous. He was dressed in a dark suit that almost matched the color of his slicked-back black hair, and when his hands moved around, she noticed that the tiger's-eye in his cufflinks seemed to match his eyes, which were still rimmed with dark circles.

"You were very good to come to me with your pictures. You wanted my daughter found."

"But you said my pictures were not of your daughter."

"I did." One eyebrow rose, while he solemnly nodded his head.

"Then why are you here?"

"I would like to have the conversation you were willing to have the day you came to me, along with the pictures you offered."

"I showed you what I had."

"Then there aren't any more of the two of them?" He hesitated slightly. "Of the man who took my daughter?"

"Mr. Vega, are you saying it is your daughter?"

He got up from the chair and walked to the window as he pulled his shirt cuffs out of his suit jacket sleeves. Then he began a measured pace in front of her desk. Maggie could imagine him using this same walk in front of a jury. She wondered if his thinking process worked best while he was walking, as he did in a courtroom, the way her thinking seemed to work best once she lifted the camera to her eye.

"I was hoping not to involve you any further," Nestor said. "That I could find my daughter with the least amount of complications." He spoke without looking at her, pacing.

"Yet you are here."

He stopped in front of her desk, looked at her, then sat back down. He ran his hands over his face and when he looked at her again, his face seemed older, his facial muscles sagging. "I am at your mercy." He extended his hands out to her. "I need those pictures back. And anything else you can tell me, so I can find Mira."

"Even if there was something I could tell you…" Maggie pictured the woman in the cream colored suit in the park, remembered the fabulous story she had told. Maggie began to click the top of a pen that had been lying on her desk. "Why did you lie to me, Mr. Vega? I could see from the pictures in your home that she was your daughter."

"I am a powerful man, Ms. Miller. There are things the press doesn't need to know. I thought if I could hire a detective and find Mira, then my whole life wouldn't have to become fodder for gossip."

When Maggie didn't answer, he continued. "I am a very high profile person."

"I don't follow what that has to do with this," Maggie said.

"I may run for office someday. Scandals are never forgotten. 'Dirt,'" he spit out the word, "is always dug up."

"So you were protecting your privacy at her expense?"

"No, no, no." He clenched his fist tightly. "I didn't think anyone needed to know. I am protecting Mira's privacy, too." He got up again and began to pace. "The detective, he wants to speak with you. He says you may have seen things, noticed things you aren't aware of." He turned toward her. "Things that will help to find her."

"Detective Hodges has my number."

He shook his head. "Not him; he is an incompetent. I'm talking about the gentleman I have hired. He has been effective in finding the victims in several similar cases." He paused, then continued, "And he is discreet."

"Have you told the police my pictures are of Mira? I called them after I spoke to you."

"I know, I know." His eyes narrowed slightly, the right side of his mouth curled in a boyish smile. "You are persistent."

Maggie could see how Lydia had found him attractive, was taken by his charm. She looked down at her desk, moved a post-it-note pad from one spot to another. "Your reaction made no sense to me, Mr. Vega. Why would you send me away if you truly wanted your daughter back?" She looked into his face for a reaction and saw only what appeared to be measured control. "I was concerned for the child."

Nestor nodded, as if understanding. "You have a good eye. And you said you've lost a child. Maybe that makes you more sensitive."

"Would you mind if I shared my photos with the police, as well as your detective?" She had no intentions of doing so just yet, remembering Lydia's plea in the park, but she needed to hear his answer.

"Then there are more?" He edged up on the seat.

"I didn't say that." Should she tell Detective Hodges the whole story and let the police figure it out? Maggie rubbed her temples.

"There is something you haven't told me." His eyes held hers, as if he knew the truth.

Maggie looked at her desk blotter, then to Nestor. "Would you like some coffee?"

He shook his head.

"I would. Excuse me a minute." Maggie got up and walked out of her office closing the door behind her. She paused, unable to shake the feeling that Nestor Vega could see right into her mind, then she continued to the break room.

"Is everything okay?" Gerlinde appeared at the door.

"Nothing is okay," Maggie said. She opened the coffee canister and knocked some grinds onto the counter, as she aimed for and missed the filter.

"Let me do that," Gerlinde said.

Maggie got two mugs and some milk while Gerlinde made a fresh pot of coffee.

"Is he bothering you?" Gerlinde said. She folded her arms over her chest and stood back while the coffee dripped into the carafe.

Maggie watched the slow stream of coffee build to a rich, dark brew, drop by drop. "Once someone lies to you," Maggie said, "what would it take for you to trust them again?"

"I wouldn't." Gerlinde poured Maggie some coffee, then poured some for herself.

Maggie thought of how easy it had been to tell Brian she was working rather than be honest about her trips to the plazas. Weren't those lies? She would never have imagined she would do something like that, yet she had.

"What about intent, if you have a good reason?" Maggie said, putting four spoonfuls of sugar into her coffee.

Gerlinde sipped her black coffee. "Sounds like splitting hairs. A lie's a lie."

Maggie nodded. There was a time when she had believed that, too. She thanked Gerlinde for the coffee and walked back to her office.

Before she went in, she took a deep breath. *Relax*, she repeated to herself every time her right foot hit the floor.

Back at her desk, Maggie held the hot cup of coffee in her hands. "Mr. Vega, I took pictures at a service plaza that I believe were of your daughter. I showed them to the police, then I showed them to you. There is no more." Maggie willed her face to remain neutral while Nestor Vega stared at her. She felt as if her thoughts were being displayed across her face the way stock quotes run across the bottom of certain TV channels. Even though the coffee was far too hot, she brought the mug to her face and sipped.

Nestor Vega began to nod slowly. "I read people for a living, Ms. Miller. I can look at a juror's face and know if they believe what I am saying, how I need to tailor my argument. I can see you do not believe my story, my motives."

"I find your reaction strange," she said. "You say you want your daughter back, but you don't want the police involved." His behavior was suspicious and made her wonder about Lydia Vega's claim. *Could* he not want anyone to know she is the kidnapper so he could dispose of her?

"It's not that I don't want them involved. I would just prefer to step up the investigation…" his words ran off. He twirled his cufflink around, as he appeared to be thinking. Finally he said, "You leave me no choice."

He slumped back, putting his elbows on the arms of the chair and his hands together in front of him. "I didn't want to tell you the truth, because I tell no one, but perhaps you will understand, when I explain." He thought for another minute as if changing his mind, then continued, "Even my wife doesn't know the whole story. I didn't think anyone would ever need to know, especially Mira. In fact, I've told her that her mother is dead."

So that much is true, Maggie thought.

He cleared his throat and continued. "It is better that Mira think her mother dead than to know the truth."

"I don't understand."

"My first wife Lydia, Mira's mother, is very ill, Ms. Miller. Psychologically disturbed. She tried to cause Mira harm in the past, and after I saw your pictures, I fear she is the one who has her now."

Maggie held the coffee mug tightly and continued to will her face to remain calm.

"I thought I had found a queen among women." A sad smile crossed his face. "She was beautiful, intelligent, so witty. But shortly after Mira was born, Lydia started to act strangely. She would go into violent fits of rage for no reason. She accused me of things I was not guilty of. No matter what I said, she did not believe me. Then Mira began to get sick. Lydia would call me home from meetings, from trials, from client dinners, because Mira was sick. She knew I would always come for Mira. The child would have diarrhea, vomiting. I thought an inordinate amount sometimes, but I didn't think much of it at first. What did I know of children? I had been an only child.

"Then I began to realize that Mira always got sick when I was not around. If I had a long weekend with her, a vacation, the child was fine. At first I fooled myself into thinking I had a calming effect on the child." His smile was gentle, sad.

"Why would your wife need excuses to bring you home?" Maggie remembered Lydia's story of other women. "Were you away a lot?"

"No more than any lawyer trying to build a practice. There is a lot of socialization in my line of work, and after the baby Lydia refused to accompany me to many of these parties, these dinners, these trips. She had gained too much weight from the pregnancy, she was tired. Every time a different excuse."

Where did all this fit into the story Lydia had told her, Maggie wondered.

"Do you know what Munchausen by Proxy Syndrome is, Ms. Miller?"

"I think I've heard of it."

Nestor got up and began to pace, his hands behind his back as he spoke. "It is a disease of the mind." He tapped his head. "One in which a person, many times a mother, a seemingly *good* mother," he nodded at her as if to hammer home the point, "harms another, usually a child, intentionally, in order to gain attention and sympathy from others. It's rather fascinating in that there is no clear psychological profile, no identifiable underlying cause. The American Psychiatric Association's Diagnostic and Statistical Manual of Mental Disorders lists it as Factitious Disorder by Proxy, but it is commonly called Munchausen's by Proxy Syndrome; a disease of deceit named after a German Baron who told fantastical stories." He waved his hand in the air and turned toward Maggie. When his eyes met hers, he blushed.

"I am sorry," he said. He returned to his chair. "I many times bury myself in facts when things are too painful to deal with." His smile was sad. "I have read every word ever written on the subject." He stared at her desk, but if it was as if he were seeing something else.

Finally, he cleared his throat again. "My wife has such a disease. Maybe not a full blown case, as she could control it when she wanted to. You see, she didn't do it to get attention from anyone but me. It kept me close to home. Once when I was at a conference in South America, Mira ended up in the hospital for dehydration." He shook his head. "When I confronted Lydia, she of course denied it. Said she could not control when the child got sick. She lost her temper, yelled at me, as if I were wrong to question. Then I found bottles of Syrup of Ipecac hidden in the closet. Do you know what that is?" He leaned forward.

Maggie nodded. "It used to be used to induce vomiting in the case of accidental poisoning."

"Used to, yes. But not any more. When I showed her the bottles I found, she said they were in the house as part of a first aid kit, recommended for certain overdoses, if a young child should swallow certain things. She claimed she didn't know it should no longer be used." He paused, then said, "She was an actress, you know. A very good one. Always prepared for her roles."

Maggie felt a shudder as another fact connected the web of both stories.

"For a while I didn't know what to believe. I couldn't stop picturing my little Mira in that big hospital bed, the intravenous lines going into her arm, her ankle. It haunted me."

Maggie pictured Lilly lying in the Pediatric Intensive Care Unit bed, her chest rising and falling while the respirator rhythmically inflated and aerated her lungs. How helpless her daughter had looked. How helpless Maggie had felt.

"Mira would look up and say, 'Make me better, Poppy.' She calls me Poppy." Nestor Vega abruptly got up from the chair and walked to the wall of pictures near the door. Maggie could only see his back, but she saw him take out a handkerchief and blow his nose. He stopped in front of a picture of Lilly. After a few minutes, he inhaled deeply, put his shoulders back and came back to the chair.

"Your child," his eyes stared straight into hers, "was beautiful."

Maggie drew in a deep breath. "Yes." They sat quietly for a moment, sharing a place of silent pain, and she felt that he must be telling the truth, for no one would travel to this dark place unnecessarily.

Then Nestor continued, "I confronted Lydia. Told her she must get help. She refused. Said I was wrong. I told her I could no longer take that chance. I had to err on the side of safety. She could not be trusted to care for Mira.

"There wasn't much of a marriage by this point, as you can imagine, but I told her she could stay. Family is very important to me. Mira would have a full time nurse, and Lydia was never to be alone with the child. She refused, saying such restrictions were an outrage. She threatened me, my reputation in the community. Said she would swear I did things that I had not. Finally she said she would leave if I paid her a large sum of money. An outrageously large sum of money." He looked to Maggie. "Can you imagine? Selling your child?" He shook his head. "I began wondering if that was what she had been after all along. She could have had any man. Do you think someone could be so calculating?" He didn't wait for an answer. "I was so in love with her. She was so beautiful, and I was so foolish. I never considered a prenuptial agreement. Friends told me to beware of a beautiful actress—she could convince you of anything." He looked to Maggie. "She is that good."

Maggie's head began to swim. Was Lydia good enough to fake the kind of pain Maggie had seen? Or was the pain from something else? An instability?

"She took the money and left," Nestor said. "That was almost two years ago."

Maggie wasn't sure what to say without tipping her hand. Should she tell Nestor that she'd been approached by Lydia with a completely different story? Should she tell the police? "Why do you think she has Mira?"

"I believe it was her in the picture you have."

Maggie's heart thumped. "That was a man with Mira."

"She is that good," he repeated, then shook his head. "I didn't see it at first. She looks different somehow."

He paused and Maggie wondered if he could possibly know of the plastic surgery.

Nestor continued, "But the 'man' in the picture wore a baseball cap from a small minor league team in New York, the Utica Blue Sox, a team the Lydia always followed because her brother played for them. It was just enough to make me think of her, and as I looked closely," he closed his eyes as if imagining the picture, "not so much the nose or face, but the determined set of the mouth, the eyebrows—the way they come together when she concentrates." He opened his eyes and nodded. "She must have had plastic surgery."

Maggie searched for something to say. "But you denied it was even Mira, Mr. Vega."

"I know, I know. A mistake—I panicked. I couldn't believe she would come back. She promised me." He clenched his hands into fists, then looked up. "But now I realize I need those pictures—I have none of what she looks like now, and she does look different. If you give me the negatives, I can afford the best experts to blown them up, analyze them for things that would prove it is her. They are the only current pictures of her." He took a few measured breaths. "It would immensely aid in her capture, and I want to get Lydia the help she needs." He paused, then added, "For her own safety. She's not a well woman."

Maggie drank the last of her coffee and put the mug down. She sat back in her chair. At this point she didn't know if it was caffeine or the story that was making her heart race. "But why not let the police do the work?" She needed to stall for time to decide what to do, who to believe, but she didn't want Nestor Vega to know how big of a decision she had to make.

"The police!" He stood, waving a hand in the air, his voice loud. "With their meager resources? They get to it when they get to it. I must have those negatives and the pictures. I have to find her." His eyes narrowed. "They turned you away with a picture of the child *and* the abductor. How good of a job are they doing? I have hired a very good detective."

His point was well taken. Maggie had gone to Nestor Vega on her own. "But why not have everyone looking? Increase your odds. They have the media at their disposal."

Nestor came back and sat on the edge of the chair. "That's exactly the point. If you alert the police, they will alert the media, which will alert Lydia that she has been found out. I can't risk that. I don't know what she'll do."

They were almost the exact words Lydia had used about Nestor. Maggie didn't know what to believe. Which one of them was telling the truth, if either?

"I can tell there is something you are holding back," he said. He reached into his jacket pocket and pulled out a checkbook. He opened it up and signed the top check, ripped it off, placed it on the desk.

Stunned, Maggie stared at the check. Was he was offering her a bribe?

"Money means nothing to me without my daughter. Hire as many detectives as you like, give *them* the information. Use my check, as much as you need, but please, do not go back to the police."

Maggie stared at the check, then at Nestor Vega. She had no clue as to what was the truth in all of this. Was the woman she met in the park mentally ill? She'd seen a documentary about women with Munchausen by Proxy, women who had gone so far as to kill their children. If that was the case, she should give Nestor her information and let him use all his resources to find her.

But what if the man in front of her were as volatile and conniving as Lydia made him out to be? She'd seen those stories, too, of powerful men who would stop at nothing to get what they wanted. If that were the case, she needed to keep her information as far away from him as possible.

"Help me, Maggie," he said.

Gone was the self-assured attorney whom she had met in the book-lined library of the palatial house. Gone was the calculating demeanor. Before her stood a beaten man who was on the verge of losing his daughter for good, and she knew all too well how that felt.

"Think of what it's like to lose a child, and help me," he said.

Maggie slumped back in her chair. She looked to the picture of her, Brian, and Lilly on her desk and felt the familiar dull ache in her stomach. "I've thought of nothing else for months, Mr. Vega. Way before I took your daughter's picture." Maggie rubbed her eyes and shook her head. She chose her words carefully so every word she spoke was the truth, knowing this man was a very careful observer. "I am tired. I am distraught over my own daughter." She looked him in the eyes. "I have the pictures and negatives, but I need to put it all together so you have what you need."

Nestor studied her face, and Maggie stared back without blinking. Finally he nodded. "I would like you to talk to my detective as soon as possible. To make arrangements to give him your negatives and pictures, everything you have. Everything," he said. "I am meticulous. I save everything and like to have information available right at my fingertips."

He pulled out a business card and wrote something on the back. He laid it on the desk next to the check. "That's my direct line. Call me as soon as you have it all together, and I will have it picked up. And if there is anything else you decide you want to tell me..." He held her gaze. "Anything else you remember. Please don't waste time, Ms. Miller."

Maggie nodded. As he walked out the door his posture became more erect, his head held at an angle of assurance. She wondered what it must be like to live life with a facade between you and the world. She looked down to the check and business card he had left. She had no idea who to believe, who was lying, and where she could find the truth.

**

A half hour later, Maggie sat at her desk and stared at the pile of office bills waiting to be paid, trying to concentrate on finances, but failing miserably. She looked up to see Gerlinde standing in her doorway.

"There's a Sandy Jones on the phone demanding to talk to you. She said to tell you it was the British woman from yesterday," Gerlinde said.

Maggie nodded, watched Gerlinde leave, then gripped the phone to her ear, the bottom half under her chin so Lydia wouldn't hear her breathing.

"I know Nestor came to see you." Lydia spit the words out as soon as Maggie had said hello.

"How can you know that?"

"I told you I have a source in the house. What did he want? Did you tell him about me?"

Maggie could hear panic in her voice. "I'm not sure you're in any position to ask questions."

"Did you tell him about me?"

"Was Mira sick as a baby?"

"Did you tell him?" She was yelling now. "Answer me."

"Was she sick?"

"What does that matter? If you've told him, I don't know what I'll do. He has a detective. Oh, god." Her voice broke. "I have to—"

"I didn't tell him." Maggie broke in before the woman could hang up.

"Please tell me the truth. I have to know."

"I didn't tell him." Maggie rubbed her forehead. "Now answer me."

"Mira was sick often as a baby. She had colitis; she still does. Why do you ask?"

Maggie froze. Her mother had had colitis in her later years. The stomach pain and uncontrollable diarrhea disabled her at times. "You didn't mention that."

"Why would I? Did he tell you she had strep throat quite often, too? I have medicine for her, if that's his worry."

"Let's say he painted a different picture than the one you did."

"And that surprises you?"

Maggie didn't know what to say. It *had* surprised her.

"He is ruthless. Tell me what he said so I can defend myself."

"I won't tell you what he said, but I will say that he is very anxious to have her back. He knows it was you—" Maggie heard Lydia's groan and added quickly, "I didn't tell him. It was from the picture I showed him."

"How could he recognize me?" There was complete amazement in her voice.

"He said you had a baseball cap on of a team you used to like. Some blue sox."

There was a long silence, then Lydia said, "Oh, my god," more to herself than Maggie. "How could I have been so stupid." Her voice was low and full of self-loathing.

"I didn't mention we met. He claims you are the one with…" How much to reveal? "Problems."

"I told you he threatened to have me declared incompetent so he could have sole custody."

"Tell me more."

"When he filed for custody, and I filed a counter suit, he produced a document from the psychiatrist I saw after Mira was born. I had postpartum depression and went to see a *friend* of his. I was fine in a few months, but he said he would show it to the judge and swear on his life that I had tried to take my life on several occasions, put the baby in jeopardy in other ways. Make it so I could never see her alone."

"Is any of that true?"

"I had the depression, but not the rest. Why do you think I left? If I were fighting a normal man, I would have stuck it out. But he had too many tricks. I would have lost my daughter forever in the eyes of the law."

"Kidnapping is not within the law. You'll go to prison if you're caught."

"I would risk going to hell if there was a chance to be with my daughter. Is there any law you wouldn't break if it would bring Lilly back?"

Maggie felt the familiar tightness in her chest. "Your daughter isn't dead."

"She would be to me. Listen, Mrs. Miller, I thought long and hard about this. I chose to look like a mother who abandoned her daughter, not an insane one locked away in an institution where I would never get to her. *To me, it was the only choice.*"

Maggie put her head in her hands. Who should she believe? "I don't know what to do. I would be an accessory if I let you go. *I* could go to jail."

"You can't be thinking of telling him?"

"He was very convincing."

"He *convinces* for a living. He's a criminal defense attorney."

"He says the same about your acting ability."

"Did he? It's nice to know he appreciates something about me."

"Both of your stories are plausible. I don't know what to believe." She ran her hand over her face. "If Nestor is telling the truth, Mira could be in grave danger."

"I would never hurt her. I took her to keep her safe from him."

Maggie didn't know what to say. Not even a question she could ask that would clarify things. Both were desperate parents, and at least one was a consummate liar. She could hear breathing on the other end of the phone.

"I need your help, Maggie," Lydia said. "I don't care about jail. All I want is a chance to watch my daughter grow up and keep her from being hurt anymore by Nestor."

Maggie's eyes moved to the picture of Lilly on her desk.

"You know how it feels," Lydia said.

"Stop."

There was silence on the line, and Maggie could hear Lydia breathing. Then in tired voice, Lydia said, "What are the chances? If you hadn't been at that plaza that day…" Her voice trailed off.

Maggie remembered back to the long drives on the Turnpike, to the hours spent in her car, eating junk food, looking at people and taking their pictures from the safety, the anonymity of her car, all so she wouldn't have to come home to a house without her Lilly. Mira was these two parents' Lilly, and, somehow, Maggie had become the judge and jury of this family's fate. She stared at the picture of Lilly on her desk. Just like the woman on the other end of the phone, she wished she'd never taken those pictures, never been in her car, hiding from the world. Never needed a reason to.

Maggie rubbed her eyes and said, "I wish I hadn't been there."

"I need to know what you're going to do," Lydia said. "My options at this point depend on what you do."

"I don't know what I'm going to do. I need time to think."

"Then you won't tell Nestor?"

"Not yet."

"You must decide soon, or I'll…"

When she didn't finish the sentence, Maggie said, "You'll what?"

After a short pause, Lydia said, "I'll call you tomorrow."

Maggie put the phone down. Maybe *she* should be the one to leave the country. Take the pictures and negatives and disappear for a few days and let these two bizarre adults battle it out. Then she looked at Lilly's picture and thought of Mira Vega. If this were just two angry adults fighting over property, she would let them battle it out and not care who won. But she couldn't abandon a child. And it sounded as if the wrong decision could be deadly.

Maggie felt like she was in one of those old horror movies where the walls start to close in. She had Nestor squeezing her from one side, and Lydia pushing her from the other. And both told a very convincing tale.

She stared around her office, not knowing where she would find answers, but she knew they weren't here. She gathered the bills into a pile and placed them in the checkbook, then closed the cover and put the whole thing into her drawer. Grabbing her purse and heading out of her office, she waved good-bye to Gerlinde.

"Where are you going?" Gerlinde said in an astonished tone.

"Out."

"We blocked this afternoon out for paperwork."

"It will have to get done tomorrow," Maggie said. She reached the front door. "I'll see you later."

"The bills—" Gerlinde's voice was cut off by the closing door.

Chapter Twenty

Maggie felt the cold blast of air conditioning as she walked into the South Regional Branch of the Broward County Public Library. She took the stairs to the research department, located on the second floor, and a woman with what appeared to be a large wig on her head was busy behind the desk. Maggie waited for her to look up and make some acknowledgement of Maggie's presence. After a few minutes and no eye contact from the woman, Maggie said, "Excuse me?"

The woman looked up and stared.

"I need some help finding information," Maggie said.

The woman looked back to the index cards in her hands, then back at Maggie. "I'll be with you in a minute."

Maggie watched as the woman shuffled the cards around then walked to a phone that was lying, off the hook, on the desk.

The woman looked at the wall as she said, "You'll have to go to the main library for that information, sir." She put the phone down, without saying good-bye, then turned her attention to Maggie. "Now, what can I do for you?"

"I'm looking for some newspaper articles on something that happened two to three years ago. They're probably on microfiche, but I need to find out where they are and how I search for them."

The woman's face stretched into what Maggie assumed was her version of a smile. "We no longer store information on microfiche. Information for those years can be gotten off the data base on the computer." She bent down to a drawer, and Maggie feared her wig would fall forward to meet her eyebrows. From a file, she pulled a blue sheet of paper and handed it to Maggie.

Maggie felt her face flush as she took the sheet of paper that had very explicit instructions on how to access the Info Trac OneFile and looked at the woman. No more microfiche? It had been a long time since she'd researched anything.

"You can actually access the system at home," the woman said.

Maggie wondered if the woman's personal goal was to rid the library of patrons. But, she decided, she'd rather be home anyway.

"Thank you," Maggie said as she turned and walked away.

***

At home, in front of her computer, which she had last used to find Nestor Vega's address, she followed the instructions on the sheet to access the public library database of archived magazine and newspaper articles called OneFile. After thirty minutes of going from one site to the next and having to make choices on things she didn't understand, frustration got the best of Maggie. She cursed the wig-woman and went directly to the *Miami Herald* site. Where it listed "search," Maggie clicked on archived articles of more than seven days, then typed in Nestor Vegas' name in the "for" space. She hit "go" and waited while the computer searched, hoping that there would be something that would help her and it would be easier than the last half hour. When it returned with only articles from within 180 days, she hit the advanced search button. There she specified Vega's name and dates from over two years ago.

After a short wait, a list of thirty-three articles came up. She clicked on one and then realized she would have to pay to access the articles and sign on for a "Real Cities Account." Maggie got her credit card and signed on for the twenty-five-article pack, at $49.95, good for thirty days, not because she cared about the thirty percent savings, but because she didn't want to have to pull out her credit card for each article. She was disappointed that the archived articles would contain no photos, but she was pleased to see that the article would be emailed to her, so she wouldn't have to cut and paste to save any information she wanted.

After clicking on the first article, Maggie realized that any article containing Nestor Vega's name in the text had been produced. The one she had just paid for was about an "elegant holiday party" where a guest had been punched in the nose. Nestor's only connection was that he had been a guest—one of many which included Gloria and Emilio Estevan and former Secretary of State Alexander Haig, as well as judges and city commissioners. Nestor did travel in high profile circles.

She went to an earlier article, entitled "Prominent Miami Attorney Files for Custody," and found it more on target. It stated that Nestor Vega's attorney, Sander Rodriquez, had filed for sole custody of his daughter Mira, citing the grounds as his wife's "mental instability." She continued reading articles and sorting the facts as she read them, trying to see where the newspaper facts fit with what each Vega had told her.

The articles reported that Lydia had filed for divorce first, then Nestor had countered with the custody suit. The case had been slowed down when Lydia's attorney, Abigail Lustig, was taken off the case while she was being investigated for "inappropriate finance manipulation" and possible disbarment. The accusation was that she had stole money from a client's trust account.

Then Maggie found an article that said in a "surprising turn of events, the highly publicized Vega divorce has been settled." The terms were unavailable as the case had been sealed by the presiding judge, Judge Harry Wasserman.

Maggie sat back. She had gathered a lot of information, and she could see why Nestor might want to keep the fact that his wife had taken the child from the press. He could hardly make a move without the press having a field day. Yet there was still no way to tell which of the two Vegas was telling the truth. And with the divorce file sealed, that would be of no help, either.

Maggie wondered who she could talk to in the case that might give her some information. She went to the yellow pages and got the number for Nestor's divorce attorney, Sander Rodriguez. When she tried to get Abigail Lustig's phone number she couldn't find it.

She went back to the *Herald* site and did a search on Abigail Lustig and found a small article that stated the lawyer had indeed been disbarred. It mentioned that she had represented the wife of prominent attorney Nestor Vega in their divorce battle until her disbarment. It did not say who took over the case.

While searching, Maggie had come upon an article about the Ronald McDonald House Fundraiser that Nestor had held two years ago. The function was described as "one of the most gala affairs held in Miami." It reminded her that when Vega's daughter had first been abducted, it had been an issue as to whether or not the function would proceed. She searched the more recent archives and found an article that stated, "Despite his daughter's continued disappearance, Nestor Vega would hold his gala fundraiser." She clicked on her computer calendar and realized that the fundraiser was the following day.

Maggie rubbed her eyes and wondered what it would be like to have to be festive and hospitable while your child was missing. She tried to figure out how she could get information and from whom. Because the child was missing, going up to someone and asking questions would arouse suspicion. There had to be some way to get to the real facts, not the Vega-colored versions. A glance at the clock made Maggie realize how late it was. She decided she would sleep on it and come up with a plan in the morning.

Chapter Twenty-One

In her dream, a portable phone lay ringing on the beach, dangerously close to the surf. Maggie, dressed in a ski bib and ski jacket and wearing skis, was trying to walk toward the phone, but the sand was moving backward like a reverse conveyor belt. Her skis kept sliding, and she realized she had no ski poles. The faster Maggie's legs moved, the farther away she got; the more helpless Maggie felt, the louder the phone rang. Maggie pulled herself into consciousness to realize that her bedroom phone was ringing and grabbed at it, trying to catch it before the answering machine picked up. The red numbers on her alarm clock said 4:12AM.

"Hello." Maggie pulled herself up in bed.

"This is ADT security. May I speak with a Ms. Maggie Miller?" The voice was very detached, and Maggie could hear the clicking of keyboards in the background.

"This is she."

"Ms. Miller, there's been an alarm code received for a place of business at 5555 Stirling Road, rear door. The police have been dispatched. You are listed to be notified."

Maggie wiped her eyes. "My studio?" Her muscles began to tense.

"Is it located at 5555 Stirling Road?"

"Yes."

"Then, yes, Ma'am."

"Thank you." Maggie hung up the phone and got out of bed. She stood in the middle of the room wondering what to do. She wished Brian was home; he would know what to do.

Grabbing a pair of jeans, Maggie decided to head over to the studio and see what was happening. She was already wide-awake. If the police were already there, then it would be safe to go, she assumed. She would drive over and see what was going on. It had to be a false alarm.

***

Maggie pulled into the shopping-strip parking lot that was deserted except for three Cooper City Police cars parked in front of her studio. She pulled into the closest parking spot and walked toward her studio. Instead of the low lighting that was left on every night, the studio was ablaze with light. Two police officers stood outside the door talking, and Maggie could see more moving around inside.

"What happened?" Maggie said as she walked to the front door.

"Is this your place of business?" one of the officers asked.

"Yes, I got a call from my alarm company. Was it a false alarm? Sometimes the lightning sets it off." As soon as she said it, she felt foolish. There wasn't a drop of rain or a bit of lightning anywhere in the sky.

"May we see some I.D., please?"

Maggie got out her driver's license and a business card.

The officer nodded and handed the documents back to her. "No false alarm. There are signs of forced entry."

Maggie felt her stomach sink—someone had actually broken in? She thought of all of her favorite equipment, thousands of dollars of cameras and lenses that she had spent years accumulating. Like a doting mother, she liked each piece for different reasons and wouldn't want to part with any of it. "It's only material things," she heard Brian saying in her head. She knew this was true, and maybe later that sentiment would work, but right now, she couldn't imagine losing another single thing. At least her favorite camera was in the back of her car in her equipment case.

"Ma'am?"

Maggie realized she was standing and staring off at nothing, frozen in disbelief that this was happening. "Yes, I'm sorry. What do I do now?"

"Could you go on inside and see if you can tell what, if anything, is missing?"

What, if anything. Maybe she'd be lucky and someone had simply thrown a rock through the window as a cruel joke. A glance at the panes of glass disproved that theory.

The officer next to her yelled into the studio, "Bob, the owner is here." He turned back to Maggie and said, "He'll walk you through."

Maggie nodded and walked into the studio to be approached by another uniformed police officer.

"I'm Sergeant Robert John," the officer said, taking off a plastic glove that he had been wearing and extending his hand. "Maybe you could walk through with me and see if anything is missing or what damage has been done. Do you keep any significant amounts of cash here?"

Maggie shook her head as she looked around Gerlinde's desk. "It's not really a cash business. Some petty cash here," she said as she reached down to pull open Gerlinde's top drawer.

"Wait," the officer said as he intercepted her arm before she could reach the drawer. "I'll need you to put on some gloves first." He pulled a pair out of his back pocket and handed them to Maggie. "They may be a little large for you."

Maggie put the gloves on and then opened the drawer.

A ten and some singles lie in a black drawer separator next to an assortment of pens and pencils and an opened bag of Twizzlers. "We never keep much more then this, maybe twenty," Maggie said.

Officer John nodded, and they started to walk back through the studio.

"This has never happened before. Not once in the five years I've been here. Do you get many break-ins?" Maggie said.

"Some."

Maggie wondered how many "some" were. She'd never heard of any in this strip of stores. The break room looked untouched.

"Let's go in here next." The officer nodded toward her office.

Maggie walked through the doorway and started to walk around her desk when she saw papers and other contents from her drawers on the floor. She stopped short.

"I don't keep any money in here," she said.

"Is this your office?" Officer John said.

Maggie nodded. She squatted down and ran her hand through some of her desk contents. All of her unpaid bills from yesterday, which she had piled into her drawer, were spread out before her. She felt a tinge of fear as she wondered if her liability insurance was paid up and how much her deductible was if her equipment was gone.

"Anything missing?" Officer John said.

Maggie shrugged. She would have to sit down and recreate her desk to be sure. "My equipment, the only thing worth anything, is in the studio."

They went to the photo studio next, and Maggie walked up to the first cabinet drawer with her heart pounding. She pulled open the first drawer to see three lenses, all covered in plastic and floating on gray foam the way she demanded they be stored, lined up neatly where they belonged. They hadn't even been uncovered to check their value. Inspection of another drawer, then the cabinets, produced the same results.

"Thank goodness," she said as she turned to Officer John. "I'll have to take an inventory, but they seem untouched."

"I'm not sure they made it to this room. They were gone when we got here, which means they had a limited amount of time. The back room seems to be where they spent most of their time. Come."

Maggie, feeling relief that her cameras and lenses were safe, followed the officer to her work room where the uneasy feeling immediately returned. The room looked as if a hurricane had hit. All of the file draws were open, and files that had held neatly organized and categorized black and white proofs and full color shots were dumped out, and pictures were all over the floor. Maggie tiptoed in, trying to push aside pictures with her shoe, rather than step on them. The floor looked like a montage of her photography career. Faces wearing mortarboards, first communion veils, and bar mitzvah yarmulkes smiled up at her. Couples wed, babies drooled, and retirees danced on her floor. Families reunited and minors turned of age as she stared back. Maggie shook her head in disbelief at what she saw.

"Who could have done this?" she said.

"This looks more like vandalism than a robbery. Do you have any un-happy clients?"

Maggie knew she had cancelled a lot of appointments lately, maybe disappointed some people, but she couldn't believe she had upset anyone to this point. "None I can think of," she said.

"Anyone who would steal your work?"

Maggie knelt down and let her hand sweep over the lives on the floor. "Who would want someone else's memories…" Maggie's words trailed off and her hand froze as she saw a picture of a little girl on a swing in a park shoot.

"Did you find something?" the officer said above her.

Maggie kept her head down, so as not to let her face show. Could one of the Vega parents want the pictures of Mira and Lydia so badly that they would do something like this? Both of them knew where the studio was; they had both been there in the last two days. And neither of them knew that her darkroom was at home and that the pictures wouldn't be here, the logical place for them to be. Maggie stood up. "No, I can't think of any-one," she said. "I'm just stunned that something like this could happen."

Maggie spent the next thirty minutes answering questions and filling out forms, while her mind wandered. Was this just a coincidence? Could this be random vandalism? The first and only in five years? Or was it con-nected to the Vegas? If there was any chance that it had been either of the Vegas trying to find the pictures, then she needed to get some information quickly, because someone was getting very impatient.

Chapter Twenty-Two

Maggie sat in the car with Donovan and stared at Nestor Vega's house. They had pulled off to the side of the road, and from what they could see, there were two lines of cars approaching the house. One line curved around the cul-de-sac and right in front of Ronald McDonald. The clown stood outside the Vega fence with a bouquet of helium balloons in one hand and a fistful of papers in the other. As each car stopped, children would jump out and talk to the exuberant clown. He rewarded them with his time, a balloon, and what must be the promised coupon for a free Happy Meal.

The second line of cars were stopped by a guard at the end of the driveway, then motioned through the gate and on to the valet.

Three days ago, when Maggie had been here last, the house had been somber, just one on a block of beautiful houses. But today, it was the star, the house that called out to be looked at, an occasion to be participated in. While the salmon-red sunset blazed behind the house, the walkway had been lined with low tiki lamps along the grass. Large gas torch lamps burnt on the lawn, sending flames toward the sky, knowing they would outlast the sun. Tiny colored lights were woven all through the metal gate and along the wall giving the impression that this was a fairytale house rather than the home of a still-missing abducted child.

Maggie clenched the ticket for the fundraiser in her left hand, while her right cradled her camera. She knew that the affair raised millions of dollars for charity, and she applauded Nestor for the stamina to go ahead with it. It was going to be a problem when Brian found out that she had paid $1,000 to come to the affair. It was a donation, she would tell him. A good cause—finding Mira.

She turned to Donovan. "Are you ready?"

"Are you sure you want me to come in? I don't exactly blend in." He placed his pale white hand, which stuck out of the French cuff of a blue shirt, in front of his face.

"I can't do this alone, Donovan. Thank you for coming with me." She put her camera back in her lap and placed her hand over his and squeezed.

He smiled and nodded, then adjusted his bow tie. "What do you want to do first?"

"Act like everybody else. Look rich." She smiled for the first time since she had seen him that evening. Donovan's pale coloring contrasted with the blue shirt and the dark tux to make it look as if someone had dressed a marble statue, a very handsome one. "You look nice."

"If it weren't for the tux rental company we use for shoots, I would be here in jeans." He smiled as he looked at Maggie's dress. "You look beautiful."

Maggie felt her face flush. She had on what Brian called her LBD— little black dress, soft black silk, that cascaded over her body, a style that hung limply on the hanger but acquired a different shape on each body it covered. It actually fit her better with the few pounds she'd lost since Lilly's death. She couldn't remember the last time she felt beautiful.

"You okay?" Donovan said.

Maggie shook her head.

"Would you like to leave?" Donovan said.

"No, I need to do this," Maggie said. "I'm ready." She looked toward the house and saw a security guard walking toward the car. "And a good thing. We have company." She lowered her window and turned her head, smiling, as the guard pointed a flashlight at her.

"Can I help you?" the guard said.

Maggie held up the tickets. "We're here for the fundraiser."

"Valet parking, Ma'am. Pull ahead." He made a sweeping motion with his flashlight toward the gate.

"Thank you," Maggie said as she continued her sweetest smile. She rolled up the window. "Let's go. I don't need to call attention to myself."

They pulled up to the valet, and Maggie slipped the camera strap over her head, letting her camera fall just below her breasts. They left the car and walked to the front door.

If the outside of the house had been made festive, the inside was like something from a *House Beautiful* spread. Flower arrangements stood on tall columns in the hallway and blooming orchids in every color decorated the tables. The sweet smell of roses and carnations filled the air, a smell Maggie used to enjoy, but now it only reminded her of the funeral home. She raised the camera to her face and took a picture of a woman who happened to be standing next to a flower arrangement that complimented her salmon-colored gown perfectly. The only thing there was more of than flowers were people.

"Can you imagine there are this many people willing to spend five hundred a head to be here?" Donovan said.

"It is a good cause."

"So is tuition."

They had been slowly walking toward the only room in the house that Maggie had seen—Nestor's office. Before they got there, a waiter in a tuxedo with a silver tray offered them a glass of champagne. As she took a sip, a tray of oysters appeared in front of her.

"This doesn't have to be all work," she whispered to Donovan after she had sucked the oyster out of the shell and placed it on the small plate the waiter was holding. She took a gulp of champagne.

"His tux is nicer than mine," Donovan said as he nodded toward a tall man in a tuxedo that fit him as if it had been sewn on him.

"He probably owns his." Maggie took another swallow of champagne. "He's the governor of Florida." She winked at Donovan then handed her glass to him as she raised her camera to her eye.

"I didn't recognize him all dressed up." Donovan nodded at her already half empty champagne glass. "Remember why we're here."

"I can't forget." Maggie lowered her camera and took another sip of the cool, dry bubbly and felt it ease down her throat. She hadn't eaten all day and could feel the alcohol relax her. What did they call alcohol? Liquid bravado? She could use some.

She walked to a picture of Mira on a side table and stared. She was one of the very few people who knew the child was alive, and she wished for the millionth time since the middle of May that there were some way that her Lilly could be, too. She lifted her glass to the picture. *To you both*, she said in her mind, then downed the champagne and placed the glass next to the silver frame. She squatted down and took a full frame picture of the picture of Mira. It would be good to have for comparison purposes.

She turned to see Donovan's eyes on her and saw the compassionate look on his face. She walked over and linked her arm in his. "Thanks," she said as she started to walk slowly into Nestor's study.

"For what?"

"For letting me finish the champagne without reprimanding me as if I were a child."

"You're a big girl."

"Now, don't let me have anymore." She laughed and then stopped when she saw Nestor across the room. "Oh, shit. There he is."

Donovan turned her around so her back was to Nestor. "This *is* his house, Maggie."

"I know. I'd just rather not run into him. Let's go somewhere else."

Donovan stared at Nestor for a minute before turning away. "Do you really think he was the one who broke into the studio? He looks so..." he thought for a minute, "respectable."

Maggie pulled him out of the room. "I'm not sure who it was, but it had to be somehow related to those pictures I took. One of those parents is getting desperate."

They walked down a hallway that led to a double set of French doors and out to the patio. The pool area was filled with tables covered with white tablecloths and surrounded with white slat folding chairs. Each table had an arrangement of purple roses, with a matching candle burning, but Maggie's eyes were drawn to the large yacht docked behind the house. It, too, had been covered with small, twinkling lights. Off to the side of the yard, was a large blow-up bubble ride, the kind that Maggie had never let Lilly go into because the kids either knocked heads inside, or threw up. Squeals of delight and flushed kids came through the opening. Maggie couldn't help but notice that many of the children were bald, and she realized they must be recovering from chemotherapy.

She glanced around and saw that some of the children were in wheelchairs, many with parents doting next to them, with food and/or balloons.

In her peripheral vision, Maggie saw that Nestor had just come out onto the patio. She turned around. "Let's just do what we came for. I'd rather he not see me."

"If he does—"

"If he does, I'll say just what we planned: This is a great charity and I wanted to contribute." She held up her camera and continued, "I freelance for several Broward papers and wanted some shots while I was here." She shook her head. "But I'd rather get out unnoticed. We've waited long enough. Let's go."

They walked back into the main foyer. "He told me he was compulsive, saved everything," Maggie said. "That he liked to put his finger on information when he wanted to, not have to go looking for it. But his study is too crowded, and if he lets people in there, that must not be where he keeps his personal information."

She looked toward the stairs. "I want health records, receipts, divorce documents. Prescriptions for Mira—if she really has colitis." She took his arm and started walking toward the stairs. "Let's find the master bedroom."

Maggie could feel the camera thump her chest with each step up. "If we get caught," Maggie whispered, "we'll just say I was trying to find a bathroom. The one downstairs was occupied."

"You mean, the *ten* downstairs."

"Do you have a better excuse for being up here?" she said as they turned down a long hallway.

Donovan shook his head. "I'm fresh out."

Off to the right, Maggie saw a set of double doors. She opened them and walked into a bedroom that looked as well decorated and planned as the rest of the house. There was a king-sized bed in the center of the room, and a sitting area off to the side. Around the room were four closed doors, and Maggie wondered where to start. She opened the first and felt as if she had stumbled into a tropical rain forest that had bathroom facilities. Light from the sunset seeped into the room through two large skylights. There were plants hanging everywhere and fragrant candles burned in crystal holders on the marble counters.

She opened the next door and it was a closet the size of her bedroom. She walked into the room and saw it was divided into two sides: his and hers. As she walked past the masculine clothes toward a bank of built-in drawers, her hand couldn't help but reach out and touch the suits, all lined up in color coordination. She stopped at a navy blue suit and ran her hand up and down the sleeve. The feel was nothing less than luxurious. Brian's uniform was like sandpaper compared to this. She moved along to the drawers, letting her hand trail over the jacket sleeves.

When she got to the drawers, she opened a thin one on the top first. Ties, arranged according to the spectral colors of the rainbow— ROYGBIV, she suddenly remembered the acronym from grade school— lined the drawer. Reds ties first on the left, blending into oranges, then yellows from the color of a lemon to a pale sunset all the way through to violet. She reached her left hand down to feel the soft silk as her right hand brought her camera to her face only to remember she had loaded black and white film.

"What are you doing?" Donovan's voice projected in a loud whisper.

Maggie jumped. "You scared me!" She turned back to the drawer. "This place is like a department store."

"Did you find anything?"

She shook her head. "No. I was checking drawers." She looked up to Donovan. "Go back and watch."

"Hurry," Donovan whispered as he walked out.

Maggie quickly opened each drawer, running her hand around the edges to see if there was anything hidden, but found only clothing. On the "her" side of the closet, she found a drawer of magnificent jewelry, but nothing of help to her.

She walked back into the bedroom and had two doors left. She picked one and whispered "Bingo" to herself as she stared into the small room. It was a smaller version of the large library downstairs minus the bookshelves. Her hand glided over the perfectly polished dark cherry wood desk as she made her way over to the filing cabinet. She pulled the handle. When it didn't open, she tugged harder. She ran her hand around the top and off to the side and felt the indentation where a lock waited for a key. Damn! Locked, even in his own room. She pulled again, harder, as if there were any chance the drawer would open.

She walked over to the desk, hoping to find a key. She pulled open the middle drawer, but it held only pens, pencils, erasers—the usual office supplies. She pulled open the right top draw and saw no keys, but noticed a small Rolodex. She flipped through it, not really sure what she was looking for. Then she saw a card with Abigail Lustig's name hand written in very neat print. Below it was a phone number: 888-843-5397 (888 THE LAWS). As easy as it the number was, Maggie's anxiety level was high and she feared she might forget it, so she snapped a picture of the card with her camera just as she heard Donovan's voice.

"This is a very nice function, sir." Donovan's voice was louder than normal.

Through the pounding sound in her temples, Maggie heard Nestor's voice answer: "Thank you, but the party is downstairs. May I help you in some way?"

As she strained to listen, Maggie heard the voices move toward her and she put the Rolodex back in the desk drawer, slamming it closed. She was just coming around the desk when Nestor walked into the room with Donovan close behind him.

Nestor's expression was one of disbelief mixed with anger, then his face broke into a smile. "Why, Ms. Miller. What a…" he exaggerated the pause, "…surprise," he nodded as if he liked that choice of word, "it is to find you here." He stared at the camera around her neck.

"Hello, Mr. Vega. You have a beautiful home."

"If I'd known you were so interested in it, I would have given you the full tour the day you came to see me."

Maggie started to walk toward the door. As she walked past Nestor, he reached out his arm and stopped her. "Perhaps there is something I could help you with? A reason," he tilted his head, his voice remaining cordial, "you are in my bedroom? With a camera?"

Maggie smiled but she could come nowhere near the sincerity he had managed to deliver. "I was looking for the bathroom." She reached down and ran her finger over the body of her camera. "I freelance for some newspapers so I took some shots of your guests, the governor." Her smile punctuated the end of her sentence.

Nestor's gaze studied her face. "There are *many* bathrooms downstairs."

"You're right. I'll be honest then." It was time to use one of the tricks she knew she might have to resort to, using the advice from a politician whose campaign photos she had once done: when surprised by an adversary, do the unexpected and turn the tables around. "I feel an affinity with your daughter, what with her missing and all. I wanted to be near her, somehow." She closed her eyes and took a deep breath. "The way I go into my own daughter's room, now that she's gone." She opened her eyes and waved her hands in a slow, exaggerated way. "To feel her presence."

Nestor stared at her as if trying to decide if she were dangerous or crazy. Or both.

"It's so hard to be without them, isn't it?" Maggie leaned toward Nestor, getting just inches from his face.

Nestor backed away.

Maggie took a step closer, sensing it was making him uncomfortable. "It's as if part of my daughter is still in that room." Maggie opened her eyes wide. She was sure the anxiety she was feeling was making her look as crazy as she felt. "I wanted to see Mira's room."

Nestor put his arm out in such a way as to appear to be comforting her, but keeping her at a safe distance at the same time. "Yes. But, Ms. Miller, this is *my* room, not Mira's. What, pray tell," he swept his arm grandly around the room, "are you doing here?" He fixed his eyes on her and stepped in closer. "Tell me."

Maggie swallowed hard and tried to back up. Nestor's grip prevented her retreat. She suddenly felt as if she'd been playing chicken with a rattlesnake.

Donovan cleared his throat. "We really should apologize to Mr. Vega for wandering off course."

Nestor never took his eyes off Maggie, but said, "And you are?"

"Donovan Renner." Donovan extended his hand to Nestor.

Nestor turned and grasped the offered hand. "Nice to meet you, Mr. Renner. Now, I would like you to return downstairs."

"I'll wait for Maggie, Mr. Vega," Donovan said as he leaned against the doorway.

Nestor nodded, visibly displeased. He turned back to Maggie. "Ms. Miller, I hope this sudden *affinity* with my daughter includes the act of bringing me the negatives and pictures I requested from you." His face was hopeful.

"I…" Maggie shook her head. "I don't have them."

Nestor walked toward his desk. He turned to face Maggie and Donovan. "You come into my bedroom," he paused and looked to her chest, "with a camera, looking for…" he stretched out the last word, his voice rising as if asking a question, then he looked around the room. He looked at Maggie, letting the pause get very uncomfortable, nodding at her to finish the sentence. When she didn't answer, he continued, "Looking for…an affinity with my daughter." He paused again. When he continued his voice was booming. "Yet you do not bring the one thing that could help return her home. I do not understand."

Maggie could see something she'd never seen before in Nestor Vega's face: a battle of emotions. His brows would knit and then his forehead would relax. He seemed to be balancing anger and control. He needed something very badly from her and did not want to make her angry. But this move had pushed him too far—she could see that much.

"I meant to bring them. I must have forgotten them in the rush of getting ready. When we got here, they weren't in the car," she said, shaking her head in disbelief. His expression told her that he didn't believe a word.

Nestor nodded almost imperceptibly. He stared at her, his eyes locking with hers.

Maggie shifted from foot to foot, but said nothing.

Finally Nestor said, "Come. I will show you Mira's room. Then perhaps you will feel compelled to bring me those pictures." As he led the way out of the room, he turned toward Donovan. "I respectfully ask that you return to the party, Mr. Renner. I will not harm your friend in anyway. My daughter's room is," he seemed to search for a word, "difficult for me under the best of circumstances. Ms. Miller, unfortunately, understands my sorrow." He turned to Maggie. "Please."

Maggie nodded toward Donovan. "It's okay. I'll be right down."

Donovan nodded back slowly. "I'll be right at the bottom of the steps if you need me."

Maggie walked into Mira's bedroom and knew what it might be like to be a modern-day princess. The room was decorated with pastel pinks, blues, and yellows in the background and crimson reds, royal blues, and forest greens accenting the focal points. The walls seemed to fall away making the room feel endless and allowing the contents to take center stage. Then Maggie realized that the echoes of the things she was seeing were due to every wall being mirrored. It was like standing in an open space that had no boundaries.

Maggie walked toward the canopy bed and ran her hand down the blue sway of material that billowed down the edge. The soft bedcover felt like clouds. Bookshelves, all three feet high, topped with stuffed animals looking out at the room, were filled with as many children's books as most bookstores. She took in the delicate wood furniture, then walked toward the dollhouse. The miniature Tudor house was three stories high with gabled roofs. The sides swung out to reveal perfectly decorated rooms with to-scale people inhabiting them. Maggie stared at the kitchen, where a chef with a tiny rolling pin in his hand attended a pastry rack filled with apple pie, strawberry cheesecake, tres leche, and flan. The chef had little puffs of flour on his face.

"Mira loved her dollhouse," Nestor said from the doorway, where he stood with his arms folded across his chest.

Maggie turned to scan the room again, seeing the wonderful photos she could shoot here. While she rarely took pictures without people in them, this was one place that had almost as much life as a human face.

"You can see," Nestor said, "that she wanted for nothing." His hand swept out to encompass the room.

Maggie nodded.

"She was always spoiled, but when her mother abandoned her," Nestor shrugged his shoulders in an almost apologetic way, "I think I may have overcompensated with *things*." His voice was very low. After a minute he said, "I explained to my daughter that the mirrored walls portrayed life: they reflect all the choices you've already made, yet represent the infinite possibilities still to come."

Maggie was surprised at such a sentiment coming from Nestor. She stared at her reflection in a far mirror and wondered if it was helpful to be reminded day after day of the choices you've already made. Then she turned just slightly and saw, reflected from the mirror behind her, an endless number of Maggies, an endless amount of potential choices yet to be made. It made her head hurt so she closed her eyes, then opened them, looking away from the mirrors.

She sat at a child-sized oak table that was set for tea with miniature china. She lifted the floral teapot and "poured" tea into the small cup. "Do you come in here often?"

"Never." Nestor's voice was just above a whisper.

Maggie looked up in surprise. She had spent days in Lilly's room after she had died, resting her head on Lilly's pillow to inhale the smell, rocking in the tall white chair where Lilly had been nursed as an infant, running her fingertips over the last pair of pajamas Lilly would ever wear, pajamas she refused to wash for fear they would lose their Lilly-smell. "Never?" Maggie said.

"I cannot." Nestor was leaning up against the doorframe now. "Not until she is back home."

Maggie stared at Nestor's face and saw the same pain she had seen in Lydia's face. "I'm sorry." Maggie got up. "This is insensitive of me." She walked to the door. "We should leave."

Nestor nodded his head as he moved aside to let her pass, then reached out and touched her arm, gently. "I must have your film."

Maggie reached down and held her camera.

"You must understand," Nestor said. "You have been in my room, my daughter's room. I trust no one right now. I will gladly return any photos you have taken of the party."

Maggie gripped the camera.

"The supermarket tabloids paid a lot of money for less, during my divorce." Nestor said.

Maggie nodded. She opened the camera without manually advancing the film, knowing she would ruin the roll—destroying the picture of a number in his Rolodex.

Nestor took the film and slipped it into his jacket pocket, then led her to a back staircase rather than the one in the front hall that she had come up. They silently descended the stairs, Maggie just ahead of Nester where she was unable to see his face.

He walked her into the party, his hand lightly on the small of her back.

"I must attend to my guests," Nestor said. "Enjoy yourself. Eat and be merry, as they say." Then he paused, his dark eyes staring into hers, locked as if she were the only one in the room. "I will not ask you again, but I would like to have those pictures." He put his hand on her elbow and leaned close to her ear. "I don't let myself think like this often, but they may be the last pictures taken of her that I will ever see."

"Nestor!" A woman Maggie recognized as an anchorwoman from Channel 6 news rushed up. "I've been looking for you. I have a live feed out on the patio. And a few kids that can't wait to be on TV with you." She turned to Maggie. "You will understand if I steal away the host."

Nestor nodded to Maggie. "I must go put on my camera face now. I hope to see you soon." To the anchorwoman, Nestor said, "I have one small thing to attend to. I promise to meet you out back in five minutes." His smile was charming as he bowed slightly. This was the charismatic man she would see on the Eleven O'clock news when she got home tonight. Nestor walked over to a man who was standing off to the side by himself. Maggie watched Nestor's back as he spoke to the gentleman who nodded and then spoke into what looked like a small walkie-talkie. While she knew there must be extensive security at the function, it had been nicely inconspicuous.

Maggie walked to the front staircase to find Donovan waiting for her.

When he saw her approaching, Donovan walked to meet her. "Are you okay? Did you have a chance to get anything that will help?"

"Maybe more than I thought I would."

"Meaning?"

"Whatever else he did, he loved," she paused to correct herself, "loves his daughter very much." She looked around at all the festivity. "Do you mind if we leave now?"

Donovan shook his head. "Hey, this is your party."

They headed for the front door, the opposite direction than that of the Channel 6 camera, and Maggie said, "Oh, and a phone number for the original attorney that handled his wife's case."

Donovan turned in surprise. "That's good, no? You must be excited."

"I must be," Maggie murmured. She couldn't shake the sad feeling she had felt since being in Mira's room, watching Nestor in pain.

Donovan grabbed a glass of champagne from a passing tray. He handed it to her. "Then celebrate. I'll drive home."

Maggie sipped the champagne while they waited at the front door for the valet to bring the car. Maggie could hear the circus music from the backyard. She wondered if perhaps this was really the place Mira should be growing up. She wanted to talk to Donovan about her visit to Mira's room but she didn't want to say anything until they got into the car—which seemed to be taking an unusually long time.

Donovan looked at his watch. "We must be blocked in."

"Guess they don't expect people to leave early." The words were just out of her mouth when she saw the car drive through the gate, followed by another car.

"At least we're not the only ones leaving early," Maggie said. She noticed how dirty her car looked compared to the shiny black Lexus that pulled up behind her car.

She slipped into the passenger seat and put on her seatbelt as Donovan drove out the long driveway. She reached into her purse and jotted down the phone number she had seen, 888-THE LAWS, on a scrap of paper, then put her head back on the headrest and closed her eyes trying to see answers she knew couldn't be seen.

Chapter Twenty-Three

Maggie and Donovan sat in her car in the parking lot of McDonald's on US1. Donovan had pulled into a spot in the corner of the lot, underneath a large light, and left the car running as they ate the food they had ordered from the drive through.

"I can't believe we left all that good food to be sitting here eating a hamburger and fries," Donovan said as he dipped a French fry into the mound of catsup on his hamburger wrapper.

"I'm sorry," Maggie said. "I just couldn't stay any more."

"The shrimp were about three hundred dollars each."

"No, they weren't," Maggie said.

"We each had a shrimp and an oyster. Okay, two-fifty each."

Maggie couldn't help but laugh as she bit into a dry fish fillet. "Don't forget the champagne."

"You're right. It was a bargain after all."

"I bet the desserts were great, too," Donovan said. "We could go back."

Maggie looked at him to be sure he wasn't serious. "I couldn't stay— that house became so sad to me. To have all that money, but not the one thing you really want."

"His daughter."

Maggie nodded. "And I couldn't sit in a restaurant right now. See happy people." She exaggerated a shudder.

"I know. The nerve of them to be happy."

Maggie managed a smile.

"You think he's the innocent one in all of this?" Donovan said.

She shrugged her shoulders. "Nestor was so sad when we were in Mira's room," she said. "Well, I was in her room; he stood at the doorway and wouldn't even come in." She shook her head. "This situation is going to end badly for one of those parents. One of them is going to lose their daughter forever, and I know how that feels." She put the sandwich down in her lap and swallowed the piece she was chewing. Her mouth had gone dry.

"Too bad they couldn't have worked things out between them," Donovan said.

"You should have seen this room, Donovan. Every wall was mirrored. Everything reflected endlessly. Nestor said the mirrors represent life. How the choices we make are reflected all around us, every day. I never thought of it like that."

Donovan took a sip of his vanilla shake. "Interesting way to look at it."

She nodded. "Everyday it's reflected back to me—Lilly's absence—that I made a bad choice in not coming out of the darkroom earlier that night."

"You can't keep beating yourself up over that, Maggie."

"Oh, no?" She looked out the window and saw a mother and daughter who were racing each other back to the car. She turned toward Donovan, away from the side window. "It's as if I've lost one of my arms. I'll never *not* notice."

"Do you ever think that some things are meant to be?" Donovan said.

"Like fate?"

"Yes, like even if you'd come out of the darkroom on that particular night, something else might have happened to make things turn out the way they did?"

Maggie had thought about that concept many times, even before Lilly's death, but wasn't sure she believed it. "She didn't deserve to have her life end."

"No, she didn't. Does any child? Look at those kids tonight. They don't deserve cancer or the other wicked diseases that put them in the hospital."

In her mind, Maggie pictured the dozens of families at the party that had been devastated by diseases. There were news stories every night about children being murdered, killed in accidents. Why did she think she should be immune?

"We never realize how lucky we are—going along, being busy and taking life for granted," Donovan said.

"But it wasn't a disease that couldn't be stopped. It was senseless, preventable. I should have prevented it. I'm her mother."

"That part must feel terrible."

Maggie looked up in surprise. She stared at him, waiting for the rest, the things everyone else said—"don't feel bad, it doesn't do any good to think like that, it wasn't your fault, you can't blame yourself, blah, blah, blah." When no negation followed, she said in a low voice, "It feels more than terrible. You have no idea."

Donovan wrapped the last quarter of his hamburger in the wrapper, put in on the dash, and turned fully toward Maggie. "Why don't you tell me?"

Maggie gave him a dirty look. "Don't make fun of me." She turned toward the front of the car.

Donovan reached over and tugged on her hand. "I'm being serious. I can't begin to imagine what you're feeling."

Maggie searched his face. He looked intent and interested, as if he'd just asked her directions to some place he needed to get to. "Brian always tells me not to talk about it," she said. "That it won't change what happened."

"If you feel it, maybe you should talk about it."

Maggie stayed silent, wondering if she was ready to go to that place of pain with someone else.

Donovan traced her knuckles with one of his fingers. "My mother used to tell me that when you spoke about bad things such as evil thoughts or scary ideas, they come out of your mouth and turn into icicles. Then they crumple and break away and melt, and they can't bother you any more after that."

"Your mother wanted to hear your evil thoughts?"

He shook his head. "She didn't want to, but we all have them, Maggie. Now and then. She told me the trick was if you let them out, they wouldn't affect your actions, and your actions are what really count."

"Your mother was something else." She smiled.

"A free spirit, to be sure." He smiled fondly.

Maggie thought about all the feelings she had pent up in her mind since Lilly's death. There were so many. "Does it work?"

Donovan shrugged. "That and the aroma therapy."

Maggie saw that he was trying to hide a smile and smiled back.

"Who can know for sure," Donovan said. "But I think verbalizing your fears gives them less power. She read a lot of self-help books."

Maggie realized she was still holding his hand. She pulled it away, then said, "I'm so angry, Donovan." She watched his face. "I'm angry at myself for not being there when she got hurt, but there's more." When he didn't say anything, Maggie said in a very low voice, "Somewhere, deep inside, I'm mad at her, Donovan. I'm mad at Lilly for not wearing her helmet. She knew she was supposed to and she probably would have survived that fall." She closed her eyes and let her head fall back on the headrest.

Then as if the words had a life of their own, she heard herself say, "I'm angry that she left me." Her head fell forward and she began to cry. She'd never said the words out loud before and rather than make them disappear, they seemed to hang heavy in the air, pointy icicles ready to stab her and cause her more pain. "How can I feel that? I'll never see her again; I can't hug her and make it better." She wiped her face with a napkin, starring down at her hands, unable to look at Donovan after what she'd just said. "I'm so angry, and it feels so wrong."

"It's not about right or wrong, Maggie. She died." He reached out and started to rub her shoulder. "You feel what you feel."

"I'm mad at myself for not protecting her. And I'm mad as hell at Brian for not letting me be angry." Her voice got louder. "I'm angry at everyone, goddamn it!"

Donovan pulled her closer. "Let it out, Maggie." He rubbed her arm.

"And I'm so confused about being angry!" She threw her hand in the air. "How can I be angry at a time like this?" When he remained silent, she continued, "I'm confused about how my marriage can be falling apart. After eleven years of marriage, I don't know how to behave with Brian—or how I want to behave. And on top of everything, I'm confused about which Vega is telling the truth. Who am I to decide who loses a child? One of them will feel like this, like me—how did that become my choice?" She let her head drop onto his shoulder. "I just want it all to stop."

She looked up and her face was just inches from Donovan's. His eyes were so kind. He let her say anything and never yelled at her, never told her she was wrong. Suddenly she felt as safe as she did when she was wrapped up in her favorite blue sheets.

"It's okay to be angry and confused, Maggie," Donovan said.

She moved her head closer to his and felt their lips touch. She reached her hand up to his head and pulled him to her. She kissed him hard at first, as if all her anger was focused on her mouth, where the words had just spilled out. Then she felt his hand gently caress her cheek, and she kissed him less urgently, her lips gently brushing against his. She focused on the sensuousness of the moment, letting herself get lost in the total acceptance for all her wrong thinking, letting the warmth spread all over her body. She wanted to take him home and wrap herself in him and her blue sheets. Pull the comforter over their heads and hide from the world. Tell him everything she felt in the soft darkness and not come out until it was all said.

She pulled away and looked at Donovan. He didn't hate her for her anger. Brian only comforted her when he agreed that her feelings were valid. Her stomach tightened at the thought of Brian, and she pulled further away. She squeezed her eyes shut and clamped her hand over her mouth.

"That shouldn't have happened," Maggie said.

Donovan moved to his side of the car. "It's my fault. I shouldn't have let it happen," he said. "You're so vulnerable right now." He took the hand that covered her mouth and placed it in her lap. Then he moved hair out of her face and put it behind her ear, stroked her cheek.

It felt so wonderful to be taken care of. She wanted more. Then she shook her head. "I'm so confused."

"I know, and that's why *I* should've stopped."

She looked at his blue eyes, at how sad he looked. "You make me feel so comfortable, like I can say the most outlandish things, and you won't judge me." She reached out her hand to touch his cheek, then pulled it back. "I know that's not a good enough excuse."

Donovan held her hand. "I hate to see you in so much pain. I thought it would help to let some of it out. To share it." He shook his head. "I didn't mean to add to it."

"It did help." She wanted him to hold her again, to kiss her face. Then she folded her arms across her chest. "What am I doing?"

He pulled one of her hands to his mouth and gently kissed the knuckle. "You were hurting, Maggie. I just…" His words fell off. "Neither of us meant for that to happen. We'll chalk it up to temporary insanity—for both of us—and never let it happen again."

Maggie let him run his lips over her fingers, her hand. She closed her eyes. What she wouldn't give to let it happen again. Her marriage? She pulled her hand away. She hoped the insanity was temporary.

Maggie had run out of words, run out of icicles to string in the air. She stared out the window at the advertisements on the window: Happy Meal for under a dollar. If only it was so easy to be happy.

After a long silence, Donovan said, "That new woman you hired is working out pretty well?"

"Yes." She wondered why he brought that up.

"Maybe I should take a few days off, if that's okay with you."

Maggie felt a sting in her stomach. "Sure. You deserve it. You've helped me out a lot the past few weeks."

"Thanks," Donovan said.

They drove home in silence, and Maggie wondered if she'd lost a friend.

Chapter Twenty-Four

Shortly after Donovan had dropped Maggie off at home, she sat propped up in bed holding the portable phone in her hand, the Bell South Yellow Pages resting on her lap. Her plan was to call the number she had found in Nestor's Rolodex, then look the firm up in the phone book. She'd hope to find an ad, perhaps some of the attorneys' names, and an address.

That was her plan, but she sat still, staring at the phone. She had taken off the black dress she had worn to the fundraiser and wore a soft cotton nightgown. For once she wasn't thinking of Mira Vega, nor Nestor or Lydia. She was thinking of Donovan. She had kissed him. But it was so much more than a kiss. Over the last few weeks Donovan's words had been like a comforting salve to her. His arms enclosed her in a soothing cocoon of safety, accepted in a way that she hadn't felt for a long time. When his eyes danced over her face, she felt as if she could do no wrong. And when his lips met hers it was like a circuit being completed. She wanted to tell him everything she felt, things she could tell no other human being, and she wanted to get lost in those kisses and never come back.

Maggie put the portable phone down on the bed next to her. She was thinking like a teenager. She was married, and so was Donovan. These things were supposed to happen to other people. Best friends were supposed to confide in you that they've misbehaved, had affairs, fallen in love. But not her. Maggie had always lived by the rules. And here she was sounding like a ninth grader whose books had been carried home by the captain of the football team.

"Are you crazy?" she said out loud to herself. Adults were supposed to control these urges. She knew it couldn't happen again. She closed her eyes, and remembering the way Donovan had gently kissed her eyelids, her cheeks, she sank lower in bed, wondering how she would ever do without that comfort again.

Maggie was startled when the phone rang. She stared at the portable phone as it rang again, praying both that it was and wasn't Donovan. Maggie picked up the phone on the fourth ring, right before the answering machine would have.

When she heard Brian's voice, she pulled the covers up over her and closed her eyes.

"How are you, Maggie?" He seemed to really be asking.

Maggie willed her voice to come out normal. "Fine." Her voice was far too loud.

"You don't mean that."

Maggie shook her head. "You're right," she said. "I haven't been fine for a long time. How are you?"

"Okay."

Maggie tried to remember how long he'd been gone.

"We need to do some serious talking," Brian said.

Maggie smoothed a wrinkle out of the comforter. "Life has been so serious lately."

"Life is serious, Maggie."

Even golf and poker were serious to Brian. Maggie thought of lying on her back looking at the clouds. Would he approve of such frivolous behavior? Would he "decide" it was not the way to spend her time? "Do you think you've been treating me differently since Lilly died?" she said.

"We've *both* been different since she died."

"Have you been overprotective? Trying to make more decisions for me because I've been upset?"

He was quiet for a minute, then said, "I don't think so. I've always tried to protect you. Sometimes I make decisions easier than you do, that's all."

That's all. Maggie felt her body sink into the bed. But then, she'd allowed him to do those things, hadn't she? She'd never complained before. If she were honest, maybe she even liked it when he made some of the decisions so her energy could go elsewhere. How important were most things anyway? The color of the car they bought? If they used liquid or power laundry detergent? Puffs or Kleenex? What did it matter?

Yet, there were other things she did care about. Like speaking for herself when the detective called.

Maggie sat up in bed, realizing that there was a lot she needed to be able to tell him, like all the things that bothered her so she never turned to someone else for comfort again. He was the one she was married to, the one she should be telling. He was Lilly's father.

"Do you think you could just listen to me sometimes, not try to tell me how to think or feel? Not make decisions for me?" Maggie said.

"I don't know." She could hear his breathing, then his voice was low. "I don't even know what it is that I do that upsets you."

"Maybe we should see a counselor, Brian. I've lost Lilly. I don't want to lose you, too."

"I'm not going anywhere," he paused, then added, "permanently. I just left so you could get over this missing-girl thing."

Maggie felt her stomach tighten. She was nowhere near "over" Mira; she was in even deeper. She took a deep breath. "See. Like that. I didn't want you to leave when you did. I wanted to you listen to my side. Even if you didn't agree, to support me, to try and understand."

After a few moments, he said, "I'd like to come back to the house and talk this out in person," he said. "I have a few days before I leave for South America again."

"I'd like that," Maggie said. Then she remembered Mira Vega. "Why don't you come back after your trip? That will give me a few days to think before I say something I don't mean."

"I don't understand. What will a few days do?" he said. When she didn't answer, he said, "Does this have to do with that girl? Have you let that go, Maggie?"

She shook her head no. Had he even heard what she said?

"Maggie?"

"By the time you get home, it should be done."

"What are you doing now?" His voice was more intense.

Maggie gripped the phone. "Please, Brian. I don't want this to get between us."

"Then—"

"Please. Go on your trip and when you get home, we'll start fresh. We'll wipe the slate clean, and leave Mira," she said, then thinking of Donovan, guilt ached through her body like the flu, and added, "and everything," things she could never speak of, "in the past."

After a long silence, Brian said, "I love you, Mag. I don't want to lose you. If I did, it would be as if our life with Lilly had never happened, somehow."

Maggie closed her eyes, trying to push the image of Donovan's gentle kiss out of her mind. "I don't want to lose you, either." And even though she still dreamt of another man's comfort, she meant the words. She wanted her marriage and she wanted the comfort—from Brian.

After she'd ended the call, Maggie sat in bed holding the portable phone. How had she done such a thing? Truth and honesty would have to exclude tonight. She could never tell him of her slip with Donovan—he would never understand. And she wasn't sure she would understand, if the situation were reversed. This would be a burden she would have to bear herself. And, on top of it all, she'd probably ruined her friendship with Donovan, too, and felt yet another loss.

She looked at the phone book that still rested on her lap and took a deep breath. It was time to focus on what she needed to do. She punched 1-888-THE LAWS into the phone and heard a recorded message that the firm of Deloitte, McGuire, and Wolman would reopen at 9 a.m. tomorrow.

In the yellow pages, under attorneys, Maggie found a half page ad for the firm of Deloitte, McGuire, and Wolman that said they were located in downtown Ft. Lauderdale.

Maggie put the phone book on the floor and the portable phone on its cradle next to the bed. She turned off the light and burrowed her way under the covers, surrounding herself with pillows, then willed herself to fall asleep.

Chapter Twenty-Five

The small reception area of Deloitte, McDougal, and Wolman was decorated in soothing shades of yellow and peach, with comfortable chairs that had cushioned backs and seats, for those having to wait. Behind a glass partition sat a well-dressed woman speaking into a phone, who had motioned Maggie to wait one moment while she finished her call.

Maggie had called four times this morning, only to get put through to Abigail Lustig's voice mail each time. When she'd asked the operator how she could reach Ms. Lustig, when she would be in, the operator had simply said that the best way was to leave a voice message, that she, the operator, "was not privy to everyone's comings and goings."

Growing impatient, Maggie'd gone back online to find a news article with a picture of Lustig, then hopped in her car to appear in person. She hoped that Ms. Lustig was in, or if she wasn't, that she could at least catch her "coming or going."

Maggie poked her finger through a glass bowl of wrapped candy while she waited, then picked one, raspberry with a filled center, unpeeled it, and popped it into her mouth. She ran her tongue over the bumps of the round candy, remembering that her grandmother had always had a small crystal bowl filled with raspberry candy in each room of her house.

"Thank you for waiting," the receptionist said. "How can I help you?"

Maggie pushed the candy to the side of her mouth and said, "I'm here to see Abigail Lustig."

The woman looked confused, then looked down at an appointment book spread out in front of her. She flipped through a few pages then looked back up. "Do you have an appointment with Ms. Lustig?"

Maggie shook her head.

"Ms. Lustig isn't in right now, and…" she paused, "she's one of our paralegals. We make our appointments directly with the attorneys." She poised her pen over the book. "Is there someone in the firm you prefer?"

"No, I need to see Abigail Lustig."

"Is she expecting you?"

Maggie had her story ready. She felt the candy get stuck on her tooth, pushed it around her mouth, then looked to the candy bowl.

"No," Maggie said, filling her voice with excitement. "It's a surprise. I'm her cousin here on vacation, and my grandmother gave me Abbey's number." Maggie looked at the woman's face, trying to see if she was getting anywhere. "My mother and Abbey's mother were twins, and I haven't seen her in so long." Maggie looked at her watch. "I didn't budget my time well, and this is my last day. Is there anyway I can see her, just for a minute?"

"There's really no way that I can—"

"Granny will be so mad at me," Maggie said. "To get this close—"

"She's not here right now," the receptionist cut in.

Maggie's verbal ploy stopped suddenly. "Oh."

The receptionist stared at Maggie for some time, then said, "I can take your number."

Maggie nodded, wondering what to do next, no longer acting, her disappointment genuine. How would she ever help Mira Vega? Maggie stared at the receptionist, feeling completely lost. "I need to see her today. I'll wait as long as I have to," Maggie said, turning to point to the plush chairs.

"Well," the receptionist said, "she very well may be at The Riverwalk Marina. She likes to work through lunch and sometimes stays the whole afternoon. She's not due back in the office until tomorrow."

"Thank you," Maggie said. "Where's that?"

"Right down the street." The receptionist gave her detailed directions, drawing a small map on the back of one of the attorney's business cards.

Maggie thanked her, then pushing her luck, said, "May I have her home number in case she's not there?"

The receptionist looked at her suspiciously. "Your grandmother didn't give you that number?"

Maggie realized her error. "Oh, she did, but Granny's eyesight's not what it used to be. She must have transposed one of the numbers," Maggie said.

"I'm sorry," the receptionist said. "That, I can't do."

Maggie nodded, thanked her, took one more raspberry candy, and left the office.

Chapter Twenty-Six

Maggie couldn't see a thing as she walked into the bar at The Riverwalk Marina restaurant. She blinked trying to let her eyes adjust from the bright sunlight to the darkness of the bar.

"Can I help you?" A suntanned girl with long hair and the unofficial but ubiquitous black outfit of all hostesses stood in front of Maggie. The girl's smile looked genuine, in contrast to her blonde hair.

"Restroom?" Maggie said.

"Down the bar and to the left."

Maggie thanked her and walked the length of the bar, her eyes adjusting to the darkness as she went. She looked at each face as she went, hoping she would be able to recognize Abigail Lustig. She still hadn't seen her when she got to the alcove where the bathrooms were. She sighed, pushed the door open, and stood in front of the mirror. She doubted anyone in the bar had noticed her, but she decided to wait a few minutes before she walked back out. Taking out a brush, she pulled it through her hair without much interest in the outcome. When the door opened, she jumped, startled. She willed herself to calm down as the hostess smiled at her. Maggie smiled back, washed her hands, and left the room.

Maggie didn't see any new faces as she headed into the room and walked toward an empty high-top table. Then she spotted her. Abigail, who had been leaning over a notebook, lifted her head and stretched. Her blonde hair fell in long waves around her shoulders and wire-rimmed glasses framed her eyes. Books, both opened and closed, covered the table and a backpack filled the only other chair at the table. She was sending a loud and clear signal: leave me alone. Maggie moved to a table where she could watch the woman while still pretending to watch the television.

Maggie ordered a Black and Tan and chicken wings and tried to think of how to approach Abigail. She had imagined the scene the way she had seen them in movies: she would walk in, there would an empty seat next to the woman at the bar, and they would strike up a conversation. Two women, drinking beer, falling into conversation. But there were no empty seats next to Abigail and that was clearly not by accident.

Maggie drummed her fingers on the table as the waitress put down the beer. As Maggie sipped the bitter ale, she stared at Abigail. If she had not been looking so closely, she might not have recognized her. This girl looked nothing like the confident woman in the newspaper clippings. Gone were the tight French-twist hairdo and conservative black suits. The girl across the room from her, nursing a St. Pauli Girl straight from the bottle, looked to be about fourteen. How had Lydia had had confidence in her? But then, Lydia had said Abigail Lustig was the only one willing to take her case.

Maggie took a long drink of the beer, inhaled deeply, and got up and went to Abigail's table. When the woman looked up, Maggie smiled. "You're Abigail Lustig, aren't you?"

The woman's face broke into a smile. "Yes. Do I know you?"

"I was wondering if I could talk to you."

"About…" The woman left the word hanging.

"A legal matter," Maggie said.

"I'm not a lawyer." The woman's smile disappeared as she raised the St. Pauli Girl to her mouth and took a long swallow. "Anymore."

"I know. It's about a mutual adversary," Maggie said, hoping that the common bond would get Abigail talking, even if Maggie wasn't yet sure which of the Vegas was her real adversary.

The woman set the bottle back on the table, staring uncertainly through the wire-rimmed glasses.

"Nestor Vega," Maggie continued.

Abigail's face was noncommittal. "Too bad about his daughter." She straightened up in the chair. "I have nothing to say about that man." She picked up her pen and looked at her notebook.

"Look, I know you don't practice law anymore, but I have a problem, and I know you went up against him. I know you were disbarred and you blame him. I just think you might be one of the few people I could talk to who wouldn't candy coat anything about him."

Abigail squinted at Maggie. "You seem to know a lot about me."

Maggie shook her head. "I did a lot of research. About Nestor Vega," she added quickly. "And your name came up." Maggie's voice broke. "I'm desperate. I really need to talk to you."

Abigail seemed to be making a decision. She slipped her backpack off the chair and onto the floor and nodded toward the empty seat. "Sit."

"Thanks," Maggie said as Abigail continued to pile books together. "Let me go grab my beer."

Maggie returned in an instant. "Want some wings?" she said as she placed the white plate full of chicken wings on the crowded table.

Abigail put her hair behind her ear, picked up a drumstick, and took a small bite. "Hot. Thanks." She dipped the wing in blue cheese dressing, took another bite, swallowed, then said, "So what do you need to talk about?"

"Divorce."

"You have my sympathies. And the advantage." Abigail wiped her hand on a napkin and extended her hand. "You are?" Her head was tilted ever so slightly, her thick hair falling out from behind her ear.

"Maggie Miller." Maggie felt a firm grip when she took the small hand.

"So, what can I do for you, Maggie Miller?" Abigail's eyes seemed to twinkle behind the round glasses.

Maggie imagined this woman sitting behind a big desk, asking the same question of a client. She wondered what the truth was about her disbarment.

"I need help going up against Nestor Vega."

Abigail shook her head. "He's not a divorce attorney."

Maggie noticed the way Abigail used the tone of her voice, the inflection, to add flavor to her words. The way a chef would use spices. It wasn't the "what" of her words, but rather the "how." There was nothing inviting in her voice now.

"I know." Maggie began the story she had concocted with Donovan. "My husband is an Ear, Nose and Throat surgeon. He got caught using the pure cocaine he uses for his medical practice for personal use, snorting it before hours, during. He found his way to Vega. The two of them hit it off. Our marriage was already on the rocks, but we hadn't separated at that time."

"How'd Vega get him off?" Abigail said. "He did get him off, right?"

Maggie nodded. "He was ordering much more than even a heavy patient load would call for. Vega shifted the blame to a young girl that my husband had just hired. He said she was the one that was using the cocaine." Maggie watched a dark look pass over Abigail's face.

"But your husband was the guilty one?" Abigail said.

"Part of our marital problem was his 'partying' as he called it." Maggie reached for her beer, then put it back down. She was already feeling the buzz. She grabbed a piece of celery and put a chunk of blue cheese dressing on the end.

"Sounds like Vega. Anyone is expendable to him, as long as he gets what he wants." She tilted her beer bottle up and drained it. She motioned for the waitress. "Want another?"

"Sure." Except Maggie knew she needed to pay attention. "I haven't eaten much today. Mind if I order a burger?"

Abigail wrinkled her nose up. "The burgers are terrible here. Try the chicken fingers." Without waiting for her answer, Abigail called to the waitress, "Two more beers and a large order of chicken fingers, with *all* the sauces on the side." Abigail turned back to Maggie. "Is that okay?"

"Sounds great." Maggie watched as Abigail began to clear off the table. "Looks like law books," Maggie said.

"They are. I work as much here as I do at the office."

"Do you miss practicing law?"

Abigail set her lips in a firm but not unpleasant way and pushed her glasses against the bridge of her nose. "I think *you* were the one who wanted to talk."

"I'm sorry."

"Please, go ahead."

"I'm getting a divorce, and while Nestor Vega isn't my husband's attorney, he seems to be giving him lots of pointers."

"And why did you want to talk to me?"

"You went up against him."

During the last ten minutes of conversation, Abigail's face had remained neutral. Maggie assumed it was Abigail's lawyer face.

"I did," Abigail said. She reached for the fresh beer the waitress put down and took a long swallow.

"I was hoping you could tell me what to expect from a man like that."

Abigail paused before she answered, a behavior Maggie had also noticed with Nestor Vega. She concluded they must teach the technique in Litigation 101: Think before you speak. "Let's say that that case did not turn out well for anyone involved," Abigail said, the words laced with finality.

Maggie wished she could just ask the questions she needed to, to find out what the real truth was, but she couldn't risk tipping her hand. If either Vega was telling the truth, a little girl's well being, maybe even her life, depended on Maggie's discretion. She leaned across the table. "It's my daughter." Her voice caught convincingly as she uttered the words. "It's not just the divorce anymore. Vega has convinced my husband to sue for custody."

Abigail nodded her head slowly as if she expected nothing less. "It's men like Nestor Vega who give attorneys a bad reputation."

"What can I do?"

"I don't know what to tell you. You must have a lawyer."

"I do, but I'm at my wits end." This time Maggie was telling the truth. She noticed she had clenched her hands together on the table. She moved them to her lap.

The chicken fingers arrived with six small plastic cups of different sauces. Abigail took a clean plate from the waitress and put two large chicken fingers on it. She placed it in front of Maggie. "Eat. You'll feel better, and I'm suddenly starving."

Maggie took a deep breath and tried to calm down. She would get nowhere if she fell apart. She didn't want food, she wanted answers, but she couldn't rush Abigail. Maggie watched as Abigail poured a little raspberry sauce on Maggie's plate. Then she added a bit of the garlic. "Try."

Maggie dipped the end of her chicken finger into the sauce and swirled the two around. When she crunched through the light breading, she was surprised at how good it tasted. "Nice." She would say or do anything to keep Abigail talking. She decided to try a little less direct approach. "Tell me about yourself," Maggie said.

"Not much to tell. I grew up in New Jersey. Went to William and Mary undergrad, U.M. law school. Then into practice with a few women doing divorce litigation in Miami after I graduated."

Maggie noticed how Abigail left out the part the newspapers had emphasized, how Abigail had graduated number one in her law class at the age of twenty-two and was heavily recruited at the time by top law firms.

"What about you?" Abigail said, but before Maggie could answer, Abigail added, "Want another beer?"

Maggie declined, and Abigail flagged the waitress down for one for herself.

"Back to you," Abigail said. She drained the last of the beer in her bottle.

"I'm a photographer."

"What do you photograph?"

"People. I do the usual obligatory photos to make a living, you know, memorable occasions, but what I really like is capturing a moment on a person's face—one that's full of emotion." She studied Abigail's face, knowing that under different circumstances she would love to photograph her. While guarded most of the time, Maggie could tell that this woman's face would play the full scale of emotions when given the chance.

"Are you good?"

Maggie felt her face flush. "I don't know."

"Sure you do. Either you are or you aren't. Like me: I was a great lawyer. That's simply a fact, not bragging."

Maggie thought about it for a minute. She thought of the recent shots, of some that really *were* good. "I think I could be. Lately I seem to be able to see things I didn't see before."

"What happened?"

"My daughter died." As soon as the words were out of her mouth, Maggie realized what she had said. "I had two."

"You've lost a child and now your husband wants to take the other one away? He and Vega deserve each other."

Maggie realized she could make this work to her advantage.

"Is there due cause?" Abigail said.

"What do you mean?"

"I don't know how to say this except bluntly. Is there a reason to take your child away? Did you have any culpability in your daughter's death?"

The words were as innocuous as the first breeze of a tornado. *Your daughter's death.* Her eyes filled with tears, and she swallowed hard. *Culpability in your daughter's death.* She had accused herself of that very thing from the moment she had seen Lilly's still body on the road. She could see it now, fresh and clear in her mind. *Did you?* Yet, no one had dared to ask her that before this. *Did you?* She felt as is she were swirling around the room. *Did you?*

"Maggie?"

Maggie heard Abigail's voice, then felt Abigail's hand on her arm.

"You're hyperventilating. Take a deep breath. Deep ones, Maggie."

Abigail's face began to come into focus in front of Maggie.

"I didn't mean to upset you," Abigail said. "I guess I was in attorney-mode."

"I'm okay," Maggie said. "Excuse me a minute." Maggie walked to the bathroom and let out a sob as she went into the stall for some toilet paper to blow her nose. The rolls were empty. "Goddamn it." Maggie grabbed a paper towel and blew her nose, the coarse paper chafing her nose. "Goddamn it all." She slammed her hand on the sink. She looked into the mirror. "She's not talking about Lilly," she said to her reflection. "She doesn't even know the real story." Maggie stared at herself as if she were waiting for an answer. "You have a job to do here." She straightened her shoulders. "Tell her a story that will make her talk."

Maggie began to pace around the small bathroom taking two steps to the door, then two steps back to the sink. If Abigail thought she lost a child and her pretend husband was taking the last child away, she would feel sorry for Maggie—*if she had no part in the child's death.* Maggie stopped pacing, splashed water on her face, and kept thinking. She thought of the details that both Vegas had told her and began to fabricate her tale. She wiped the mascara from under her eyes and headed back to the table.

"I'm sorry," Maggie said. "It's been such a hard time."

"We don't need to go there."

"We do. If you're going to help me at all, we do."

"Listen, you aren't my client, therefore, there is no attorney-client privilege," Abigail said. "Meaning, there is no confidentiality in what you tell me."

"I understand."

"Do you? I won't tell a soul what you tell me, but if somehow I get subpoenaed, I have to, by law, repeat anything you tell me."

Subpoenaed? Maggie's realization that this woman believed her story gave her the courage to push harder. "A child's entire life depends on what I find out here." That was the truth, but she would have to remember that this woman also studied faces for a living. Maggie had to be as sincere with her lies as she could. "This won't be easy, so if I seem a little odd—"

"Just talk." Abigail moved her plate aside, then took her glasses off and laid them on the table.

"Am I responsible?" Start with the truth, Maggie thought. "No one has ever asked me that question before, although I've asked myself every minute, of every day since she died if I could have done something differently. She fell while roller blading; she had no helmet on."

"I'm sorry."

"Everyone is." Maggie shrugged. "The very same 'everyones' say: 'there's nothing you could have done; she chose to go out without her helmet on.' But you never believe them. You see, you go back in time to the moment you said she could go and you ask yourself, if you had said, 'Lilly, wear your helmet,' would that have made a difference? Then you ask yourself, why you weren't in the same room when she went outside so you would have seen she didn't have it on. You ask yourself why you weren't outside when she was skating, like when she was five or watching through the window, like when she was seven. Why you didn't duct tape the damn helmet on her head. Why you didn't lock her in her room." Maggie shook her head. "Why, that one day, you didn't say, 'Not tonight, Lilly, you may not roller blade,' and then she would still be here. She wouldn't be dead at all." Maggie felt as if it could all have been so different.

Abigail nodded. "So your husband blames you?"

Maggie looked at Abigail, willing herself back to Mira. "I don't really know what he thinks," Maggie said. "I only know that he's trying to take my child away." She moved a chicken finger around her plate and decided it was time for a Vega tidbit. "The ironic thing is that he's the one with the temper. He didn't do it often, but there were times when he lost his cool and really let the kids have it."

Maggie paused to see if there was a reaction from Abigail, but there was none. "When I told my attorney that I thought my husband was getting advice from Nestor Vega, he told me that Vega had sole custody of his daughter. I wondered if you had any tips for me."

"Tips? I represented his wife, remember. *He* has the daughter."

"I know, but did he deserve to have her?"

"I can't talk about the case—that's attorney-client privilege." Abigail put her glasses back on.

"But you're not an attorney anymore. What are they going to do, disbar you again?" Maggie regretted the words even before the angry look crossed Abigail's face.

"I still have ethics. I don't need to act like a witch just because they burned me at the stake." Abigail stared at Maggie. "Unjustifiably."

"Who would know?" Maggie leaned across the table, desperate for answers.

"I would."

Maggie took a lesson from Litigation 101: think before you speak. She told herself to remember to incorporate a kernel of truth into the lies. "I'm scared." Truth. "I don't need you to tell me particulars about the case." Lie. "I just want to know what kind of man he is." Truth: A lie sandwich. She took a deep breath. "When it became apparent that someone, other than his own divorce attorney, was giving my husband advice, I went back and read some old newspaper accounts on the case. My attorney said if Vega was helping, I was in trouble. I guess I want to know to what lengths Vega went to get his daughter—to what lengths he will take my husband."

Abigail thought for a moment. "Why is Vega helping your husband?"

More lies. "When I found out about the cocaine, I found out about a lot of other stuff I never knew about. My husband sees a lot of young woman as patients who come in for facial plastic surgery. A lot of them don't have the money it takes to pay for that kind of surgery, and insurance doesn't cover elective plastic surgery." She looked at Abigail. "He, shall we say, barters his services, for theirs."

"Jeez. Your husband is a gem. What does that have to do with Vega?"

She shrugged. "I assume he introduces them to Vega, a big time lawyer." Maggie waited for a response to see if Abigail would comment on his womanizing.

"Vega wouldn't want that."

Lydia was lying, then. "He's not interested in other women?"

Abigail's deep laugh rocked the table. "Oh, he's interested. But for him, I hear, the chase is half the fun. The conquest. Being handed a woman would be no fun for him."

So Lydia wasn't lying. "How did a man like that get custody?"

"Being unfaithful doesn't make you an unfit father."

Maggie leaned forward. "Was his wife unfit? Did she hurt the little girl? Did she deserve to lose her daughter?" Maggie realized how adamant she was getting and sat back in her chair. "I need to know how bad it can get. How much can be made up about a person and the lies believed?"

"In order of presentation: bad," Abigail took a sip of her beer, "and a lot."

"If Lydia Vega deserved to lose her daughter, I won't be as afraid as I am now. Whatever advice Vega gives my husband, I'll know won't matter because I'll know I should win. But if he's underhanded, if he can make things real that aren't…"

"Be afraid, Maggie. If Vega is in your husband's corner, be very afraid."

Maggie ran her finger down her sweaty beer mug. "Did you believe Lydia's story?"

"You sound as if you know her."

"I guess I got so into the stories about their divorce, trying to find a parallel to mine. I feel as if I know them both, but not the real truth."

"You're talking to a lawyer about real truth?" She shook her head. "Yes. I believed my client in this case."

"You don't believe she had Munchausen by Proxy syndrome?"

Abigail took a small bite off the tip of a chicken finger and studied Maggie before answering. "I can't tell you anything that she told me in private, but there is much that was brought up in court…made public. People don't have that syndrome and direct it at just one person. Meaning, I had experts testify that it is a disease of lack of control. You can't have lack of control in such a controlled manner. They do it for the attention, not the attention of one particular person." She picked up her beer.

"He had an expert testify she was unstable," Maggie said.

Abigail nodded, but said nothing.

"Did Vega hit the child?" Maggie said.

Abigail's eyes narrowed at Maggie. "That part never got to court."

"My husband used to talk about Vega when he first got to know him. Before we split. He said he had a real temper."

"I wish I could have found someone like your husband to testify in court. The one person who agreed was suddenly on a plane back to Santiago, Chile."

"Who?"

"A Vega with honor. His brother."

Maggie seemed to remember that Vega had made a point of telling her he had been an only child. "Would it have mattered?" she said.

"After all was said and done, probably not."

"Why?"

"One way or another, he would have gotten what he wanted. What he did to me alone proves that he would stop at nothing to halt an adversary."

"What he did to you?"

Abigail took off her glasses and rubbed her eyes. "This is not privileged information; this is my life." Abigail thought for a moment. "To cover his bases, Vega didn't just attack his wife, ship off his brother—he neutralized me, too." She looked at Maggie. "You mentioned my disbarment."

"I read about it in the papers."

Abigail nodded. "Early in the Vega divorce case, he called and politely asked me to talk Lydia into concessions that would be favorable to him—to throw the case his way, you know." She looked closely at Maggie. "Or maybe you don't. Deals are struck every day. Lady Justice is blind to a lot more than she should be. Vega said he would make it worth my while in the future, promised me a lucrative career, important cases going my way. He was close to a lot of people. I could call in the chit many times over. Of course, I refused."

"Good for you."

"Yeah." She motioned to her backpack. "Now I'm a paralegal; good for me."

"What happened?"

"Later, during the case, when we were making headway, my partners came to me and said it would be better for the client if they finished the case. I disagreed. A few weeks later, they took it from me—started the disbarment proceedings. Obviously, they liked Vega's deal." She took a long pull on her beer. "I would never have expected that of them." She studied the label on the beer bottle.

"It said in the paper you embezzled money from a client."

"I have a large trust fund from my parents, to begin with, and even if I didn't have money, I would never do that." She looked at her law books. "I believed in the law back then."

"What happened?"

Abigail was quiet for a moment, and Maggie realized the crowd at the bar had thinned out considerably.

"Vega happened. Money disappeared from one of the firm's trust accounts—one of *my* client's trust accounts. A large amount of money."

"They accused you?"

"The money showed up in one of my personal accounts. The exact amount, to the odd little penny, on the same day."

Maggie didn't know what to say.

"I am, *was*, a very good lawyer, but not a very good bookkeeper. My bank statements sit on the desk for months." She shook her head. "I never realized the money was there until it was too late."

"You couldn't prove you didn't take it?"

"I had the money. What more did they need? How could I prove I didn't do it?"

"What happened?" Could Nestor, the sincere man she saw in Mira's bedroom, have been involved in such a thing? Or could Abigail really have been guilty?

"The rest, as they say, is history." Abigail stared at her pile of law books, but seemed to be distracted. She looked up. "Lydia was one of the few people who did believe me."

"She had faith in you."

"Little good it did her." Abigail looked around the bar. "She had a lot of fight in her. I never would have believed she would leave her daughter for any amount of money." She shook her head sadly. "I've learned everyone has their price."

"Was she a fit mother?"

"Yes, but we never got to prove it—she settled, soon after I was removed. I still think we had a chance to win. They would never have been able to repudiate the psych eval we had done of Mira. Even with everyone in their pocket they couldn't get that child to lie on video." Abigail smiled slightly and shook her head. "She was a trip, that little girl. Very precocious."

"What was the psych eval?"

"We requested a psychological evaluation as part of our custody case. Mira managed to let them know that she was hit, even when being led otherwise. That's when Nestor turned up the heat. Suddenly he had testimony that Lydia was unstable—should be put away. I became an embezzler."

"Mira told the truth?"

Abigail stopped with her beer midway to her mouth and stared at Maggie. "Why are you so interested in this case?"

"I told you, I'm in a similar situation."

"Bullshit." Abigail leaned in closer.

Maggie felt the chicken tenders going the wrong way in her stomach. She leaned back in her chair. She'd promised Lydia that she would tell no one, but there was no way that she could make a decision without the facts.

"You don't have anything to do with the kidnapping, do you?" Abigail continued.

"No!" Maggie couldn't let anything slip. What if Abigail went to the police? "I'm just curious as to who you think the child should have been with."

"Why? What does it matter now? Who she *should* be with never did seem to matter. It was who could fight longer and dirtier. Lydia gave in. I was so naive. I shouldn't have been surprised that everyone has their price, even my partners." She took a long swig of beer. "But surprised me, it did."

"But Mira—"

"Don't you get it?" She banged her bottle on the table. "All anyone ever had to do was ask the child. She'd tell you. You didn't need to believe Lydia or Nestor." She pulled her hair back with both hands as if making a ponytail, then let it drop. "But it never got to that."

Maggie stared, letting what Abigail said sink in. That was the only way to know the truth. Maggie would have to insist that she meet Mira and listen to her. Not to Lydia, not to Nestor, not even Abigail. The only way Maggie could live with this decision was to meet Mira and find out for herself.

With the tip of a fork, Abigail swirled the white ranch sauce into the deep red raspberry making it a pretty color of pink. She stopped suddenly, and her eyes lifted toward Maggie. "Mira's kidnapping." Her head started to move from side to side slowly. "My God. It isn't for ransom or an enemy trying to get back at Vega." She dropped her fork on the plate. "Lydia got her back. That's what this is all about."

Maggie tensed. "What are you talking about?"

"Now it all makes sense." Abigail pushed her plate away from her and folded her arms on the table. "I was so bitter, so ready to believe the worst in everyone when it happened, that I believed she sold out, too." A big grin spread across her face. "She hired someone to snatch her daughter—make it look like a kidnapping."

"She wouldn't do that," Maggie snapped, too quickly.

"Why not?"

"It's illegal."

Abigail burst out with one of her deep laughs and leaned back in her chair. "And all that shit Vega did was by the book, right? Give me a break."

"Will you go to the police with your suspicions?"

Abigail became serious. "How do you fit in?"

"I don't fit in."

"Is that what this is all about?"

Both women stared at each other. Finally Maggie said, "I asked if you'll go to the police."

Abigail looked intently at Maggie, as if making a decision. "No." Then she waved her arm in the air in an exaggerated motion. "I've had too much beer. I really don't even know what the hell we're talking about."

Maggie stared at her. "That's probably a good thing for everyone involved."

"I only pray that's where that little girl is. And," her eyes seemed to pierce through Maggie, "I hope you're on the right side of this."

So did Maggie. She stood up and extended her hand. "Thank you, Ms. Lustig, you've been a big help."

Abigail held on to her hand. "Maybe someday you'll tell me about it."

Maggie nodded as Abigail let go of her hand. "Maybe I will." She walked out looking at her watch, wondering when she'd hear from Lydia again.

Chapter Twenty-Seven

Maggie waited in a pavilion at Long Branch Park in Boca Raton the next day, the place she and Lydia had agreed to meet when they spoke on the phone the night before. Once again, she was early, but she was so anxious to meet Mira that she had left her house early, unable to sit there and wait. Instead, she sat in the park and waited.

Maggie watched as Lydia finally appeared wearing a wide brimmed beach hat, holding the hand of a small girl with curly red hair. The girl, who wore a pair of denim overalls with a large paisley cotton purse slung across her chest, constantly turned and lifted her face up to talk to Lydia. The child did two small skips to each step of the woman's.

As they got closer, the little girl focused her eyes on Maggie.

"Ms. Miller, this is Mira," Lydia said.

Mira's eyes grew wide, and she turned to her mother.

"It's okay," Lydia said. She played with one of the child's curls. "I told Ms. Miller your real name."

"My name that goes with the red hair is Shirley," Mira said to Maggie.

"Mine is Maggie," Maggie said. She held out her hand. "So what shall I call you?"

"Shirley." She shook Maggie's hand, then ran her fingers through her curls. "My mommy and I are playing a game to see how many people we can be. I'm winning 'cause Mommy has very short hair, and I can keep cutting mine."

Maggie watched the animation in the face, the eyes, and there was no doubt this was all the same girl: the one from the paper, the news, the plaza, the Vega house.

"I'm going to be an actor like my Mommy so we're practicing. Want to play Go Fish?" She dug into the cloth purse that dangled on her chest. She held out a worn set of colored fish-shaped cards held together by an elastic band.

"Sure. I used to play with my daughter," Maggie said.

Mira walked toward the picnic bench. "My Mom said not to mention your daughter because she died, and that it would make you sad." She sat down. She peered at Maggie. "You look okay."

"Some days I am," Maggie said as she smiled at the little girl.

Mira spread the cards out on the table and swooshed them around, the child's version of shuffling. Then she divided the cards into four unequal piles, putting one in the middle. She caught Maggie's look. "It's faster than dealing."

Maggie laughed. She was drawn to the precocious child but at the same time she couldn't stop comparing everything about her to Lilly. She didn't know how long she could bear this. She sat down at the table.

Lydia remained standing. "You don't have to play."

Maggie picked up her cards. She smiled at Lydia. "I'm fine."

Lydia nodded and sat down. She picked up her cards and turned to Mira. "I told you Maggie would be asking you questions, just like the psychologist did for court. Be just as honest with Maggie as you were with the doctor, okay?"

"Sure," Mira said. She turned to Maggie. "Do you have any reds?"

Maggie pulled one from her pile.

"Any blue?" Mira squirmed in her seat.

"Go fish."

As the game went around the table Maggie watched Mira and her mother. She recognized that special banter and the looks between them that had built up over the years. She remembered how Lilly and she would say just a word or two and laugh over something that had happened in the past.

"You have fun playing with your Mom," Maggie said to Mira.

"I do now." Mira nodded. "We had a soap-opera miracle."

"You did?" Maggie said.

"That's what Mommy calls it. Everyone thought she died, but she didn't, and so she came back to tell me. I saw it happen on the soap opera Yayee watches when she baby-sits me." Mira leaned in and whispered to Maggie. "I'm not supposed to watch, but I do."

"Really?"

"Yep." She put her cards down. "I don't really understand how it happens, I'm just glad she's back." Mira put her cards back in her hands. "Any yellows?"

"Go fish," Maggie said.

"Maybe your daughter will come back in a soap-opera miracle." Mira's eyes were wide, her small face raised toward Maggie.

Maggie began to blink back tears. Her hand reached for the angel pin on her collar.

Mira looked to her mother. "I thought it would make her feel better," she whispered. "To know it could happen." She leaned into her mother, anticipating the hug that would come.

"I know," Lydia said. She kissed the mop of red curls.

"I'm sorry to make you sad," Mira said to Maggie. "Did she make that pin for you?"

Maggie nodded her head, her fingers rubbing the pin. "She…" Maggie wanted to tell her that was a Mother's Day gift from Lilly. She wanted to say that she would cherish it forever because it was the last gift Lilly would ever make her. That she was sorry she'd abandoned it in the drawer while Lilly was alive. Her fingers closed tightly around the pin as her throat closed around the words. "Yes."

Lydia looked at her watch, then to Maggie. "We can't stay long. Maybe we should get to your questions for Mira." She looked to her frowning daughter. "Er, Shirley."

Mira rolled her eyes as she looked at the cards. "We didn't finish the game." She looked to Maggie. "You get to be the fault winner."

"*De*fault," Lydia said.

"De-fault winner," Mira said as she leaned toward Maggie. "That means you get to win because we stopped the game."

Maggie looked at Mira. "We can play while we talk." She needed a few minutes to regroup. "No fun winning by default. Any greens?"

The game continued as Maggie wondered how to phrase the question of Nestor hitting Mira. Should she be direct, or mention it in conversation? She was no psychologist, not trained to ask these things. "Can I ask you something serious?" she said to Mira.

"Sure," Mira said as she laid down cards.

"Did your dad ever hurt you? I mean—hit you or anything like that?"

Mira's face scrunched up. She picked up her cards and brought her hands close to her chest. She stared down for a long time. "They were accidents. He didn't mean to." She looked up, her eyes sad. "Do you have any blues?" she asked of Maggie.

Maggie shook her head. "Go Fish." She watched Mira reach for the pile and draw a card. "I'm sure he didn't mean to," Maggie said.

Lydia gave Maggie a look over Mira's head, as if asking her to stop, but Maggie needed to be sure.

Mira was much quieter than she had been since she arrived. She ran her finger around the round curve of the fish card. Without looking up, she said, "Dr. Diane said that if someone does something wrong, even if they say they're sorry, it's still wrong." Mira looked up at Maggie. "And it's wrong to hurt people like that."

Lydia reached out and rubbed Mira's shoulder. "Dr. Diane is right."

Mira nodded. "Hitting never solves anything," Mira said as if repeating a truism she'd be taught to recite, her look now a little distant.

"Does he still do wrong things when he's angry?" Maggie said softly.

Mira nodded her head. "Sometimes." She rubbed her shoulder. "I try not to get him angry." She looked to her mother. "I try to be good."

Lydia pulled her daughter to her. "You are good, baby." Her voice caught in her throat. "It's Poppy's problem."

Maggie stared at the confusion, the hurt in Mira's face and felt sorrow for the little girl in front of her who tried to be "good enough." She hadn't yet learned that trying to prevent that kind of rage was like trying to hold back a tidal wave.

"Anything else?" Lydia said.

Maggie had decided she needed to ask all the questions just to be sure. Making Lydia's story about Nestor right, didn't negate the accusations Nestor had made. This time she decided to be indirect. She rubbed her stomach. "Ow. My stomach hurts. Must be from my breakfast." She looked to Mira. "Do you ever get stomach aches?"

Mira nodded. "I get a lot. I have colditis. Do you have that, too?" She sat up in her seat.

Maggie shook her head.

"Colitis." Lydia corrected.

"Whatever," Mira said. "I like to call it cold-itis because it's like a cold in your stomach. Instead of a sore head and runny nose, you get a sore stomach and runny…" She looked at Maggie. "You *know*. The other end runs." She started to laugh at her own joke, her mind adjusting to another topic, the resilience or apparent resilience of a young mind. "Mine's a lot better now. I hope you don't catch it."

"I hope not, too. Did the doctor tell you that you had it?"

Lydia's eyes narrowed at the question.

"I had tons of tests," Mira said. She rolled her eyes. "I had to drink this stuff that tasted like melted chalk, and then they put me to sleep and stuck a camera inside my butt." She giggled as she said the last word.

"But he told you that's what you had?" Maggie said. "Colitis? That's what was wrong with your stomach?"

"Yes. The doctor gave us a book on it and Mommy read it to me. I have to eat a lot of very small meals. Often," she said as she looked to her mother. "In case you forgot."

Lydia shook her head. "I haven't forgotten. Are you hungry already?"

"A little. Maybe a Happy Meal with catsup and fries."

Lydia had been telling the truth, and Nestor had been lying.

Suddenly Mira turned to Maggie. "Would you like to come to our house to meet Pepper?" Mira sat up tall, anticipation on her face.

"Pepper?"

"He's my imaginary black cat. I also have a white Persian named Salt. They lived with me when I was with Poppy—because I couldn't have real pets. But when we get to our farm, Mommy said I can have as many real cats as I want. I'll get a real Salt and Pepper. Next, I'll get a tabby named

Relish. I'm going to call them my condiment kitties. Isn't that funny?" Her nose crinkled up. "I'll use hair dye like Mommy uses and make one yellow and call it Mustard." She began to giggle uncontrollably, and Maggie was reminded how young she was.

"You have a very vivid imagination," Maggie said. She reached out to touch Mira's face, but stopped short, not sure she would be able to handle a cheek that was soft and warm when she was so used to cold, flat resin paper.

"My Mommy reads to me a lot," Mira said.

"Maybe you'll be a veterinarian, a pet doctor, when you grow up, instead of an actor," Maggie said.

"Maybe. Poppy wants me to be a lawyer like him, but now that he's having a new baby, Nicole says that her baby can be the lawyer for him."

"Your dad's having a new baby?" Maggie said.

"Yeah. It's still a secret. I found out from Hattie, my nanny. I'm very good at finding things out, you know." She moved curls around her head. "I might be a spy when I grow up. Maybe…" She looked mischievously at her mother. "Maybe a pet-doctor-spy. You know lots of people tell their pets secrets, and I can invent a way to get the secrets out of the dogs and cats. I can be rich like Poppy!" She giggled, then sobered. "Poppy says it's important to be rich because then people won't walk on you." She arched her back. "I think it would hurt to have someone walk on you."

Maggie stared at the little girl. She no longer wanted to rush this visit. She wanted to soak up the little girl's vibrance. She wished Mira lived down the street and could come over and make her laugh. They would bake cookies the way she had with Lilly, eating one cookie from each batch as they came out warm from the oven. The edges would crunch and the soft centers would melt in their mouths.

"Do you bake cookies?" Maggie asked Mira.

"Not since my Mommy left. Hattie buys hers," Mira said. She put her finger in front of her lips, giving Maggie the universal "secret" gesture. "Some times she warms them in the microwave to fool Poppy."

Lilly, who had always wished for a sister, would have loved Mira. Maggie looked to Lydia who beamed with that special pride that one takes in having produced such an offspring. She couldn't imagine how empty

Lydia's days must have been without this chatterbox of enthusiasm. But then, she could.

Mira squirmed on the seat, and Maggie recognized the childish impatience setting in.

Lydia turned to Mira. "Why don't you go play so I can talk to Maggie?"

"But I never get to talk to anybody anymore, and I like her," Mira said.

"Mira?" Lydia said firmly.

"Adult stuff?" Mira said as she scanned the park. "I'll go play on the swings."

Lydia seemed to be taking note of the playground's proximity to where she was. "All right, but don't leave the play area."

"I won't."

Lydia looked at Maggie intently. "We have to go. Are you convinced Mira is where she should be?"

"She's incredible," Maggie said as she watched the girl pump her legs on the swing.

"I mean, we have to leave the county. The paperwork is ready. I wanted to be sure I have your word that there won't be any surprises as we travel," Lydia said.

Maggie took a deep breath, but the question was no longer a question. As she nodded her head, she heard Mira cry out.

"Mommy!"

Both women turned. Maggie quickly looked down, wondering how long it would take before she stopped responding to that name.

"Watch this, Maggie," Mira yelled. She started up the ladder of the slide, then turned around toward the women. "I'm going to go down with no hands." Mira let go of the ladder and put both hands in the air, a preview of her feat.

Maggie watched as the gesture of throwing her arms into the air sent the little girl off balance. Gravity pulled Mira's body toward the earth. Almost as if in slow motion, Maggie saw the girl's eyes widen with fear as she yelled out for her mother. Mira grabbed for the ladder, but she was too far away. With a dull thud, Mira fell into the sand and lay still.

Maggie ran toward Mira who was whimpering and reaching for her arm that had been caught underneath her body.

"My arm, Mommy," Mira said. She broke into sobs as her mother reached down to pick her up.

"Don't touch her," Maggie said.

"It's only her arm," Lydia said. "She broke the fall with it." She lifted Mira and pulled her close to her. Mira held her left arm with her right hand. Lydia gently lifted Mira's arm to look at it.

"Ouch," Mira yelled. She pulled her arm away from her mother. She breathed heavily from the crying.

"Mommy has to check it, baby." Lydia waited a minute, then ran her fingers over Mira's forearm. "There're no cuts," she said to Maggie. "I'm sure it will be fine."

Maggie watched Mira wince as Lydia touched the limp arm. "It could still be broken."

"It can't be broken," Lydia said. "It just can't." She tried to move the arm again, and Mira let out a more persistent yell. Lydia shifted the child on her hip and pulled her close. "A sprained wrist, is all."

"Can I look, Mira?" Maggie said.

Mira shook her head and pulled her arm away, wincing in pain.

"Please? We have to make it stop hurting, and the only way is to know exactly where it hurts so it can get fixed," Maggie said.

"Don't touch it," Mira said. She extended her arm. "Just look."

Maggie noticed how it hung limp, the way Lilly's had, but the difference was that Lilly's arm had been twisted back and Mira's hand seemed to hang from her forearm as if it didn't belong. "I'm going to touch it here, really softly, okay?" Maggie pointed to a spot right below the elbow.

"Please, Mira," Lydia said.

Mira nodded and closed her eyes.

"Tell me where it hurts." With one finger Maggie touched the arm, starting from the elbow, moving down toward the wrist. About half way down, Mira's eyes flew open and she yelled. Maggie stopped immediately. Then she held the little girl's wrist still and moved her hand. Mira watched without saying a word.

"It's not her wrist," Maggie said to Lydia. "I think it's broken here." She pointed to Mira's forearm.

Lydia began to pace, holding the child on her hip. "What am I going to do?"

"We have to take her to an emergency room," Maggie said.

Lydia turned to Maggie. "I can't take her to the hospital. You know that."

"It hurts so bad, Mommy." Tears rolled down Mira's face. Her legs were wrapped around her mother's waist.

"We can't just let her hurt like that," Maggie said.

"It could be just a sprain." Lydia said the words as if wishing them true. "We'll go home and put ice on it."

"You can't take that chance. I know a good orthopedist. Maybe—"

"Maybe, what? What am I supposed to do? Walk in and say, 'this is my daughter, the missing child?'" Lydia yelled with anger. "With the fake ID I just got? I have no insurance card, no checks, no credit cards. Don't you think that will be a little suspicious?"

"I could say you're a friend from out of town."

"I'm sorry, Mommy," Mira said. She wiped her nose with her good hand. "Will I have to go back to Poppy now?"

"No. I won't let that happen." Lydia kissed the top of her head. "How's the arm? Any better?"

"No," Mira said.

Lydia looked as if she were ready to cry. "How could this happen? I got away with all the hard stuff. First your pictures, now this." She gave Maggie a look as if this was all her fault.

"I'll take her to the hospital," Maggie said.

"If I wanted her to go, I would take her myself."

"I'll say she's my daughter."

"What are you talking about?" Lydia said.

"It hurts when you move, Mommy," Mira said.

Lydia gently put Mira down to a standing position.

"Come back to the table for a minute," Maggie said. The three walked back to the sitting area. Mira sat on Lydia's lap with her arm resting on the table.

Maggie pointed to Mira's arm. "It's already starting to swell and bruise. She has to be taken care of." She took a deep breath. "I'll take her to the emergency room and say she's Lilly."

"But your daughter is..." Lydia's face turned red as she let the sentence trickle into nothing.

"No one ever asks you for I.D. for your child when you take them to the hospital—who even has any? I have insurance; I'll register her as my daughter."

"But they'll figure it out."

"How?"

"You don't have a daughter anymore." Lydia pronounced each word as if Maggie would understand it better.

Maggie winced. "But they won't know that! I've never taken Lilly to a hospital in Palm Beach."

"I don't know." Lydia reached for her purse, then seemed to think better of it.

"Think about it, Lydia. Have you ever taken Mira to the emergency room?"

Lydia nodded.

"They didn't ask you to prove it was your daughter, did they?"

"No," Lydia said. "I guess they didn't."

Maggie turned to Mira. "You've been lots of people lately. Think you could be my Lilly for a day?"

"They'll figure it out. Eventually—" Lydia said.

"Eventually, yes," Maggie said. "I'll say it was a mistake. How could I have taken a daughter who doesn't exist to the ER? Or, I'll just pay the bill; that will keep the hospital quiet." She shrugged her shoulders. "I'll have to deal with it then, but you won't. You'll both be gone."

Lydia stopped and stared at Maggie, hearing the words she said. Then she looked around the park, then at Maggie. "This isn't a set up, is it? A way to get us caught? You won't turn us in while we're there, will you?"

"How could I plan this?" She pointed to Mira's arm. She looked at the serious look on Lydia's face. "You don't trust anyone do you?"

Lydia shook her head. "Not anymore."

"I'm sorry. No. I won't turn you in. I want to help."

Lydia took a deep breath. She looked at Mira's arm. "Okay, let's get it done."

Maggie dialed 411 on her cell phone and received the name of the nearest hospital along with directions.

"You could drive with me," Maggie said.

Lydia shook her head. "I'll take my car. This way none of us have to come back here."

Chapter Twenty-Eight

In the Emergency Room parking lot at Boca Raton Medical Center, Maggie locked her car and walked to where Lydia was parked. She got into the front seat and turned to talk to Mira who sat in the back. Maggie saw that Lydia had fashioned a splint of sorts; Mira's arm was suspended in a gold and turquoise silk scarf.

"How's your arm?" Maggie asked Mira.

"Okay if I don't move it." Mira shrugged her shoulders. "It's worse than cold-itis and my broken pinky put together, and that's pretty bad."

Maggie smiled at the little girl. "You're very brave."

Mira nodded. "So I've been told."

Both Maggie and Lydia laughed.

"Are you ready?" Maggie asked them both.

"I've been rehearsing with 'Lilly,'" Lydia said. She nodded to her daughter.

"My name is Lilly Miller. We were visiting with my Aunt Sue," she pointed to her mother with her good arm, "when I fell off the slide at the park."

"Good." Maggie turned forward. "Let's go." Her heart was starting to race.

"Mommy?" Mira said.

This time Maggie willed herself not to look.

"Mommy?" Mira repeated, only this time with an insistent tone.

Maggie turned toward Lydia to see why she wasn't answering.

Lydia motioned to the backseat. "That's you."

Maggie turned around.

"You need practice, Mommy," Mira said in an exaggerated voice.

"I guess I do…" She tried to call the little girl Lilly, but her eyes welled up with tears.

"Would you rather I use a different name?" Mira said.

Maggie took out a tissue and blew her nose. "You can't. I only have one daughter." She shook her head. "Had. Today you're her."

"Doctors and nurses like to ask children a lot of questions. They think it takes your mind off the pain, but it doesn't." Mira said. "Is there anything I should know about Lilly?" She thought for a minute. "Where did she go to school? Did she like to color?"

Maggie looked at Mira sitting in the back seat. So little, so grown up. "She liked to color very much. And play Go Fish. You can say you go to Rock Creek Elementary, if they ask you. As for anything else, you decide. Okay?"

"I want to play her right," Mira said. "The trick is to use a little truth when you lie. Poppy told me that for lawyering, but it works for acting, too. And Mommy taught me to put on the role like a Halloween costume. You step into it with your whole mind and body, and then you become the person. You can do the same thing. Today you wear the costume of my mother." She nodded confidently at Maggie.

"We'll both do just fine," Maggie said. She got out of the car and opened the back door. When Mira moved her arm, she cried out in pain.

"I'm sorry, Mira—" Maggie started.

"Maggie," said Lydia in a hushed voice.

"I'm sorry," Maggie said. She took a deep breath. "I guess I'm not as good at this as you two are."

"You'd better be," Lydia said. Her face was grave.

Maggie took a deep breath, nodded to Lydia, then turned to Mira. "Are you okay?"

"It hurts so bad when I move it."

"Let's get this taken care of," Maggie said. As she helped the little girl out of the car, she could feel her shaking. "Are you scared," she paused, "Lilly?"

Mira nodded her head vigorously.

"You'll do fine," Maggie said.

"Not about that. I can pretend to be anybody," Mira said. "I'm ascared of needles," she whispered. "Do you think they'll give me one?" She swallowed hard.

Maggie thought about it. "I'm not sure."

"I really don't want a needle, Mommy." She looked to Maggie, but then her eyes drifted to Lydia.

"I know, baby." Lydia kissed the top of her head.

Maggie remembered the angel pin on her collar. "Would you feel better if my angel was with you?"

"But Lilly gave that to you," Mira said.

Maggie took the pin off her shirt. "And today, you are Lilly." She pinned the angel on Mira's shirt. It hung off balance, the one larger wing pulling the angel to one side. "Beautiful," Maggie said.

The three walked to the Emergency Room door, and as the electric doors swhoosed open and cold air hit them, Maggie remembered the last time she had walked through door like this.

She shook her head and focused. She signed Mira in as Lilly and sat down. After a half hour's wait, they were called to a registration desk, where all three played their parts well. After another hour in the waiting room, Lydia began to get nervous.

"What if they're checking?" Lydia said.

"Checking what?" Maggie said.

"If she's your daughter?"

"How are they going to do that?"

"What if they call to verify the insurance, and they're told that your daughter died?"

Maggie shook her head. "They won't. They'll just verify that I have—"

"Lilly Miller?" A nurse holding a metal clipboard, stood beside the door to the treatment room.

"Showtime," Lydia said under her breath.

The three walked to the door. The nurse bent down and said to Mira, "Are you Lilly?"

Maggie's heart thumped in her chest.

"Yes," Mira said. "And this is my broken arm."

The nurse laughed. "We'll see about that. Come on back." She held the door open for Maggie and Mira, but when Lydia started through, the nurse said, "I'm sorry. We're really busy right now. Only immediate family. You can wait out here."

"But…" Lydia started.

"Can't she come? She's my sister," Maggie said.

"I'm sorry. Just you and your daughter." The nurse began to close the door, with Maggie and Mira on one side and Lydia on the other.

"I'll be good, Auntie Sue. I promise," Mira said to Lydia.

"I know," Lydia said. "I love you." There were tears in her eyes.

The nurse patted Lydia on the shoulder. "We'll take good care of her."

"I love you, too," Mira shouted as the door closed.

The nurse led them to a stretcher, then pulled the curtain to enclose the three of them in a tight cocoon that gave the illusion of privacy. Maggie noticed she could hear the conversations from other parts of the room and realized she would have to be playing her part, even when it seemed they were alone.

The nurse started asking questions about how the accident happened, sprinkled with personal questions, just the way Mira told Maggie she would. Maggie hid a smile as the nurse asked "Lilly" if she liked to draw and color. When Mira answered that she did, the nurse pulled out two crayons, one orange and one blue, and a small note pad.

"Are you right-handed or left-handed?" the nurse asked Mira.

Mira held up her left hand. "Left."

"Lucky break," the nurse said. "Oops. Bad joke. Sorry." She winked at Mira.

Mira smiled, then said, "Very unlucky break."

The nurse put the crayons and pad down on the over-the-bed tray table. "My daughter is in her first year at the University of Florida, so I carry these colors." She looked to Mira. "Your mom will really miss you when you go away to college."

"I know," said Mira quietly.

Maggie nodded.

"You get used to it," the nurse said.

Maggie forced a smile, the "you get used to it" comment ricocheting around her head. "I hope so."

She patted Maggie on the arm. "You can color or play Hang-Man. That's one of my daughter's favorite games. She even plays it on her cell phone. The doctor won't be too long." The nurse turned and pulled the curtain closed behind her.

***

Maggie looked around the small cubicle and out into the examining room of the emergency room. Mira had just been taken for her X-ray, and because they were so busy in X-ray, they had pressured Maggie into staying behind. She decided it was a good time to give Lydia an update, so she walked out into the waiting room.

Lydia jumped to her feet when she saw Maggie. "Where's Lilly?"

"They're taking her for an X-ray."

"Why aren't you with her?"

"They wouldn't let me. I tried."

Lydia's voice was loud. "She shouldn't be alone. What if someone—"

"Sue." Maggie grabbed her arm. "Calm down." She noticed some of the people in the waiting room looking at them. "Let's go outside and get some fresh air."

When Lydia hesitated, Maggie added, "They said it would be a while. Up to thirty minutes."

Lydia nodded and the two women walked outside. The blast of humidity seemed to unleash Lydia's tongue.

"You have to understand," Lydia said as soon as they got outside. "What if someone recognizes her?"

"Shush." Maggie once again took Lydia's arm, continued walking and didn't speak until they got to her car. "Get in."

Once inside the car, Maggie turned to Lydia. "Now, go ahead."

"What if they recognize her from the pictures in the paper and on the news?" Lydia said.

"Why would they? She doesn't fit the general description of Mira Vega, and she has a wristband on that says she's Lilly Miller. Here with her mother. Photo ID, insurance, the whole bit."

"Still, to leave her alone…"

"Lydia, I had no choice, and there's no reason to call attention to ourselves."

Lydia bit her fingernail. "How's she doing? Does it hurt much?"

"Yes, but they said after the X-ray they'll probably give her something for pain."

"A needle?"

"I guess," Maggie said.

"I should be with her. I can't believe this is happening."

"I'll be with her for that. It'll be okay. Her arm will be fixed, and then you can continue with your plans."

"What if she needs surgery?"

Maggie hadn't thought of that.

"I didn't bring it up because I didn't want to scare Mira," Lydia said. She slammed her hand on the dashboard. "How did this happen?"

"It just happened."

"I should have made her sit next to me—not move—the whole time."

"You couldn't have known what would happen." .

Lydia shook her head. "If you would have backed off from the beginning, this never would have happened."

Maggie felt a mixture of guilt and anger. "I couldn't just decide something this important without meeting Mira. I had to know which of you was telling the truth."

"If we hadn't been in that park… How could she let go?" Lydia was beginning to get frantic. She turned toward Maggie. "You and your damn pictures." She reached for the door handle. "I can't take this chance. I'm going to get her."

"Lydia," Maggie yelled. "You can't. You'll ruin everything."

Lydia turned to look at Maggie. She was breathing heavy and her eyes were narrowed at Maggie.

"We'll get through this," Maggie said.

"It's all my fault. I should have been watching her."

"Even if you were watching her, you wouldn't have gotten there in time to catch her."

Lydia began to cry. "She knows better. She knows never to let go when she's climbing a tree, or riding her bicycle, or on a Merry-go-round. She's such a careful child."

"Even careful people make mistakes." Maggie looked Lydia in the eye, held her hand, trying to calm her down. They couldn't afford Lydia losing her cool now.

"I'm just so scared." Lydia took a deep breath. "I have to get her away from him. The past two years were hell. I don't know what I'd do if I had to spend the rest of my life without her."

Lydia, lost in her own pain, seemed oblivious to Maggie's loss. But Maggie was unable to bring forth any platitudes of encouragement. She had found none that would help her. "Let's hope you don't have to." She nodded toward the hospital. "Let's get back inside."

***

Maggie sat on the plastic white chair next to the stretcher, her head even with Mira's. The arm was broken, and they were waiting for the cast to be put on. Maggie had held Mira's good arm and looked into her eyes, telling her it would feel better soon, as the nurse gave her a shot for pain. One small hurt to make the big hurt go away, Maggie had said.

Maggie stared at the little girl holding her arm close to her. The pain medication was making her drowsy, and she had begun to hum. Maggie moved the perspiration soaked red-ringlets away from Mira's face.

Mira looked up and smiled. "Thank you," she said.

Maggie ran her hand through the little girl's hair.

"Feels good," Mira said.

"Do you like hair-thingies?"

"What are hair-thingies?" Mira asked. She turned her face toward Maggie.

Maggie realized it was a phrase most people wouldn't understand. She lowered her voice and leaned close to Mira's ear. "My little girl used to love when I played with her hair. She used to ask me to do 'hair-thingies,' meaning to comb my fingers through her hair." Maggie stood and did the motion from Mira's front hairline to the back of her head, realizing that she would stumble on such words and phrases for the rest of her life, words that only she and Lilly had shared.

"It's putting me to sleep," Mira said.

"Then go to sleep, pretty girl." Maggie leaned down and kissed Mira's forehead.

Mira closed her eyes. "Will you come and visit us in Brazil?"

Maggie stiffened at the information. "Is that where you'll be?"

Mira's head bobbed slightly. "Mommy showed me on a map. It's far, far away." Her head fell slightly to the side. "It's a secret," she said before she dozed off.

Maggie stared at the soft white skin, the thin fragile eyelashes, the lips, just slightly parted as Mira breathed gently in and out. Maggie wondered what it would be like to have this child for the rest of her life. She could sneak out the back door, get in a cab, and go far away with her new Lilly. Mira was already missing, and Lydia couldn't come forward and ask for help, could she? She ran her finger along the high cheekbone, so much like Lilly's. Mira twitched in her sleep. They could play Go Fish and bake chocolate chip cookies with twice as many chips as the recipe called for. They would eat them until their bellies were bursting and never worry about a balanced dinner.

Maggie sat back down on the chair and leaned her head onto the stretcher, letting the tears fall quietly, as she stared at the red ringlets of a child she knew wasn't hers to dream about. She wished for her real Lilly to come back. She closed her eyes, listening to Mira's breathing, and imagined a world where such things could happen. In this illusory world, Lilly would pop out from behind a corner one day and yell, "Surprise!" Lilly would tell her it had all been a mistake and she'd been written back into Maggie's life. Back because it was realized that Maggie couldn't go on without her. But Maggie knew such a place didn't exist; what did exist was a world that let beautiful creatures come and go arbitrarily. She knew it would be easier if she believed in something—anything—but nothing made sense to her. She opened her eyes and put her hand on Mira's arm. It was warm and real and alive, and Maggie knew somehow she would have to get used to the world the way it was.

Maybe someday she and Brian could have another child. Some day, when she could stop comparing every child to her Lilly.

"She'll be okay, Ms. Miller." The nurse had come back in. "The doctor is ready for her in the cast room."

Maggie nodded.

"You can come with her this time."

In the casting room, the doctor was brusque, all business. It seemed that to him it didn't matter if he was setting a five-year-old arm or a seventy-year-old arm. Mira's charms were lost on him. In a way Maggie was glad. She didn't need this visit to be memorable.

"Simple break, really," Dr. Madison said.

"How long will she need the cast?"

"You'll need to go see an orthopedist within three days. I'll refer you to one, if you don't have one. Be sure to pick her X-rays up before you go and take them with you. He'll want to X-ray it again to compare, then decide how long the cast stays on."

Maggie wondered how Lydia would get the cast taken off. "But what's the usual?"

"There is no usual. People heal at different rates." He looked at Mira as if realizing for the first time that she was a child. "Someone her age could probably throw enough calcium onto the fracture in a few weeks. You'll see the patch on the X-ray." He looked at Maggie. "Ask to see it. Fascinating."

Maggie nodded her head. She could tell that facts and tests were the "fascinating" part of his job.

"You will always be able to tell the bone was broken," he said. "After a break, bone is never the same."

"Will she be okay?"

"Oh, sure. The bone will actually be stronger, less vulnerable in that part. From the outside she'll look the same as always—but inside, the evidence will always be there. Fascinating."

"And the cast?"

"About six weeks max." He smoothed the plaster wrap on Mira's arm. "Nice hair." He looked to Maggie. "Must come from your dad," he said to Mira.

Mira nodded quickly.

"My daughter has red hair," the doctor said. "From her mother."

"How old is your daughter?" Maggie was happy to change the subject.

"Two." He moved to the sink. "No, wait." He turned the water on with the foot pedals and lathered his arms from his hands to his elbows. "I'm in my third year—she's three." He looked embarrassed as he grabbed paper towels.

"Cute age," Maggie said.

"Yeah." He wiped his hands on the towels and tossed them in the metal garbage can. "The nurse will give you a referral to an orthopedist. Be sure to check her fingers." He picked up Mira's hand. "Make sure they don't get discolored, especially in the nail beds. And make sure there isn't a lot of swelling. It may hurt to move them, but she should be able to wiggle them." He looked at Mira. "Go ahead and wiggle them, Hon, just a little."

Mira moved her fingers slowly.

"Good," Dr. Madison said.

Lydia would have six weeks to figure it out.

"Oh," Dr. Madison said. "Don't get it wet—I used the stuff that dissolves in water. The nurse will tell you all that, too." He turned toward the door. "Tah."

"Tah," Maggie said as she watched the door close.

Chapter Twenty-Nine

Maggie was helping Mira put her casted arm through her shirt and then her overalls. She straightened the angel pin, but the left wing continued to sag back down. "As soon as we get you dressed I'll take you out to your mom," Maggie said close to Mira's ear.

"She's mad at me," Mira said.

"No, she's not. She's just upset."

"She is. I can tell."

Maggie saw that Mira was very agitated and wondered if there were more secrets she didn't know. "Will she yell at you? Spank you?"

"No." Mira shook her head of red ringlets. "My Mommy never hits. When she's mad, she does this for a few hours." Mira squeezed her lips together into an exaggerated grimace. "Then she tells me how disappointed she is about what I did."

Maggie stifled a laugh. "What will she say?"

"She'll make her voice very low and say, 'Mira, you should know better. You know you always use two hands when you climb or swing or ride a bike. I'm disappointed that you didn't listen.'"

"I see," Maggie said.

Mira suddenly looked serious. "She won't send me back to Poppy, will she? Because I disappointed her?" Her face was full of fear. "I didn't mean to."

"Your Mom wouldn't do that. She went through a lot of trouble to get you back."

"I was just showing you how I'd go down the slide." She began to whimper. "I wanted you to like me so you'd let me stay with my mommy."

Maggie felt her stomach tighten at the words. "Oh, Mira." Maggie put her arms around the little girl and pulled her close, being careful of the cast. "I like you very much."

"Promise she won't send me back?" Mira said.

"You've been so brave." Maggie pulled her closer. "It all must be so scary. She won't send you back. This isn't your fault. You didn't know that you'd fall." The angel pin was poking her in the neck, but she didn't want to move.

"Even careful people make mistakes." Maggie's voice was even, soothing, rhythmic. "You didn't mean to do it." She felt the small body melt into hers, begin to calm down. Closing her eyes, she rocked her and could feel the small heart beat against her own. "It's okay, Lilly."

The words began to swirl in her head as the picture of Lilly on the black asphalt filled her mind. She saw the stillness, the blood. She heard the sirens as she leaned so close to Lilly she could feel her breath. She saw Lilly's head with no helmet lying on the hard pavement. She began to think harder as if something was on the tip of her consciousness, but she couldn't reach it. Weightless and fleeting a thought danced around her mind. Then light as a butterfly it landed. Maggie feared that if she reached for it, it would disappear. "I'm angry that it happened, but I know you didn't mean for it to happen." Her words were soft and hushed, pushed past her lips with great effort.

The curtain flew open and Lydia burst in. Her face was a mixture of anger and fear. She pulled the curtain closed behind her.

"Let's go, baby," Lydia said, pulling Mira away from Maggie.

"Lower your voice. They'll hear you," Maggie said.

Lydia turned quickly and faced Maggie. She stood inches from her face and said in a hushed voice. "You'd like that wouldn't you? Are the police on their way, too?" She turned back in the cramped space.

"What are you talking about?" Maggie said.

"Are you mad at me, Mommy?" Mira said.

Lydia kissed the top of her head. "No, baby."

"What's going on?" Maggie said.

Lydia ignored her. "We have to hurry, Mira. Poppy's here."

Mira let out a gasp. "You're sending me back?"

Maggie felt the blood drain from her face. "Nestor?"

"God, no," Lydia said to Mira. She put one hand on each side of the little girl's head and looked at her. "We, you and me, have to get out of here before he sees us."

"Where is he?" Maggie asked.

"He'll probably be in here any minute." She was wildly looking around the small cubicle as if she were missing something. "I was outside having a cigarette when I thought I recognized him. I came back inside and watched. It's him. I've seen him everywhere, imagined him every place I've been for the past few days, but this time it's really him." There was sweat on her face.

"How did he find us?"

She turned to Maggie. "He must have been following you."

Maggie looked at the frantic woman and tried to understand. "Wait." She grabbed Lydia's arm. "Just for a minute."

"I can't wait any more. He's here. Don't you understand?" Lydia looked at Maggie, then shook her head. "He never would have known it was me. Never would have known what I look like now." Her face began to crumble, then she looked at Mira and a strength came into her face, her whole body seemed to straighten. "You and your pictures…"

Lydia didn't finish the sentence, but she didn't have to. This woman might lose her child because of her. Maggie watched as Mira hooked her good arm around her mother's neck, "Lilly Miller" staring at Maggie from the small white armband.

"Let me help you," Maggie said.

"Thanks, but I'm done." Lydia reached for the curtain.

Maggie grabbed her arm before she could pull it open. "I mean—let me help you get to safety."

Lydia tried to get her arm free.

Maggie grabbed Mira's arm and pointed to the armband. "I can pretend she's my daughter again. I'll take her out of the country. Meet you somewhere."

Lydia hesitated, then shook her head. "He's following you. That will never work."

"My husband's a pilot. There must be something—"

"I have to go," Lydia said. "Just burn those pictures."

"Wait." Maggie reached into her bag. "Take this." She handed Lydia her cell phone. "Please. I'll call you in a few hours. There must be a way."

Lydia looked confused—as if she were trying to make a decision.

"They're looking for a woman with a small child," Maggie said. "If you're alone…"

"I don't know."

"Just take the phone. Answer it. Let me think of something."

Lydia grabbed the phone.

"I really want to help," Maggie said. "Wait here and I'll get rid of him so you can leave," Maggie said.

Lydia's eyes narrowed. She walked away from Mira and whispered in Maggie's ear. "You are the only one that knows I have her. He will kill me this time. Think of life with a man like that—a man that would kill your mother." She backed away from Maggie and looked into her eyes. "Please understand that is truth, not melodrama."

"I'll go talk to him." Maggie rushed out of the curtained area to see that the ER had become even busier than when they had arrived. She walked out the door that separated the treatment room from the waiting room to find Nestor Vega arguing with the admitting nurse.

"I told you, sir, I can't let you back there."

"There." He pointed to Maggie. "She has my daughter."

Maggie took a deep breath and remembered the words of advice from the backseat. *The trick is to use a bit of truth when you lie.* And *to put on the role like a Halloween costume. You step into it with your whole mind and body, and then you become the person.* She put her shoulders back and "became" a person in control.

Nestor rushed up to her. He lowered his voice. "I don't want to have to make a scene. Just give her to me."

"I don't know what you're talking about."

"You came here with a woman and a small child."

"I was on a shoot and the child got hurt," Maggie said.

"I will get her back."

"What are you doing here?"

"I'm here for my daughter."

Maggie's heart was beating and all she could think about was ways to get Nestor to go away. "I have the pictures at home. Follow me back, and I'll give them to you." She started for the door.

Nestor grabbed her arm and spun her around. "I'd rather have the real thing." He looked past Maggie. She turned to see what he was looking at and saw that the E.R. nurse had come out to call in the next patient. Nestor rushed to the door and pushed the woman to the side.

"You can't go in there!" the nurse yelled.

Nestor didn't stop and Maggie was right behind him.

"Call security," the nurse yelled.

Nestor stood still and looked at all of the closed curtains. He turned to Maggie. "Which one?" When Maggie didn't answer he pulled open the first curtain to reveal a tiny woman with thinning white hair. Her johnny-coat had fallen off her frail shoulder, and thin, bony fingers were grabbing and missing, grabbing and missing, trying to pull it back up.

"Son," the old woman said, "you're back. Help me with this." The woman reached out for Nestor.

Nestor stepped away and turned to Maggie. "You can make this much easier."

Nestor pulled back the next curtain and the space was empty. Next he grabbed the curtain that separated him from Mira.

Maggie was right behind him. "No." She tried to grab his hand but he shook her off.

A large orderly grabbed Nestor at the same time but not before he whipped the curtain open.

Maggie stared at the rumpled sheets on the empty stretcher.

The muscular security guard placed himself between her and Nestor and spoke to Nestor. "I'm going to have to ask you to leave, sir." He rested his hand on his gun.

"She took my daughter. She's here somewhere." His head spun from side to side.

"Sir, this is a hospital," the guard said.

Nestor took a deep breath and suddenly became very calm. "I'm sorry, Officer. I'm rather upset. This woman is here with my daughter who has been kidnapped, and I'm trying to find her." He reached into his pocket.

"Put your hands at your side, sir," the guard said.

Nestor put his hands into the air, a pleading looking on his face. "I'm an attorney. I was going to show you my card."

"That won't be necessary right now. Please step outside."

The nurse that had taken care of Mira came up beside the three. The guard looked to Maggie, then to the nurse.

"Do you know either of these people?" he said to the nurse.

The nurse nodded toward Maggie. "She's here with her daughter. Broken arm."

"Her daughter is dead," Nestor said.

Maggie felt a wave of terror at being found out.

Nestor began to speak, calmly, convincingly. "I'm an attorney in Miami, and recently my daughter was abducted. Mira Vega, I'm sure you've heard it on the news."

"Just a moment, sir." The guard put his hand up.

For the first time she could remember, Maggie was silently thankful for the battle of testosterone she was watching. Rather than being impressed by Nestor's status, the guard seemed anxious to prove who was in control here.

"You say she's here with her daughter," the guard said to the nurse. "Have you seen this man before?"

"No, she was alone. Maybe a relative in the waiting room."

"Let me just see *her* daughter, then," Nestor said. "Prove it."

Both the nurse and the guard began speaking at once.

"We don't need to prove anything to you, sir," the guard said.

"Her daughter was just right here," the nurse said at the same time as she nodded to the stretcher, then ran her hand over the sheets, smoothing them out. She lifted her hand, and Lilly's angel pin was in it.

"Lilly's pin," Maggie said as she reached for it.

"Who does that belong to?" the guard said.

"It's my daughter's." Maggie's voice was low.

Nestor turned to Maggie with his eyes blazing as he realized he had found the place, but Mira was no longer there.

"Do you know this man?" the Security guard asked Maggie.

"Where *is* your daughter?" the nurse asked Maggie.

"What have you done with Mira?" Nestor asked.

Maggie felt the questions hit her like physical blows. She had answers for none of them. Maggie rubbed her fingers on the pin as she said, "This man's daughter is missing; he's telling the truth. But it must be getting to him—he's stalking me." She began to let the upset out. "He's crazy. I guess I need to get a restraining order." She turned to Nestor. "You have to leave me alone." She began to shake from all the adrenaline and didn't try to hide it. "I'm so glad you're here," she said to the guard. "Please make him leave me alone."

Nestor's eyes blazed, but he stayed calm. "You won't get away with this."

"Where is your daughter?" the guard asked.

"My sister took her. She recognized him in the waiting room." Maggie nodded to Nestor.

"Will you be okay?" the security guard asked Maggie. "Would you like me to escort you to your car?"

Maggie shook her head. She wanted to give Lydia time to leave before Nestor went back into the parking lot.

"Just a glass of water, please," Maggie said.

"Why don't you all step out into the waiting room," the nurse said.

Chapter Thirty

Maggie sat in the corner of the crowded waiting room, sipping water from a small conical paper cup. She had long since quenched her thirst, but from this vantage point she could see everything she needed to see. A glimpse to the left showed Nestor leaning against a wall, holding his cell phone close to his ear, but his lips never moved. Nor did his eyes, which stayed zeroed in on Maggie. To her right was a clear view of the parking lot and Lydia's car that hadn't yet disappeared, as she had hoped it would. By now, she assumed Lydia and Mira had abandoned the car and found another way to get away from the hospital.

Maggie got up, wishing she could magically get to her car without having to deal with Nestor, tossed the cup in the garbage, and headed out the automatic doors into the heat. Her heart pounded.

Just a few steps out the door, Maggie felt a grip on her arm, just above the elbow and heard Nestor say into her ear: "I want to know where my daughter is."

Maggie looked him right in the eye. "I don't know where your daughter is."

"How do you contact Lydia?"

"I don't know what you are talking about."

"You are not a very good liar," Nestor said.

Maggie didn't answer.

"I want to know what you know, and I want those negatives, Ms. Miller. I will find Lydia if it is the last thing I do."

"I don't have them anymore."

Nestor stared for a minute, then said. "Again, you lie." He laughed. "You have no idea who you are dealing with."

"I'm beginning to realize."

Nestor adjusted his sleeves, twirled his cufflinks, and his smile became friendly. "Do you know how I knew you were here?"

"I have no idea."

"I had you followed. Once you showed up at my house with a camera, I became suspicious. I confess, I never thought you would lead me to them—that was more than I ever dreamed."

Maggie's stomach tensed. There was no denying he was this close to finding Lydia and Mira because of her.

"But you were reluctant to hand over the pictures, and I wanted leverage."

"What are you talking about?"

"Leverage. It is what the law is really all about, you know. Positional advantage."

"I don't want a lecture on law." She started to walk away.

"Perhaps not. But you might want these."

Maggie turned around. Nestor waited until he had her full attention, then pulled a picture out of his inside jacket pocket. He waved it in the air. "A twist on the biblical phrase...a photo for a photo. Justice, no?"

Maggie turned back and started walking to her car. "You have nothing I want."

"Not want, Ms. Miller, maybe need is the more correct word. If you can't use them, I know a few other people who would be interested: Your husband, or," he paused for dramatic effect, "your lover—the very white man."

Maggie stopped in mid stride and bit her lip. Her lover—*the very white man*. She turned slowly.

"Come see." His words were so sweet, so inviting. The short walk back to Nestor was like walking through molasses, each step an effort, fearful of what she would find.

He held the picture up and in it Maggie saw herself and Donovan in her car. He had his hand on the back of her neck, and they were kissing. She closed her eyes tightly, but then she could see the moment as it happened, feel Donovan's hand on her neck, feel the warmth as it spread through her body, feel her heart flutter. She opened her eyes again and stared at the picture. How different the moment looked in Nestor's hands; it all looked so wrong, so calculated. Her head fell. They had only kissed that once, and here it was caught for eternity on a piece of high gloss paper.

"I'm not judging you, Ms. Miller. I have 'indulged' a time or two myself."

Maggie grabbed the picture out of his hand; she couldn't stand to look at it any more. "You bastard."

"I don't have to be. You see—it's very simple. You give me all your pictures, all the information you have—details about what the two look like now, how she contacts you, what their plans are, and these pictures," he nodded to her fist that gripped the crumpled picture, "will disappear."

Maggie couldn't believe what was happening. After Lilly had died, she couldn't imagine her life could get any worse.

"Add the reward money, and you will come out fine."

Maggie stared at Nestor, not wanting to say a word, give anything to this man.

"I don't want to hurt you. I only want my daughter. Surely you understand that," Nestor said.

Maggie wasn't sure what she understood anymore. She glanced at Lydia's car, still sitting empty in the parking lot, and wondered where the two were. She imagined Mira, happy and vibrant in Brazil with her kittens. She thought of the moment in her own car with Donovan, imaging Brian's reaction when he saw the picture. Saw him walking out of the house, suitcases packed. No daughter, no husband. She walked slowly to her car with Nestor close behind her. She needed time to think. The more time, the farther away Mira got. "I did throw the prints out, but I can develop more. I need time."

"I don't have time, Ms. Miller. My daughter slips away as we speak. I will follow you and take the negatives now."

"My husband will get suspicious."

"Your husband," Nestor tilted his head, "hasn't been around for a while."

Maggie felt angry, realizing how much of her life Nestor had violated.

"He's a pilot. He has the ability to show up at the most unexpected times."

Nestor nodded. "That's your problem."

Maggie thought for a moment. "If you're serious, that you will leave me alone if I give you what you want, then you can't make a scene in my life," Maggie said. "Or," she waved the crumpled picture in the air, "I have nothing left to lose, and in that case, you have no leverage." She looked him full in the face. "Give me twenty four hours. I'll call you and tell you where and when—away from my house and my husband."

"I will give you until tomorrow morning at ten, no more. You may pick the place."

Maggie was having trouble thinking, but she knew if she were to meet this man, it must be some place public, some place crowded, somewhere she could find help if she needed it. "Sawgrass Mills Mall," she finally said.

"That huge mall in Broward near the hockey arena?"

Maggie nodded.

"Where?"

Maggie wanted some place she knew there would be people by ten. "The coffee shop right inside the book store."

"If you don't show up, the pictures will be hand-delivered to your husband the next time he arrives home."

Maggie's hand shook as she tried to put her key in the lock, missing the first two times. She got into the car and started the engine. Nestor knocked on the window. She lowered the window and looked at him.

Nestor bent down, his face just inches from hers. His breath was foul, laced with peppermint. "You don't want to make an enemy of me, Ms. Miller. Surely Abigail Lustig would give you the same advice."

Maggie's face flushed as she realized her every move for the past few days had been done under Nestor's surveillance. "Bastard." She stabbed her finger on the button that made the window go up and willed it to go faster. She wanted as much distance between her and Nestor Vega as she could get.

Maggie pressed her foot on the accelerator and sped out of the hospital parking lot. Her mind jumped from Donovan to Brian, Mira to Lilly, Lydia to Nestor. She couldn't seem to slow her thoughts down. She was two blocks from the hospital when she almost hit a pedestrian crossing the street. Maggie gripped the wheel as her whole body started to shake, and she pulled into the parking lot of a Wendy's restaurant. She parked her car in the corner of the lot, away from any other cars and began to cry. She looked around, wondering if one of Nestor's men were following her now, then screamed at the top of her lungs, "Fuck you, Nestor Vega." She pounded the steering wheel until her hand hurt, then she slumped back into her seat.

After a few minutes, she looked into the rear view mirror, wiped her eyes, and started the car. She needed to think, and she needed to be home.

Chapter Thirty-One

Maggie drove her car around the cul-de-sac and took her foot off the accelerator when she saw Brian's car in the driveway. There was a loud honk from behind her, and she realized she had stopped still in the middle of the road. She waved into her rear view mirror to a neighbor, one who had moved in next-door two months ago and whom she still hadn't met, and eased her foot off the brake. In the driveway she put the car in park and took a deep breath. Her fingers found the angel pin that she had tucked into her purse. She held the pin in her hand, moving her fingertips over it delicately. Not ready to face Brian, she put the car in reverse and started to back out of the driveway. The car stopped short as she slammed on the break. She couldn't hide forever.

As soon as she opened the front door, Brian called her name from the kitchen.

"I'm glad you're home, Maggie," Brian said as he walked toward her, wearing an apron and drying his hands on a kitchen towel. He slowed his pace as he looked at her face. "Are you okay?"

Maggie shook her head as her hand went to her eyes; she knew her make-up was all smeared. Then she looked at Brian again. "What are you doing wearing an apron?"

"Sometimes people do surprising things," he said, smiling.

Maggie searched his face. Could he already know about the pictures? He wouldn't be smiling if he did.

"What's wrong?" Brian said. The concern on his face made her burn with guilt.

Maggie pushed the picture of her and Donovan to a corner of her mind. She couldn't be distracted right now. She needed every available brain cell to figure out how to get Mira to safety. She could deal with the insanity of what she had done later.

Maggie held out her clenched hand and opened it slowly to reveal the pin. "I found her, Brian."

Brian looked at the pin, then back at Maggie. "Lilly gave that to you." His voice was wary as he said, "You found who, Maggie?"

"I found Mira Vega." She looked away from Brian's face.

"You found the pictures you were looking for?"

Maggie shook her head. "I met her."

Brian's expression was one of doubt mixed with surprise and fear. "Let's go sit down," Brian said. "We can talk over there." He nodded toward the family room as he pulled the apron over his head.

In Maggie's mind, Lydia's fear and Nestor's threats began to swirl, fused and inseparable, like the colors on a candy cane, and the last thing Maggie wanted to do was sit. "So much has happened, Brian." She walked into the kitchen with Brian following her and saw the flour canister and a mixing bowl on the counter. Two sticks of butter sat next to a large package of chocolate chips. "What's this?"

"I was going to bake you cookies."

Maggie turned to Brian.

"You haven't baked any since…" his voice trailed off. "You used to bake them with…" he stopped again. Then he shrugged, "The recipe's right on the chocolate chip bag. I just thought some homemade cookies would make you feel better."

Maggie fought back tears. "You don't bake."

"Apparently I do, Mag," Brian said as he picked up a spatula off the counter and posed with it.

Baking her cookies was such a considerate gesture. She wouldn't tell him that the smell of a chocolate chip cookie caused an ache so deep and painful it was like inhaled air rushing over an exposed nerve in a tooth. She took a deep breath. "That was so nice of you, Brian. Maybe we can bake another time, but I need to think right now." She reached for the coffee carafe, filled the pot, and added grinds to the filter. She pushed the start button, turned toward the table, sat down, and then popped back up.

"What's up, Maggie?"

"I have to get her to safety," Maggie said. "It's my fault Nestor knows Lydia took her." She paced the kitchen floor. "I have to make that right." Then the thought that had been snaking around her mind came out of her mouth, "I'll fly her out as Lilly." She stood perfectly still for the first time since she'd entered the house. "It's perfect."

Brian ran his hand through his hair. "You're scaring me again, Maggie, and I—"

Maggie's thought process was stopped by the apprehension on Brian's face. She realized that if she was going to pull off what she needed to do, she couldn't have Brian against her. "Let me start from the beginning." She walked to the coffee maker and poured two cups of coffee, added milk to both, sugar to hers and placed them on the table. Her deliberate movements belied the manic state of her mind, but she knew if she was going to convince Brian, she needed to appear calm and sane.

"It really was her. *Is* her," Maggie said as she led Brian to the table and sat him down. She pulled her chair close to the table and leaned over the bare wood surface. "Not only is she alive, Brian, she's with her mother." She saw the surprised look on his face and said, "Just bear with me and listen, then ask me anything you need to ask me." She looked at the clock. "But we don't have much time."

Maggie went through a thorough but brief account of what had transpired over the past days, recounting with great detail her separate meetings with Lydia and Nestor, as well as her confusion over who had been telling her the truth. She told him of the fundraiser, not mentioning the cost; of being found in Nestor's bedroom, where she found Abigail Lustig's phone number and their subsequent meeting; and of meeting Lydia and Mira Vega. She ended with the scene at the hospital, leaving out the picture of her and Donovan and the threat of blackmail.

"I'm going to give Nestor Vega a doctored-up picture of Lydia, and then his detectives will be looking for a woman with different features. It will just take a few hours on Photo Shop."

Brian stared at her, clearly confused. "What do the police say about this? Don't they want the real picture?"

"They didn't believe me, remember?" Maggie said.

"Weren't they at the hospital when all this was going on?"

"No, and I don't want the police to find her, now," Maggie said, waving her hand in the air, thankful that she didn't have to contend with the police, too.

"If this Vega guy believed his daughter was there, why didn't he have the place surrounded by a SWAT team?" Brian said. "I would have."

"He thought his detectives could do it better. And he claims he's worried about negative press."

"Negative press? What about his daughter?"

The words "negative press" sounded so hollow when Brian said them. Nestor's words ran through Maggie's mind: *Is there anything you wouldn't do to get your daughter back?* She shook her head, trying to clear it. Like the pieces of a puzzle spread out in front of her, Maggie thought back over the last few days. Nestor had her followed, which is how he had the pictures of her and Donovan. He showed up at the hospital, convinced that Mira was there, which he could only have known because his detective must still have been following her. Yet he *hadn't* called the police.

She could feel the blood drain from her face.

"Are you okay?" Brian said.

She held her hand up, letting the pieces fall into place in her mind. After a few minutes she stared at Brian. "Brian, you're right. If what he really wanted was his daughter found, he would have called the police. I've been so caught up in their stories…" her words trailed off as Lydia's words rang through her head: *He will kill me this time.*

Her hand covered her mouth, but the words snuck through, "He really wants to kill her and take his daughter back. That's the only explanation of why the police weren't there."

Brian stared at her. "Now you're talking insanity, Maggie," Brian said. "A well respected attorney is going to kill his wife?"

"*He* won't do it, but he'll see that it's done. He'll just have her disappear. As long as Lydia is alive, he can never be sure what she might do. It's the only way to ensure he will keep his pristine image and have sole custody of Mira—forever," Maggie said. "Don't you see? It's a mixture of things. This man has a huge ego. He makes things happen on a daily basis...in court, with his power, with his money. He even 'fixed' his divorce! Think of the things you hear on the news that people do because they think they are justified, or above the law. Men like him don't defend the law, they manipulate it."

"But murder?"

Maggie stood up and looked around the kitchen as if she'd find the answer hidden behind the stove or tucked into the toaster. "I've got to get them out of the country. Brian, you have to help me, please. Mira deserves a normal life with her mother."

"Maggie—"

Maggie turned back toward Brian. "I know, I know. It's hard for you to buy all of this, because you didn't think I was right to begin with. It's pretty outrageous to me, too, but think about it. First Nestor Vega tried to 'fix' his divorce, and when Lydia's attorney wouldn't go along with it, he had her disbarred. Then he was going to prevent Lydia from having visitation rights by having her declared mentally incompetent." Maggie shook her head. "All the while, he was the one endangering Mira. Hitting her when his temper got out of control. He even broke one of her fingers in a fit of rage."

She stared at Brian, letting it all sink in, then said, "I can't even imagine what life would be like for Mira if she ends up back with Nestor. Lydia will end up in prison, or worse, and all she wants is a life with her daughter." She looked into Brian's eyes. "Imagine if you could have a second chance with Lilly?"

Brian winced, averting her gaze. Then he looked back at Maggie. "You know all this to be true?"

"I've done almost nothing but track down facts since I recognized her."

Brian got up and paced around the kitchen.

"If I let you talk to them, will that convince you?" she said.

Brian spun around to face her. "You can contact her?"

"I gave her my cell phone," Maggie said.

Brian walked over to Maggie and held her head between his hands. His voice was slow, as if speaking to a child. "Maggie, if you really believe he would kill the mother, and you have proof that he knows it's her who has their daughter, then you're in danger, too."

"Me?" She hadn't had time to think that far ahead.

"You should go to the police," Brian said.

"And tell them what?" Maggie leaned back against the kitchen counter. "They would only believe me if I turned in Lydia and Mira, and I can't do that."

"But if you are right about all of this, what will stop him from harassing you? Doing something like he did to that lawyer? Or even hurting you?"

Maggie thought of Nestor's blackmail plan, of the picture of her and Donovan, and knew Brian was already right, more than he knew. "I can't think of that now, Brian!" she said, her voice rising, knowing it wasn't Brian she was angry with. "The first thing I have to do is get those two to safety, and quickly. I'll worry about the rest later."

Brian shook his head. "I don't know..." His voice trailed off.

Maggie couldn't slow her thoughts down. "Did you ever take Lilly off the airline's dependents-eligible list?"

Brian shook his head. "I meant to." He shrugged his shoulders. "I liked seeing her name listed with ours—I couldn't make her disappear like that just yet."

Maggie looked at Brian with surprise and nodded her understanding, then went on. "Good. Then I'll fly her out of the country as Lilly," she said. "Lydia will have to meet us somewhere." Maggie stopped and looked into Brian's face. "You don't need to help me. I'll do it myself. Just don't try to stop me this time."

Brian stood still.

Maggie reached for the portable phone, then pulled her hand back. "Can I use your cell phone?"

"What's wrong with that phone?"

"I'm getting paranoid."

"You think it's bugged?"

"I never would have believed I was followed, either."

Brian walked to the hall table and brought back his cell phone.

"I'm going to let you talk to them, Brian." She punched in her own cell phone number and waited while the phone rang. On the last ring before the message would have picked up, Lydia answered. "Yes?"

"Lydia, it's Maggie. Are you two okay?"

"As good as could be expected."

"I'm still working out all the details, but tonight I'll fly Mira out of the country and you can meet us somewhere."

Maggie saw Brian's eyebrows shoot up and he mouthed the question, "Tonight?"

Maggie nodded to Brian, then said into the phone, "I just have to find out what flights are available, to where, and how many open seats on each," Maggie said. "Details like that."

"What are you talking about?" Lydia said.

"We don't have much time," Maggie said. "My husband is a pilot for TransGlobal Airlines. I can pass-ride Mira on the plane as my daughter. All I need to do is present her birth certificate."

"Maggie—"

"It will be just like today. Think about how ridiculously easy that was." When Lydia didn't answer, she added. "No one will even question it."

"I don't know."

Maggie could hear Lydia breathing into the phone. "Lydia, even if I don't give him a picture of how you look now, I'm afraid he may already have one."

"What?"

"If he was following me when we met in the park," she said, "his detective could well have had a camera with him."

"Oh, god." After a long pause, Lydia said, "Where and when do I meet you?"

"I don't know yet, but ask my husband any questions you may have. And then let him talk to Mira."

Brian took the phone. "This is Brian Miller."

Maggie watched Brian's face as he listened to Lydia.

"Maggie pass-rides all the time. It's a very common practice." He nodded his head. "Yes, so did our daughter. There's only the usual security.

Maggie needs picture ID, but someone under eighteen wouldn't..." His shook his head, listening for a moment. "That's right."

Brian paused as Lydia spoke. "I'm not sure I agree with what Maggie wants to do, but, yes, I do think it would work." He nodded. "You're welcome," Brian said as he looked at Maggie. Then his face softened, and Maggie assumed Mira was on the phone. Brian nodded and spoke soft, affirmative answers into the phone. She saw tears in his eyes. He looked at Maggie, but spoke into the phone, "We'll do what we can so you can stay with your mommy." Then his face broke into a sad smile. "I'm looking forward to meeting you, too. Tell your mom we'll be calling back soon."

Brian snapped his cell phone closed and looked at Maggie. "She's adorable." He pulled Maggie to him. He stuck his face into her neck as if trying to hide the words he said, "I miss her so much, Mag. Some days I just ache."

Maggie held tight, knowing exactly who he was talking about. "I know. I miss her, too." They stood silently for a while, and then Maggie pulled away. "When this is over, let's start missing her together."

Brian nodded.

"Do you think there's a flight I can get on with Mira tonight?"

"We can check my flight to Santiago," Brian said. "It's off season which usually means plenty of open seats."

Maggie grabbed Brian's hand and led him to the small office with the computer. After checking seat availability on all of TransGlobal's Miami flights out of the country, Brian made a few phone calls, checked crews, then listed Maggie and "Lilly" on the stand-by list for the midnight flight to Santiago, Chili. They called Lydia back, filled her in on the details, and gave her specific instructions on what to do and where to meet.

Maggie looked at her watch, then went into the bedroom to pack her carry-on bag.

Chapter Thirty-Two

Maggie and Brian stepped out of the cab outside the TransGlobal Airline terminal at Miami Airport. Unsure as to whether or not they were being followed, she and Brian had driven their car to Ft. Lauderdale Airport, parked, gone into the terminal, through security, then walked back out quickly, catching a cab to Miami, keeping a close eye out for anyone who might have been following them in the crowds and traffic.

Brian, who was in full uniform, paid the cab driver, then stood up and nodded to Maggie. He pulled his carry-on suitcase with his pilot's case piggy-backed on top, and Maggie pulled just a carry-on. The airport was less crowded at night, but this just made all the security more obvious. Maggie couldn't help but notice the police strolling the lighted walkways outside the terminal. She forced herself not to look away as they passed.

As they walked through the automatic doors into the terminal, she bent down, pretending to fix her shoe, trying to see if anyone was following them. Several people were moving through the terminal behind them. What did she think she might see? Any one of them—the overweight man with the shoulder length black hair who was wearing a Hawaiian shirt and florescent green Bermuda shorts, the tall stately gray-haired woman who rhythmically stretched her fingers as if getting ready to give piano lessons, or even the frazzled-looking twenty-something mother who pushed a stroller with a sleeping toddler—could be watching *her*. She concentrated on what they were wearing, so she could see if any of them showed up again at the gate.

When they got to the security checkpoint, Maggie took a deep breath and told herself to relax. She put her purse and shoes into a plastic bin, then followed Brian through the metal detector. When the alarm when off, Maggie jumped. Off to the side, the security guard's wand found that the angel pin Maggie had on her blouse had set the detector off.

Once they were through security and began the long walk to the gate area, Maggie was torn between looking around and keeping her eyes glued to the gray carpet. She chose to watch the area just a few feet ahead of her, staring at people's ankles.

She had made this walk dozens of times, yet she never realized what a long walk it was. Every time she allowed herself to make eye contact, she imagined that it was a plainclothes FBI agent who was going to slap her in handcuffs. But not yet, she realized. She had done nothing wrong, yet. For now they would only stop her, question her, and ruin the plan. Even one of Nestor's men would do nothing now. They would all just be watching, so she began to look people squarely in the face to see if they would look away.

When they got to the end of the long hallway, where the gates for the international flights were located, Brian went to the men's room while Maggie took out her passport and Lilly's birth certificate and waited in line at the desk to check in as a pass-rider.

The woman at the desk took Maggie's passport without saying a word. Maggie watched the woman's fingers fly over the computer keyboard and realized that her own fingers were drumming on the counter and held them still.

"You and your daughter, Ms. Miller?" The woman glanced up, and then moved her eyes to the screen.

"Yes," Maggie said.

"And where is she?" The clacking of the keyboard continued.

Maggie's eyes searched the area near her. Before approaching the desk she had located a woman with two small children, one boy and one girl, both around Lilly's age.

The woman looked up.

"Over there with my sister," Maggie said as she nodded into the crowd.

The woman smiled and looked back to the computer screen. "Thank you." More clacking. "You're all set," she said.

Maggie thanked her and turned to see Brian leaning against a column near a large window. He smiled as she walked toward him.

"I've got to go preflight the plane," Brian said, rubbing Maggie's arm. "Are you okay?"

"I'll feel better once this all gets going," Maggie said. She looked at her watch, then at the crowd, and every person now looked suspicious.

"The flight is still wide open," he said. "When they start to call the stand-bys, you should be one of the first called. Go get your boarding passes first, then go to the ladies' room. I'll see you on the plane."

Maggie nodded. Her armpits were wet and her head was pounding.

"Relax, the plane won't leave without you." He rubbed her arm. "I'll see to that." Then he kissed the top of her head and walked away.

Maggie watched Brian's back until she couldn't see him anymore. Then she turned to the crowd again, looking, but not wanting to make eye contact.

General boarding of the plane began, and Maggie was sure that the people around her could hear her pulse beat as it pounded through her body. She almost felt as if she were going to faint and willed herself to take deep breaths. *Mira and Lydia are counting on you,* she said to herself. *You can do this, you can do this,* she repeated as she got up and pulled her carry-on behind her toward one of the large windows. She looked into the darkness at the massive airplanes, all going to different parts of the world. She found herself repeating the same word she had used when she sat next to Lilly in the hospital: please. Please, please, please make this work. She wasn't even sure who her single-word prayer was going out to, but it helped her stay focused some how.

Then she heard her name over the microphone. "Passengers Miller and Miller, please come to the desk."

Maggie walked to the small counter and smiled. "Miller," she said as she pushed her passes across the counter to a middle-aged woman with black hair. "Maggie and Lilly." Maggie remembered the dozens of times she had done this before and tried to act like she had those times: excited, tired, bored.

The black-haired woman clicked on her keyboard for what seemed like an eternity to Maggie, and she was sure something was going to go wrong. The woman had never even looked up after Maggie said the names. Normally Maggie would make polite conversation with the gate agent, but she felt it would be better to keep conversation to a minimum. Finally, the woman slid across the boarding passes with seat assignments. "Have a pleasant flight, Mrs. Miller."

"Thank you," Maggie said. She turned around, and instead of heading for the gate, she walked toward the ladies' room. Once inside, she leaned into the mirror, pretending to fix her mascara as she waited for a young girl to finish drying her hands. Then Maggie walked to the handicapped stall, placed her bag outside, and knocked on the door.

When the door opened, Maggie thought she had made a mistake, then realized the woman with the long, dark, Cher-like hair was indeed Lydia. And standing next to her was an almost-as-unrecognizable Mira.

"I—" Maggie started to say she hadn't recognized her, but stopped when she saw Lydia's hand come up to her lips as she shook her head.

Maggie nodded. She walked into the stall, and Lydia closed the door. Mira's transformation was more subtle, but just as complete. Her hair which had been red and wildly curly was now brown and combed close to her head with gel, the way people with naturally curly hair try to tame their curls. But what really made her look different was the dark brown eyes and deep tan.

Maggie panicked at first because Mira looked nothing like Lilly, then realized that anyone who would know her well enough to know what Lilly looked like, would also know that she was dead. Besides, Brian had checked the flight crew and there didn't seem to be anyone she knew on the flight.

Maggie felt a genuine smile cross her face for the first time in hours. "Are you ready, Lilly?" she whispered. She put her hand out to the little girl, and then noticed that a long-sleeved peasant blouse covered the cast nicely.

Mira took Maggie's hand, but looked up to her mother.

Lydia squatted down so she was eye level with her daughter. In a low voice, she said, "Do exactly what they tell you, no matter what. Okay?"

Mira nodded. Maggie could see tears in her eyes.

Lydia hugged Mira to her and held her tight. "I'll see you soon."

When she stood up, Lydia turned to Maggie. "I can't tell you how much this means to me. For some things, there are no words."

Maggie nodded. "I know."

The three looked at each other and nodded. Mira flushed the toilet and a few seconds later, Maggie and Mira walked out of the stall, hand in hand.

Maggie felt a stab of fear when she recognized the stately, gray-haired piano teacher from the entrance to the terminal standing at the sink washing her hands. Maggie kneeled down to adjust the hem of Mira's skirt to regain her composure. She stood, smiled, and looked the woman in the eyes, looking for a reaction and following her gaze.

The woman smiled back in the mirror and said, "Hola." Then she looked down and continued to soap up her hands.

Maggie gripped Mira's hand as they walked out of the restroom into the terminal, telling herself that this *was* a large airport and several flights *were* leaving the terminal tonight. The Piano Woman could simply be going on a trip.

Maggie took the boarding passes out of her purse and held on to Mira's hand tightly. They walked directly to the gate at a pace fast enough that Mira had to skip to keep up. If anyone was going to stop them, if she was going to be arrested as a kidnapper, now was the time.

Maggie turned to look behind her as they got to the gate, but didn't see the Piano Woman anywhere. She turned back and smiled as she handed the gate agent their boarding passes and watched the two white stubs get sucked into the electronic machine and pop out the top. The gate agent handed them to her and smiled back.

Maggie had time to listen to their feet make only a few hollow thuds as she and Mira walked down the jet way, when she heard the gate agent's voice say, "You just made it, sir."

"Last minute change of plans," the man said. "Clients!"

Maggie turned to see a middle-aged man in a suit and carrying a portfolio scurrying up the jet way behind her. She felt yet another wave of panic as he sped toward her. He slowed as they reached the door of the plane.

"I thought I'd missed this by a mile," the man said to Maggie. "Must be my lucky day."

Maggie nodded, hoping it was hers, too. She and Mira stopped at 2A and 2B in the first class section, while the businessman moved pass them into the coach cabin. The Piano Woman had not boarded the plane.

Maggie and Mira settled themselves into the spacious first class seats, Mira looking somewhat lost in the wide seat. They said little to each other and Maggie thought of how different it was than the other times she had been with the child.

Maggie heard the familiar click of the PA system, then Brian's voice.

"Good evening, ladies and gentleman. This is Captain Miller up here in the cockpit along with Co-Captain Safra. We have a small maintenance delay; however, it should be resolved quickly, so I'm asking you to remain in your seats, as we will be closing the door and departing shortly."

The PA system clicked off, and a few minutes later the cockpit door opened and Brian walked out. He nodded to the flight attendant, who was busy getting the first class passengers their preflight drinks, and walked over to Maggie and Mira and smiled. "Small maintenance delay. We shouldn't be too long." He leaned in and ruffled Mira's hair.

She smiled up at him.

"Oh, god," Maggie said. "I left my carry-on in the bathroom. What was I thinking?"

"You have time," Brian said. "Go get it. I'll watch out for Lilly."

Maggie turned to Mira. She reached for her hand and held it, then reached over and kissed her on the cheek. "Mommy will be back soon." She fought back tears and took strength from the courage in the little girl's eyes. She leaned over and whispered in her ear, "I will miss you."

Maggie turned and started to get up.

"Mommy?"

Maggie froze at the word…the right name, but the wrong voice. She turned around to see Mira motioning her closer. Maggie sat back down and leaned toward Mira.

Mira threw her good arm around Maggie's neck. "You make a good Mommy. Lilly was lucky, like me," Mira whispered.

Maggie sat for a minute, trying to regain her composure. Then she reached into her purse and pulled out the angel pin. She pinned it on Mira's blouse and smiled. "You be a good girl for Mommy."

Maggie got up, mumbling about being so stupid as to have forgotten her bag. Brian walked her off the jet way, explaining her forgotten bag to the ticket agent. Maggie watched him get back on board the plane and then walked toward the ladies' room. The bathroom was empty and miraculously, her bag was still where she had left it, next to the handicap stall. She wheeled it out of the bathroom, straight down the hallway, past security, and out the front door of the airport, while tears rolled down her face.

Chapter Thirty-Three

Through the front-glass windows of Books-A-Million, Maggie saw Nestor sitting at a small wooden table as she rounded the corner into the bookstore. It was a few minutes after ten, and she saw him look at his watch impatiently as she approached. There were some people browsing, and a few having coffee. Just enough for her to feel safe, but no one was close enough that she and Nestor couldn't talk freely.

Maggie sat down, put Brian's cell phone on the table, off to the side, then put the manila envelope with the picture she had brought on her side of the table, folding her hands over it.

"I'm glad to see that you made the right decision," Nestor said. He reached for the envelope.

Maggie held it captive under her hand. "You have something for me?"

Nestor took out a white, business-sized envelope from his jacket pocket. He waved it at her, then put it down on the table.

"One more thing," Maggie said. "Why do you really want these pictures?" She wasn't sure what she expected Nestor to say, but she needed to hear what he would say.

Nestor shifted in his chair. "I have told you, Ms. Miller. I want to find my daughter and get her mother the help she deserves."

Maggie nodded. "So you need these to identify Lydia and Mira—how they look today."

"Yes." Nestor's tone was full of impatience at having to explain things repeatedly.

"How is it that if you had me followed and took those pictures," she nodded toward the white envelope on the table, "that you don't have pictures of Lydia and Mira from the day you had me followed to the hospital?"

Nestor's eyes narrowed as if trying to see her more closely. He twirled his black onyx cufflinks around, and then a small smile crossed his lips. He nodded, and Maggie wasn't sure if his look was one of admiration or amusement. "I told you when we first met. I like to tie up all the loose ends." He reached for the envelope and pulled it from her hands. "I don't need you running back to the police with these."

He opened the envelope and dumped out the contents. One single 8 x 10 picture fell onto the table, face down.

Maggie could see the anger seeping into Nestor's face.

"What is this, Ms. Miller?" He looked at her as if cross-examining her. "The deal was the negatives and all the pictures you had." He reached for the photograph.

Maggie willed her heart to slow down as he turned the picture over.

Nestor stared at the picture, anger no longer disguised in his face. "You are playing games with the wrong man." He threw the picture toward her. Face up on the table was a picture of Mira's hand being held by Lydia's hand, but Lydia's face had been replaced by the head of Bo Bo the smoking Clown.

"I will not be made a fool of." His leaned forward, his voice low, full of forced control. "You lose all around." He pointed to the white business envelope he had brought. "I will send these pictures to your husband and the white man's wife."

"And your daughter?"

"Did you really think I would sit still and wait for these useless pictures? I only wanted them because it was cleaner if they were destroyed, once and for all." He shook his head and studied her. "This was to be a simple matter. I ask you for the pictures, you give them to me. But it has become way too complicated because you became stubborn." He moved to get up.

"And what if I go to the police with my pictures?" She needed to get him to sit back down, to bait him. "What if I told them that you had known where your daughter was and didn't notify them for help? How could you explain that?"

"Why should I have to explain myself? It's my word against yours."

"Is this really about getting Mira back, or do you need to win, too?" She stared at his face. "You can't stand the thought of Lydia outsmarting you."

Maggie watched as he clenched and unclenched his hands.

"When these pictures of you kissing another man surface, you have no way to link me to them," he said.

"But it will create quite a scandal if I go to the media with my pictures and give them my story of your involvement."

Nestor thought for a minute, his fingers rubbing the flat surface of his cufflinks. "You are either very stupid or you just don't think." He stared at her for a minute then said, "Ironically, I should be getting a call any minute saying that my daughter and her mother are in very safe hands."

Maggie felt a tightness in her throat. "What are you saying?"

"I am saying that I had you followed. I know you put my daughter on a plane to Santiago, Chile last night. Then you got off and went home."

Maggie thought back to the "businessman" who had boarded the flight when she had. How many others had been watching?

"Unlike you, my man remained on the plane. He will follow Mira and Lydia through customs in Santiago, then…" He waved his hand in the air. "Let's just say that my daughter will be returned home safely, and Lydia will get…" he looked around as if choosing his words, "just the *help* she deserves."

"She said you would kill her." Maggie's heart pounded.

"She is very bright for a woman, brighter than I ever gave her credit for. But details like that you don't need to know. What you do need to know is this." He leaned across the table and lowered his voice. "If you go to the police, say a word of this to the press, I will have you arrested. A federal kidnapping charge has a maximum penalty of life in prison and a $250,000 fine." His voice became melodic, and he moved his hands through the air as if he were creating a story. "Perhaps," he paused, "you were the kidnapper all along. You went to the police, came to me, for attention. Who knows how a sick mind works? You had just lost you daughter—you wanted another one. The police will even testify you acted bizarrely."

Maggie tried to keep her anger under check, her mouth closed.

"*Why* doesn't matter," he added smugly. "I have proof you sent my child out of the country."

"You seem to have thought of everything," Maggie said. "But Mira will tell everyone if something happens to her mother. How will you keep her quiet?"

"Give my associate some credit. It will be a 'terrible accident,' what I should have done the first time. I won't be fooled by Lydia again."

Maggie wanted to hear more but wasn't sure how far to push him. When Nestor's phone rang, it startled her.

Nestor looked at his cell phone. "You and I were to have concluded our business by now," he said. "I had no intentions of sharing this call with you, but now, why not?" He flipped his phone open and said, "Yes?"

He listened intently for a few seconds, his face filling with anger. "What? Check again." He listened again.

Maggie wished desperately that she could hear the conversation on the other line.

Nestor's voice was low and angry as he spoke into the phone. "You are sure?" He paused. "Say it one more time." Then he nodded and hung up. Rage showed on his face, and Maggie remembered the story of Nestor's temper and Mira's broken finger.

"Where is my daughter?" Nestor said. His voice was low, growling, his nostrils flaring.

"I don't know what you are talking about."

"She wasn't on the plane you put her on, so where is she?" He reached over and grabbed her forearm.

"I don't know what you're talking about. I put my niece on a plane last night—"

"Stop this!" he yelled and slammed his hand on the table.

Maggie was stunned into silence.

Nestor looked around the bookstore. Then he took several deep breaths, took his hand off her arm, and twirled his cufflinks. He appeared to regain his composure, but his words were spit out between clenched teeth. "Tell me, or I will ruin your life. Not just your marriage."

"Are you threatening me?"

"Do you take me for a fool?"

"Or are you talking about the way you ruined Abigail Lustig's life, setting her up to look like a thief so she'd be disbarred, when she wouldn't cooperate with you during your divorce?"

"That's nothing compared to what I am capable of. You will not have one moment's peace until you tell me where my daughter is. You will—"

"There's nothing you can do to me, Mr. Vega," Maggie said with a bravado she wasn't feeling. "I don't care about those pictures—"

"Those pictures are child's play," he cut in. Nestor's breathing was getting heavy.

"If you kill me, then you'll never find out."

"Kill *you?*" He shook his head. "But you have a business you cherish. Perhaps the next break-in won't be so benign. An arsonist, perhaps; everything you value destroyed."

"That was you?" She tried to appear more surprised than she was.

"Did you think I was really *waiting?*" He laughed. "And, you have people you love, I'm sure. You just had a loss. How would another one feel?"

Maggie stared at Nestor, wondering just how much this man was capable of.

"I will give you one last chance," Nestor said. "An offer you shouldn't refuse, as they say." Nestor once again leaned into the table. "Tell me where my daughter is and you walk away from here and from me forever. Not only will you avoid being charged with a felony, but all those you hold near and dear will live long and healthy lives."

"You *are* threatening me," Maggie said.

Nestor's smile made her stomach lurch.

"What if I go to the authorities and say that you are planning to kill Lydia and threatened to kill those around me until you got what you want?"

Nestor made a deep, throaty noise, a cross between a snarl and a laugh. "Who would believe you? I will say your story is in retaliation for my turning you in."

Maggie looked down at her hands, gathering her thoughts together. "I have a different deal," she said.

Nestor laughed. "You are in no position to make a deal."

"My deal is this. You mourn the loss of your daughter and move on. If any harm ever comes to anyone that I love, or Lydia is injured, or if Mira ever shows up in your custody again, the authorities will know all about this conversation."

Nestor contemplated her for a minute. "They'll never believe you over me."

"No, they won't. But they will believe this." Maggie reached into her pocket and pulled out a small tape recorder, her finger rubbing the glowing red power button.

Nestor stood suddenly, tipping his chair to the ground, and jabbed his hand toward her, reaching for the recorder. Maggie jumped up and out of his way. The people at the other tables turned to look.

"Sit down, Mr. Vega," Maggie said. "Or, would you prefer to make a scene and get the police involved right now?"

Nestor picked his chair up, adjusted his collar, and sat down.

Maggie waited until she had her composure, then started talking. "Right now in a safe deposit box at the bank are all the photos and negatives of your wife and your daughter, along with a detailed account of all the times you called and came to see me, trying to get them. There are also several letters in the box, with all the details I've mentioned, to be mailed if I should meet with an untimely death. One is to the FBI, one to the Coral Gables Police, one to the Florida Bar," she said. "Did I leave any out? Because I can add another when I put copies of this tape into the box with them."

"You are insane to threaten me like this." Nestor's words were like hisses.

"You gave me no choice." Her heart was pounding. "Do you understand the deal? You leave me and my loved ones alone—and that includes those pictures you took—forever. Even if my husband's plane should randomly crash, life as you know it is over, so you'd better pray that doesn't happen. And," she took a deep breath, "if Mira ever shows up in your custody again," she paused for effect and then repeated, "*ever...* I will release all of this information to the people I listed."

Nestor remained silent.

"I suggest you cut your losses and leave her alone," Maggie said. "I'm only sorry that I can't turn you in now, but then they'd know your wife took your daughter, something you've worked very hard to keep a secret."

Maggie reached for her cell phone as if getting ready to leave. "Oh, one more thing." She held the phone close to her head and said into it, "Did you get all that?"

"Loud and clear," came Donovan's voice from the cell phone's speaker.

Nestor inhaled loudly as his nostrils flared. His head seemed to twitch just slightly, while the rest of his body was as still as set cement.

"So, should you choose to do anything to me on the way out, or on the way home, the tape from the other end of this phone will hit the media and the police immediately," she said. She adjusted her purse on her shoulder, and then stood to leave. "I think you and I are finished, then." Maggie walked toward the door, hoping that the trembling in her legs wasn't noticeable.

Chapter Thirty-Four

Maggie walked into the diner and straight to the back, where Donovan was waiting for her in a booth. She slid into the seat across from him, waving at Ethel who stood a few tables away.

"Thanks," she said, smiling.

He nodded.

"Do you have the tape?"

Donovan handed an envelope to Maggie. "Did you get the original into the safe deposit box?"

"Yes. I was jumping at my shadow the whole time," Maggie said. She looked around the diner. "I still am." She looked back at Donovan. "I can't thank you enough. I couldn't have done this without you."

"That man was evil," he said.

"He still *is* evil."

"And your...niece?" Donovan lifted his eyebrows. "You said you'd explain all that."

Ethel showed up at the table and looked closely at the two of them. "How 'bout letting me choose the pie today?"

Maggie and Donovan nodded.

"I'll only be a minute," Ethel said.

Maggie watched Ethel walk away, and then looked back at Donovan's questioning face. "Let's wait for the pie."

Donovan nodded. Maggie rearranged her fork, knife, and spoon on her napkin. After a few minutes, Ethel put down two coffees, a milk for

Donovan, and two pieces of chocolate cream pie. "Comfort food—today you kids look like you both need it," she said as she walked away.

"Thanks, Ethel," Donovan yelled after her.

"Welcome, kiddo," Ethel yelled back.

Maggie looked down at the pie, which was really chocolate pudding in a crust with whipped cream. She remembered the "skin" of the top of the pudding being her favorite part when she was a child. Maggie moved the whipped cream off the top of the pie, but there was no skin, just silky mousse-like chocolate.

"I should be hearing from my niece shortly" she said, checking her watch and looking at Brian's cell phone. "She should be calling me at one o'clock our time."

"But how did you manage it? I heard Nestor say he had you followed and that he had a man on the plane."

Maggie thought for a moment. "I'll tell you the how, but not the where. How's that?"

Donovan took a big bite of pie, leaving a small dab of whipped cream on his lip. Maggie smiled and pointed at it, and Donovan licked it away, looking ten years old.

"Did I tell you I took Mira to the hospital as Lilly?" Maggie said.

Donovan shook his head. "All you told me this morning was to go buy a very reliable tape recorder and be at the office at 9:30."

She explained in detail how she'd made prior plans with Lydia and took Mira aboard the plane as Lilly and how she got off and went home to take care of the evidence that needed to go into the safe deposit box before her meeting with Nestor.

Donovan shook his head, confused. "If you left Mira there, what happened to her? Nestor said Mira wasn't there when it landed."

Maggie felt a stab of old fear. "I know; when he said that this morning, I wasn't sure how many people had been watching us.

"I got off the plane and left Mira there with Brian, who had a small maintenance delay, not just by coincidence, mind you. He explained to the flight attendants that I wasn't coming back and that Mira wanted to be with her mother." Maggie paused to smile at Donovan. "Then Brian took Mira off his plane and on to the plane where Lydia was waiting in first class with two full-fare tickets. He was simply escorting a passenger onto a flight where she belonged…where she was united with her mother. Both Lydia and Mira had valid tickets and legitimate, albeit fraudulent, ID, which Lydia had been waiting for so she could leave the country. Brian's plane landed without Mira. The flight they really *were* on, landed in a destination that shall remain nameless. Now they can go anywhere without being noticed—you can get on a train in, say Europe, and travel between countries and there's no record of your trip. You just need proper ID, which they have."

"What about the police? The FBI? Weren't you concerned? If you'd been stopped, you'd have gone to jail as a kidnapper."

"It was a risk I had to take. It was the only way to assure that they would get out," she said. "I was scared out of my mind in that airport, but I had to figure that Nestor hadn't called the cops or they would have been at my house before we left for the airport." She shook her head. "I was praying we'd only have Nestor to contend with, and we had to move fast.

"I thought I could buy some time, by telling him I'd give him the pictures this morning, but couldn't rule out the possibility that he would have me followed. Which, as you heard, he did." She shook her head. "He was so convinced he could have it all, doing it his way. Find Mira and get Lydia out of the picture for good. No scandal, and life goes back to the way it had been just a week or so ago."

"And his man he had on the plane?"

"There was a man that got on right after we did. He must have bought a gate ticket, but waited to board to be sure that we got on."

"Why didn't he just stop you there?" Donovan was leaning over the table and had forgotten about his pie.

"If he tried to stop us there, it would have involved the police, and it's clear from what he said this morning—that was never part of his plan. You heard him. He planned to have his man follow them out of the airport in Santiago and resolve the issue in his own way."

She took a deep breath and leaned back in the booth. "Can you believe how much has happened?"

"You look tired," he said.

"I was up late writing the letters and making copies of all the pictures for the safe deposit box. I had to get all that done before I met Nestor this morning."

"Did you actually give him a picture? He sounded furious, from where I sat."

Maggie laughed. "I gave him a picture, all right. I wanted to be sure I could set his temper off, so I used Photo-shop to create a picture with Lydia's body and BoBo the Clown's head." She shook her head at the memory of Nestor's angry face.

"Weren't you afraid you'd put him over the edge?"

"That's exactly what I needed to happen. He needed to think I was cocky *and* stupid. I wanted him to threaten me."

They sat for a long time without saying anything.

"A lot has happened," Donovan said. He looked at Maggie and reached out and squeezed her hand, then let it go. "How are you holding up?"

Maggie looked at Donovan. "I have something else to tell you, and it's not good."

Donovan nodded. "About a picture?"

"You know?"

Donovan shrugged. "I heard what Nestor said about a picture going to your husband and 'the white man's wife.'"

Maggie groaned. "I forgot you heard that." She looked at the uncomfortable look on his face. "I'm sorry."

"Tell me."

"In the car at McDonald's, after the fundraiser, when we kissed—"

Donovan nodded.

Maggie felt awkward. "It was his way of getting 'leverage,' as he called it, on me."

"I wanted to talk to you about that." He took her hand and looked her full in the face. "In some ways, I'm not sorry it happened," he paused, and then continued, "but it was a mistake. It never should have happened."

"I know." Maggie's voice was barely a whisper. "I'm sorry that I got you involved in this," Maggie said. "I don't think he'll do anything with that picture."

Donovan shook his head. "For me it doesn't much matter. I've already told Julie."

"You told her?" Maggie pulled her hand away. "Told her what?"

"The night I got home after the fundraiser, I guess I was acting kind of weird. The conversation took a lot longer than this, but the bottom line is that I told her I kissed you."

Maggie felt shame ooze through her body. "Oh, god."

"She was upset, needless to say, but we talked for a long while."

Maggie looked up, surprised, and realized she knew so little about his relationship with his wife.

"She asked me if I was falling in love with you," Donovan said. His eyes seemed to search her face for a reaction.

Maggie looked away from his stare. When he didn't say anything, she looked back.

Donovan reached over and took her hand. "I told her you were like a damsel in distress and things got carried away." He brought her hand to his mouth and kissed it ever so lightly. "And, I told her I was going to give you my two weeks notice." He placed her hand back on the table.

Maggie wondered why she felt such surprise at the inevitable. "Will she forgive you?" she said in a low voice.

"She's going to try."

Maggie nodded.

They sat in silence for a while, Donovan running his fork over the whipped cream, and Maggie holding tight to her coffee cup.

"What about you?" Donovan finally said.

"I hired that new photographer." She shrugged.

"I meant, will you tell Brian?"

Maggie slouched down into the booth. She had been so busy the last twenty-four hours that she hadn't had time, hadn't wanted to have time to think about it. "I honestly don't know." In the days after the kiss, she had had no intentions of telling Brian. She knew the kiss was a mistake and had hoped it would just go away. "I don't know if he'd understand."

She thought about total honesty, something she'd always believed in…before this. It was a wonderful concept as long as you didn't screw up and hurt the people you loved. Once you did, was cleansing your own soul to feel the relief of not harboring a secret worth hurting someone else? Was it just a transfer of the burden?

"If Julie had kissed someone," she said, "if she thought she might be attracted to someone else, would you have wanted to know?"

"I thought about that," Donovan said, "after I told her. I'm not sure I did the right thing. I hurt her by telling her." He thought for a moment. "I think we always *say* we want to know, but I'm not so sure about this. It wasn't an affair; it's not ongoing. It wasn't exactly a fall from grace, just a stumble, a misstep." He looked at her as if looking for agreement. "It was wrong, but it's done." He shook his head, picked up his fork and stabbed the crust of his pie. "Maybe I'm just rationalizing, trying to minimize things, but I don't think I'd want to know."

Maggie looked at his face, knowing how much she would miss his honesty, his wisdom. "I'm sorry we crossed that line, Donovan," she said. "You've been such a good friend to me."

He nodded slowly. "We might have been crossing the line even without the kiss."

His gentle look made her realize how much she would miss him. She suddenly felt incredible fatigue. "I'm too tired to think straight, maybe that's my problem." The lack of sleep, combined with the highs and lows of the last few days were now taking their toll.

"Maybe there is no one right answer, Maggie, only the one you can live with. My answer may be different from yours."

"I will miss you, my skinny white Buddha with the long flowing ponytail." She started to laugh. "Could you look any more un-Buddha like?"

"Ah." Donovan placed his hands in prayer-like fashion in front of him, taking on an Asian accent when he said, "Buddha come in many forms. Maybe it is time for Maggie-san to be strong and lean on self now."

"If Maggie-san lean on self *now*, Maggie-san fall down."

"'Fall down eight times, get up nine.' Famous proverb."

"Stop," Maggie said. She had started to laugh, but the tears in her eyes weren't from the laughter. Maggie looked at Donovan's smiling face. "I just want to feel normal again. I want to stop waking up every day aching for something I can't ever have again, feeling sad or scared or worried."

"With Mira safe, that should help, right?"

Maggie nodded.

"And as far as Lilly is concerned..." He took her hand again. "There's some powerful hurting going on inside of you—as there should be. Stop trying so hard to feel better. It will come. Do you know the fable about the jackass and the cow?"

"Did your mother tell you this one?"

He nodded his head.

Maggie leaned back and settled into the booth. "Tell me one last story."

"A jackass and a cow are trying to cross a wide river one day, to get to some food on the other side. They are doing just fine, swimming across the river together, braying and mooing, when they come across a powerful current that begins to toss them around the water. The eddies swirl them in the wrong direction, threatening to smash them into the bank of the river or against the jagged rocks on the bottom. The jackass is just ahead of the cow as he gets to the most powerful part of the current, and he begins to swim as hard as he can, fighting the current with all his might. He pumps his fore legs, kicks his hind legs, breathing hard, and fighting until he begins to tire. He never gives ups, but the current doesn't seem to end. Sadly, the cow sees the jackass go underwater, fighting until the last minute, but finally having no strength left to keep his head above water.

"The cow begins to feel the pull of the current and becomes petrified. She knows she's not nearly as fit as the jackass. How will she ever survive? Then she turns on her back and lets the current take her. She is tossed wildly around the river, holding her breath when she gets pulled under, gasping for air when she can, and being thrown against sharp rocks, causing her intense pain. All the while she is questioning her decision, wondering where she will end up or if she'll even survive. After what seems like a cow lifetime, she finds herself floating down a quiet part of the river, not at all where she intended to be, exhausted but alive." Donovan smiled at Maggie.

Maggie smiled back at the face that always managed to make her feel better, yet she felt the pull of all the sadness around her. "A cow lifetime?"

Donovan shrugged. "I just added that part."

Maggie laughed, then sobered. She shook her head, thinking of Donovan's story. "Just how long is a 'cow lifetime'?" she asked.

Donovan studied her face, and then tugged on her hand. "As long as it has to be, Maggie, and not a minute shorter, no matter how much you'd like it be."

They sat in silence for a while, and then Maggie looked at her watch and saw she only had ten minutes until Lydia's call. "I'd better go."

"Me, too."

Maggie nodded. "I will miss your wisdom, Donovan." She looked at his clear blue eyes. "Can I have your mother's number?"

Donovan laughed. "I wish. She died a few years ago."

"Really? You talk about her as if she's still alive."

"In a lot of ways she still is…to me," he said. "I still hear her stories in my head. At first I would push them away because they would make me sad, but now I fear her voice is getting dimmer and dimmer, and search for the memories so I don't lose them."

Maggie thought about that. Right now the pain from the memory of Lilly was so intense that she couldn't wait for it to lessen, but was that the trade off? Could Lilly's face ever get so faded in her memory that she couldn't picture it? Or her voice so low that she couldn't imagine it? She prayed not.

"Do you think we could meet for pie, now and then?" Maggie said.

"Sure."

They looked at each other for a moment as if each believed the answer. Maggie wished it could be so, but felt somehow that it would never happen and knew it was better for both of them if it never did.

"Let me leave first," Maggie said. "I don't want to watch you walk away."

"I'll do that if you remember one thing," he said.

"What's that?"

"Regardless of how you feel right now, you are a strong woman, Maggie Miller. Just don't be a jackass."

Maggie smiled. "I will miss you," she said. She started to walk away then turned back. "Do you think cows can really float?"

"Oh, yeah," Donovan said. "In a world where clouds fall to earth, anything can happen."

"If only that were true," Maggie said, "I would be living a soap opera miracle right about now." She smiled, and then walked away, willing herself not to look back.

Chapter Thirty-Five

Maggie sat in her car fixating on her watch. It was 1:15, and Lydia should have called fifteen minutes ago. She checked the battery on Brian's cell phone and it was fully charged. Then she checked the service and saw that there were five full bars of service. She could start driving, but didn't want to be in traffic when she heard from them.

Then the phone rang.

"Hello?"

"Hello, Auntie Angel."

Maggie recognized Mira's voice. She closed her eyes and held the phone close to her lips. "Are you two okay?"

"Yes! We had the best flight. They gave me pretzels and chocolates whenever I asked."

Maggie smiled and nodded, then said into the phone, "I'm glad you had a good time."

"Mommy says I have to go now. Here she is. Thank you, again."

Maggie heard the exchange of the phone, then Lydia's voice. "Maggie, I can't thank you enough."

"Everything is okay?"

"I think so. As far as I know there's been no one following us, and we've made a few…changes…already."

"I think you're clear. There was a man on the plane to Chile. They were convinced that's where you were."

Maggie heard Lydia suck in her breath. "Someday, I will thank you. It may take a while, but one day, you'll get a surprise, and you'll know it came from us."

"Just enjoy your daughter..." Maggie's voice broke. "Enjoy each other. That is thanks enough."

After a short silence, Lydia said, "We'd better run now."

Maggie searched for words to say, something to prolong the conversation, to keep the connection alive, but could think of nothing. "Take care of yourselves."

"You, too."

Maggie hit the end button on the phone and sat in her car, listening to the silence. She started the car and headed for home, wishing there was someplace, anyplace, she wanted to be other than with Lilly or Mira Vega.

Chapter Thirty-Six

Maggie stared out the kitchen window watching a small gray squirrel run over her screen. The squirrel would run quickly, and then stop suddenly, his tail flailing behind him. Maggie could see his underbelly, his rapid breaths when he stopped. He jumped to a nearby palm tree and was gone.

Maggie turned toward the coffee maker and poured herself another cup of coffee. Brian had called from the airport a half hour ago, his trip from South America completed, and she had showered and waited. While he'd been away, their conversations were polite, brief, a few details of Lydia and Mira's escape and the fact that they were safely "somewhere." They both seemed to be avoiding anything that might cause a fight.

When she heard the front door open, Maggie went to meet Brian. She held him close. "I can't thank you enough," she said.

Brian nodded and kissed her neck. "I can't believe you pulled it off."

"Not just me," she said. "And I mean thank you for believing me when you really had no reason to—except I was asking you to."

"I never meant to not believe you." Brian put his arm around Maggie as they headed for the kitchen. "Things have been so hard since Lilly died."

Maggie noticed that he had used "died" instead of referring to it as "the accident," or Lilly being "gone." "You must be so tired. Can I get you something?" she said.

"Just a shower and a nap," Brian said, kissing the top of her head. He poured himself a large glass of orange juice. "I'm beat."

"I bet."

They walked to the bedroom, and Brian sat on the side of the bed. Maggie could see the fatigue in his face and didn't think it was solely from the night flight back from Santiago.

"Things are different between us, aren't they?" Brian said.

Maggie sat down next to him, and he pulled her close.

"I knew it would be hard after she died, but not between us," Brian said. "I never expected that."

"I didn't, either."

"I was just trying to make you feel better, but I can't seem to do anything right," he said.

Maggie thought for a moment, and then said, "The thing is, you can't make me feel better. I have to get there myself." She felt her eyes start to tear. "And I don't think you feel better for a long time after something like this." She looked up and into his face. "She's never coming back, Brian, and that's a terrible thing to try to reconcile in my mind."

Brian thought for a minute. "Maybe I was being selfish anyway—trying to fix you for *me*, not for you." He lay down on the bed and turned onto his side, facing Maggie.

"I don't understand."

"I've been thinking a lot on this trip. I realized you always make everything right, and this time—you wouldn't, no, couldn't do it."

Maggie leaned back, propping herself on one elbow, and looked into Brian's eyes. "*I* make everything right? You're the one that always tries to fix things, Brian."

"I try…" His voice cracked. "But you do it."

"When do I ever try to fix things?"

"I just thought you knew you were doing it." He shrugged. "You would walk into a room and put your spin on things, and everything seemed better for me," he nodded and added, "and for her. Your smile, your laugh would always cheer us both up." He looked at her, studying her face. "When she was gone, you stopped. It was as if your light had gone out, too."

"I'm hurting, Brian."

"I think I was scared," he said in a hushed voice. "It was as if what I wanted didn't matter. As if *I* didn't matter anymore."

Maggie suddenly felt heavy with a different kind of sadness. She knew the effect she'd had on Lilly's life; Lilly made it so obvious with her laughter, her responses, but Brian's demeanor was always so regulated. How could they know each other so little after all these years?

"You did matter." She hugged him. "As much as anything could have mattered after losing her—but when you pushed me to do things I couldn't..." She thought hard, making sure she her words didn't come out hurtful. "I had no energy—for anything."

Brian was quiet for a long time, staring around the room, then he turned to Maggie, and there were tears in his eyes. "That little girl Mira broke my heart, Maggie."

"She got to me, too," she said, "but she's okay now. Thanks to us." Maggie managed a small smile.

Brian shook his head. "Not because she was in danger." He thought for a minute, and then his voice was low, "because she was alive." Brian leaned back on the bed and turned his face from her. "How terrible a person am I to say that?"

Maggie looked into Brian's face. "You're not terrible. You miss Lilly."

Brian turned his head away again, so Maggie snuggled into his shoulder.

After a few minutes, Brian said, "I don't know what to do with it, Maggie—all this pain." His voice was hushed, barely audible.

"Feel it," Maggie said.

"Oh, god," Brian said. "I can't." He shook his head.

"It won't just go away."

He pulled his arm from around Maggie and turned onto his side, his back toward her. "If I let it in, it may never stop, and I can't bear that much pain."

"She was a part of you, Brian. You can't lose a part of yourself without feeling pain." She searched for words, concrete words he would understand. "Imagine if you'd lost your arm or your leg. It would hurt and your whole life would be different."

"I have to be strong."

Maggie chose her words, trying not to shut Brian down. "If you'd lost your leg, would you expect to get up and walk the next day?"

"That's different. That's not possible."

Maggie put her hand on Brian's arm. "And maybe what you're trying to do isn't, either." She felt his muscles tense. "Lilly was our daughter, and she's dead, Brian, and there's no way that I can just walk on without stumbling and falling down for a while."

Brian groaned. "But I always keep going. It's what I do."

"Maybe not this time." She moved close and held him from the back. "This time is hell."

She heard him inhale deeply, and then felt his body shudder. He sobbed quietly, then after a long while he said, "Do you think we'll make it, Mag?"

"Other people do. I guess we can, too."

"I mean *us*. Do you think we'll come out of this together?"

Maggie took a deep breath. A black and white question, but not a black and white answer. She thought of Donovan, of laughing on the blanket in the park, of picking pie by the state, of telling him every secret in her soul and his acceptance. She had glimpsed a picture of a relationship the way it could be—albeit a brief snapshot—but she knew those were the kinds of memories she wanted to build. Could Brian be that man to her?

Maggie held her husband. "I don't know, Brian." She felt him shudder. "Let's not make any decisions right now. Let's just be here for each other now. Later, much later, we can talk about it."

Brian nodded, and then turned around to face her. His face crumpled, giving way to all the pain that was finally oozing through his body.

"It's okay," she whispered, moving in to hug him. "I'll hold you."

She wrapped her arms around him and kissed the top of his head. After a few minutes she heard Brian softly crying.

For all the times she had cried alone, seeing Brian give in to his pain made her hurt so much more. She rubbed his back while he cried, making soothing noises like she used to for Lilly. She nestled her face against his shoulder and let herself cry with him. She cried for her little girl, she cried for the adult daughter and friend she would never get to know, and she cried for the loss of the life she had planned and thought she would have. She cried for the man she held, for how much he was hurting, for not realizing sooner how hard he worked to keep his pain bottled up inside. She cried because she couldn't be sure they would make it together, but they would try. And for the first time since Lilly died, she knew that each of them *would* make it. She cried until she was exhausted, then let herself slip into her memories—the one place she could always be with Lilly.

CPSIA information can be obtained at www.ICGtesting.com
Printed in the USA
LVOW11s0858301115

464655LV00001B/4/P